To Bind a Dark Heart

BOOKS BY KATHRYN ANN KINGSLEY

THE IRON CRYSTAL SERIES

To Charm a Dark Prince

KATHRYN ANN
KINGSLEY

TO BIND A DARK HEART

SECOND SKY

Published by Second Sky in 2023

An imprint of Storyfire Ltd.
Carmelite House
50 Victoria Embankment
London EC4Y 0DZ
United Kingdom

www.secondskybooks.com

ISBN: 978-1-83790-478-5
eBook ISBN: 978-1-83790-477-8

PROLOGUE

Mordred flew high above the woods on the back of his dragon, watching as an ever-expanding circle of light flowed over the landscape far beneath him, turning the brown and faded colors brilliant and sparkling.

Avalon was truly like nowhere else he had seen, across the realms and worlds he had visited. It was a thing of beauty.

When it was not devoured by war and suffering.

The peace and sense of wonder would only last long enough for the elementals to catch their breath and begin their backstabbing and warmongering.

He would strike before they had a chance to gather their wits. Before old alliances and grudges reared their heads. The dragon circled lazily as it climbed higher in the updraft. The weather was warmer, the season having quickly changed from its perpetual autumn to spring.

He had let Gwendolyn escape. He had refused to answer the questioning of his knights as to why. The reason was simple. Obvious, really. But he did not care to explain it to them. He barely wished to explain it to himself.

He loved her.

And killing her—or sending her into the Iron Crystal—would shatter what was left of his heart. Her betrayal had wounded him enough. To see her rid from this world... would be what destroyed him in the end.

Luckily, he had somewhere else to focus his attention, away from his love and her betrayal. A far larger threat than Gwendolyn could ever claim to be.

Somewhere, there was one elemental, who was now freed, who must be found and stopped at all costs—the demon Grinn. Wherever he was, Mordred did not know. But somewhere on the island, a true monster was loose.

The Ash King must be captured and stopped. Or all the world would burn before Mordred had a chance to save it for a second time.

He could only pray that Gwendolyn would never find herself in the presence of that treacherous bastard. His jaw ticked at the very idea of it.

The Ash King would be found and captured first.

Then his war on the others could commence.

He would postpone dealing with Gwendolyn for as long as he could. But the matter of what to do with the young woman would arise sooner or later.

He could only hope that she kept her head down. If she were smart, she would hide in the mountains or lie low in a small village somewhere. But while the girl was certainly clever... she was not precisely *wise.*

Then, it hit him. A solution to his problem named Gwendolyn Wright.

Perhaps there was another path ahead for them. Perhaps he was uselessly bargaining with himself, trying to find ways around that which he dreaded. But it was the best way forward that he could see.

Who was to say that he could not simply keep her as he had

originally intended? Who was to say he could not keep her as his prisoner?

This time, he would ensure she stayed in iron chains.

She had thrown his hospitality back in his face once before. She betrayed him, seemingly not believing his threat to simply rebuild the Crystal once it was destroyed. It was almost as though she wished him to be the cruel prince they all claimed he was.

He smirked. Well, if she wished him to play the tyrant, he would oblige her. He knew, deep down, that he would do whatever she wanted of him. And this was no different.

He was Mordred, the Prince in Iron.

And the Iron Crystal would reign again.

Run, Gwendolyn Wright.

Run as far and as hard as you can.

Because when I catch you?

You belong to me.

ONE

This is some serious monkey-paw-level shit.

It was hard to imagine that just over a week ago—maybe two weeks, if she was being generous—Gwen had been sitting on a bale of hay in her barn, remarking to her angry stray cat that she wanted an adventure—telling him what she wouldn't give to go anywhere, do *anything*, other than stay in her sad and boring life on the farm.

Pushing herself up from the ground, she groaned in pain. She was really sick of waking up in ditches or other weird places. Usually after something terrible had happened to her. Which she supposed made sense. People generally didn't wake up in ditches because they'd just had a great time.

It took her a long moment to remember what had happened. Mordred had destroyed the Crystal in a fit of rage. She had run for the forest. A shockwave, and then—yeah, that would be why she hurt everywhere. She had been knocked through the trees like a pinball before ending her trajectory by smashing into a rock.

Standing, she staggered a few steps and put her hand on the trunk of a tree to keep from falling over. Rubbing her temple, she winced. "Can we stop being a punching bag? That'd be nice, I'd like that." She didn't know who she was complaining to. She didn't know if she really cared.

A cloud moved, and a ray of bright sunlight streamed through the leaves in the trees, momentarily blinding her. Lifting a hand to shield her eyes from the glare, she blinked, trying to clear her vision.

She gasped.

The world around her had... changed. Avalon was nothing like it had been only a few hours earlier. With the passing of the shockwave, it was like someone had reset the contrast and saturation on everything. Not only reset it—cranked it up. The trees around her were no longer faded, with half-bare branches shedding their last browning leaves. They were in full spring bloom.

The air was sweet with the smell of flowers. Birds chirped merrily in the branches. Leaves of every shade of green surrounded her. Some of the trees were even flowering, branches overfull with pink and purple blossoms. Petals rained down to the forest floor like beautiful, slowly drifting snow.

Dead grass was now bright and crisp, swaying in the breeze around her.

She gaped at what she saw. Birds flew overhead—all in wild colors like parrots. It took her breath away.

This was what Avalon was meant to be like?

Was this what Mordred had really robbed from the world?

It was beautiful. Beyond beautiful, actually—it was a paradise.

She walked deeper into the woods, marveling at everything she saw. At lady slipper flowers and colorful orchids, to buzzing, brightly colored insects that zipped from flower to flower like hummingbirds.

She watched as one of those insects flew close to a vaguely circular shrub, packed with large, thick green leaves.

A tongue darted out from the shrub and snatched the bug

out of thin air with a loud *glomp*. It had looked like a frog's tongue. But it had been *huge*—easily the length of her arm. Unable to help her curiosity, she tiptoed closer to the bush, hoping to see whatever odd creature was hiding inside.

When she got within a foot of the bush, she leaned in closer to see if she could spot the creature hiding in the branches. It was then that she realized the creature wasn't inside the shrub—the creature *was* the shrub.

Each thick green leaf of the shrub opened into a bright green frog's eye.

Squeaking in surprise, she fell back onto her ass, staring at the shrub-of-frog-eyes-on-sticks that was now looking at her, blinking its eyes in random patterns. Each time it blinked, the eye would look like a leaf again before opening and revealing its true shape.

It looked almost like a sea urchin. Only with *eyes*. On the end of sticks.

It stared at her. A lot.

And she stared right back. "Hey, buddy. Hey. Sorry. Didn't mean to get in your personal space. We're good."

Eyes kept blinking, watching her, as if she were a threat.

She had no idea if the thing was sentient enough to have a conversation. Standing back up, she retreated away from the eye-shrub and raised her hands in a show of harmlessness. "I'm gonna just... leave you to your froggy monster business, okay?"

The eyes began to close until the shrub once more looked like any other normal bush. Even if it was a little too round. She couldn't help but stare at it still as she walked away, almost afraid to turn her back on the eye-shrub. But it didn't seem to want to mess with her in any way, so she turned to keep wandering through the forest, taking in the sights and sounds of the new world around her.

She came to the edge of a pond, and watched as large, shimmering shapes dashed beneath the surface. They were like fish, but way too big. At least too big for a pond. But it didn't seem to bother them, as they seemingly blinked in and out of existence.

Teleporting, magical fish.

That was *so cool.*

She sat down on the edge of the pond, watching them dart around, fascinated by them, for a good long while before she decided it was time to get up and keep moving. She couldn't just sit in the forest forever, right? She should probably *do* something. Go somewhere.

And it was that realization that made her mind wander to Mordred. Her heart suddenly ached, and she turned her gaze in the direction of his keep. Wrapping her arms around herself, she frowned.

She felt terrible for what she had done. Had it been the right decision? Was it only going to lead inevitably to death and war? Or had she given Avalon a second chance? She supposed only time would tell.

But one thing was certain. She wished she could ask the Prince in Iron for advice, which was hysterical given the circumstances. *He'd know what to do. He always knows what to do. Too bad I don't think we're exactly on speaking terms right now.* And she didn't blame him. She had betrayed him—tricked him—and poisoned him with a muffin laced with sleeping powder.

If anything, he probably wanted to kill her or imprison her. Or worse. She didn't know what "worse" was, but she was pretty sure he'd figure something out.

Letting out a breath, she turned away from the keep and began to walk in the opposite direction. No, no matter how hard she wished she could just hug him and beg for forgiveness, to feel his kiss and hear his deep, rumbling voice, she had slammed the door on that. It was her fault, not his, that she was on her own now.

God, she missed him.

Letting out a long sigh, she shook her head, only idly wondering where she was going. It didn't really matter, she supposed. Away from the keep. Away from the mess she'd made. And away from Mordred.

Something rustled up in the branches, and she stopped to see what it was. A large lizard, the size of an iguana but resembling a bright teal gecko, was staring down at her. Spines jutted out from its back like a porcupine. It raised them in a wave before flattening them down, which Gwen assumed was some kind of freaky lizard warning. It flicked out its tongue into the air like a snake.

She smiled. "Oh, hey there little buddy. Little being relative."

It watched her, curious but wary, and turned its head to the side to peer at her with a bright purple eye.

"Aw, you're cute." She chuckled.

It ran off, leaving her alone once more. Then loneliness hit her, as fast and hard as a train. She wanted to ask Mordred all about the weird lizard and the frog-shrub. She wanted him to give her a tour of the new world, to show her all of Avalon the way it was supposed to be. Y'know, before he ruined it. Or saved it. Jury was still out.

She sighed.

How long until I bump into somebody? I hope they're friendly. Is that too much to ask?

It was another hundred yards before she got her answer.

More or less.

"Where do you think you're going?" It was a gruff voice, coming from behind her.

Turning, she blinked. She knew the voice, but she certainly didn't recognize the man that stood before her. He was a little over six feet, his skin was the texture it has when people spend a long life out in the sun and blistering weather. She knew a few farmers who looked like that as they got on in years—the decades of hard labor catching up to them. The man had salt and pepper hair with a black beard. There was a long, jagged scar that took up the left side of his face, the eye that it crossed being white and sightless. And he looked extremely cranky.

Oh, shit.

Gwen stared. "Merlin? Is that... you?"

"Who else would it be?" He rolled his good eye.

"What do you mean? I thought—" To be fair, she hadn't checked to see if she still had her fiery powers. One glance at the color of her hair told her that yeah, she did. She had been trying to grapple with how wild and magical the world looked and she hadn't really thought about it. "Wasn't this supposed to give you your powers back? Why are you a human now?"

Judging by how angry he looked, something told her things didn't exactly go as planned. Her shoulders drooped.

Merlin grimaced. "Come on, we have work to do." With no further explanation, he started walking away.

"Where are we going?" She followed after him.

"Doesn't matter."

"But what're we doing?"

"Doesn't matter."

She stopped walking and folded her arms over her chest. "I blew up the Iron Crystal for you. I feel like I'm owed an explanation."

With a ragged, annoyed sigh, he turned to face her. "You didn't do anything. Mordred blew up the Crystal. And you didn't do it for *me*, you did it for *Lancelot*." He said the name both overdramatically and somehow full of revulsion at the same time.

"I'm not going anywhere with you until you explain to me what's going on, and why."

Merlin stared up at the sky, clearly begging for patience from someone, somewhere. "Can I at least explain it to you on the way? We're wasting time. And standing in one place is going to get us caught by Mordred and his damnable knights."

She supposed that made sense. "Fine."

"Good." He turned on his heel and started off again into the woods. "Now shut up and follow."

God, she hated that cat. Person. Whatever he was. "Can you please be nice to me? Even a little?"

"No."

Well, at least it was definitely Merlin. At least she didn't have to worry about *that*.

* * *

Lancelot was unsure of how long he had been walking when he became aware of himself for the first time. In ages past, when he had been a mortal man, he had commanded a soldier who had been prone to walking in his sleep. It had puzzled Lancelot at the time, curious as to how something like that might feel.

Now he knew.

He was walking on the side of a dirt path through a glade. He paused and looked up at the sky—at the beautiful sunlight filtering through the leafy trees. Laughing quietly in disbelief, he rubbed his eyes. Was he still dreaming? Had imprisonment in the Iron Crystal sent him mad?

The world around him was beautiful—beyond beautiful. It caught his breath in his lungs as he took in the sights. It almost made him wish to weep in joy. In relief. The world had been mended—or perhaps it was all in his mind. He was not so certain he cared.

If this was insanity, he would take it over what he had just endured. He shivered from the memory of the emptiness—the *cold.* The sound that had once been whispers had become the deafening cries of others trapped with him but still separated. Surrounded by a crowd and yet entirely alone.

Had Gwendolyn truly succeeded? Or had he been trapped in that cursed place for a thousand years, until Mordred died?

It was impossible to know how much time had passed. All he could remember was the feeling of being ripped apart, then the horrendous cold and the screaming. He scratched at his chest, over where the crystal was embedded into his flesh, and—

He paused. Pulling aside his shirt, he looked down at his chest.

"Gone," he whispered to himself before breaking out in a disbelieving laugh. "Gone!" He was free. *Free!* The iron that Mordred had used to corrupt him—to keep him obedient—was missing! He had a scar where it had once been driven into his flesh, but that was the least of his concerns.

Looking down at his hands, he summoned his armor. Silver covered him, glistening in the beautiful glow of the sun. He was still an elemental. And he was *free*.

A sound from overhead that he recognized sent him ducking under the branches of a nearby tree. It was the creak of metal wings. Sure enough—an iron dragon soared over him, blotting out the sun briefly as Mordred's enormous minion swooped over the landscape.

That answered his question.

Mordred was still alive—and therefore, Gwendolyn was likely dead, having sacrificed her life to destroy the Crystal. Lancelot could not comprehend a world in which the Prince in Iron let the young woman live.

His next step was to make himself a steed. Focusing, he summoned his power, glad to feel the world flex beneath his will. There was comfort in it. The armor took shape before him until it resembled a horse. It shook its head, shining silver hoof stomping at the ground.

Climbing atop his horse, he commanded it forward. He needed to find the nearest town. He needed information—and he needed allies. He would have to discern where he was in order to locate the nearest elemental who might aid him in his new quest.

Gwendolyn was dead. The Iron Crystal was gone. And Mordred was still alive.

But not for long. He clicked his tongue, urging his creation to gallop faster.

Justice would finally be done.

Mordred would finally die.

TWO

Gwen walked beside the disgruntled old man that was, apparently, Merlin. He wasn't looking at her. He wasn't talking to her. He was just staring ahead as they made their way through the woods.

She walked along with him in silence for about ten minutes like that before she couldn't take it anymore. "Okay, so where are we going? What're we doing?"

"I don't have my power back." Merlin somehow managed to look even more put out than he had a moment before. "We're going to go fix that."

"So... we're stuck."

"Yes."

"I don't want to be stuck." She glared at him. "I *really* don't like you."

"The feeling is mutual. And if you would shut up and let me think, I might be able to come up with a solution for our problem." He grimaced, baring jagged and broken teeth.

"Mordred might know how to—"

"You really are an idiot, aren't you?" He shook his head. "Do you really think he'd help us? Yes, what could possibly go wrong with a suicide march back to the man who you just *betrayed*?"

"Whatever." She frowned. He really was an asshole. "So, if we're stuck, where are we going then? How do we get ourselves unstuck?"

Avalon's skies were clear for the first time in three hundred years. Sunlight and spring were back, and it seemed like every living thing in the forest had come out to celebrate. At least the view was nice, even if her current company was sorely lacking.

"Where are we going?" She followed after him.

"There's a town not far from here. We will take what we need for travel, and you will burn the rest." He said it so matter-of-factly, as if pointing out the obvious to a child.

"Wait, what?" She jogged to walk beside him. "You skipped, like, eight steps. What're we doing? Where're we going?" She stopped walking. "I'm not taking another step until you tell me."

He rubbed his hands over his face, muttering in a language she didn't understand. "If you wish to return home, then you will keep helping me."

"And what if I decide I don't want to go home?" She lifted her chin in defiance. Sure, she missed her parents—and she'd miss her own world. But Avalon was full of so much more. Here, she might have a chance at being someone. Or at least living an interesting life.

He stormed up to her, trying to use his grizzled appearance to intimidate her. "What is your grand plan, then, little human?"

"I just take a left and walk somewhere else. If we're stuck together, that means you're just as bound to my decisions as I am to yours. Lancelot must be out there somewhere. Maybe I could make friends or allies." She held her ground.

"Think it through, girl. The Crystal is broken. Magic has returned. And with that, a new struggle for power. Forces will rally against Mordred before he can capture them all again. The elementals will rise to fight, and if *we* do not help them, then Avalon will never be free."

"Try harder. Not good enough. I can lie low. Find friends."

"Friends?" He sighed heavily. "Consider this—without me, you know nothing of where you are. Where you're going. Who could be a danger and who could be an ally. You would fall prey to another elemental in moments. They will not take kindly to you."

"Why not? I'm the one who set them free."

"You clearly do not understand the nature of this place." He turned and began walking into the woods again. "I am done with this conversation. It is a waste of time. I'm going this way. The farther away we become, the more pain you will experience until it blinds you. I expect my tolerance for such things is higher than yours."

She frowned. That sounded miserable. "You could have just started with that."

"I foolishly thought you might have some sense in your head."

She sighed.

Go it alone.

Or follow a jackass cat turned... whatever he was now.

"How do you plan on fixing this?" She jogged after him. Fine. She'd tag along for now while she tried to come up with a better plan. "Where're we going after the village?"

"To the mountain. There is a wizard there who might be able to help us. If the crazed bastard is still alive." He snorted.

"A wizard? Is he the real M—"

"I don't know!" Grinn cut her off. "But probably not. Stop asking if everybody is Merlin."

"Damn." It was her turn to sigh. She was really hoping to meet the real Merlin. Maybe she still could, some day. Nobody knew what happened to him, but he was probably *super* dead. "So... you think a mage can help pry us apart?"

"I have no other bright ideas. I certainly do not wish to have you in possession of my power for any longer than I can help it." He bared his teeth again, almost looking feral. "And I will not go back into that Crystal. I will *not*."

Frowning, she didn't know what else to do. She had no other bright ideas either.

She couldn't go back to Mordred. She couldn't stay in the forest on her own. She couldn't even stay separated from Merlin for too long without it hurting her, apparently. *Great. Just fucking great.*

Now, she was in a foul mood. Which was in stark contrast to the beautiful array of colors in every tree they passed. They hopped over a small brook that was glittering with more of those strange, shimmering fish.

Avalon really was a paradise.

And she wanted to scream.

A little while later, they came to a road. Merlin seemed to have no problem walking on the street, and it was definitely better for her bare feet. The knights would probably all be flying around on dragons, so she didn't expect to find them on the road. Besides, it wasn't like Merlin and Gwen had any other choice. They couldn't trudge through the underbrush forever. "Hey—"

"Whatever it is, I don't care."

She glowered at the back of his head and tried to set him on fire with her mind. Unfortunately, it seemed she couldn't. *I hate all of this.*

Her mood changed when she heard a bark from behind her.

Turning, she felt her heart lift. "Eod? Eod!"

The hound was galloping down the packed dirt surface, tongue hanging out of his mouth. He nearly tackled her as he hit her, jumping up to lick her face.

"Oh, *great*." Merlin grunted. "The mutt."

Eod barked at Merlin, his ears back.

"It's okay, doggo." Gwen petted Eod, kneeling to hug the animal. "It's all right. He's fine." It was a lie. He wasn't fine, and none of this was fine, but there wasn't anything that was going to be done about it with barking.

Eod growled, not believing her at first. But as she kept petting him and quietly assuring him that the scary man wasn't going to hurt them, he finally calmed down.

"I don't like him either, but it is what it is." She smiled at the dog. "I know, he's mean and ugly, but he can't help it. Well, he can't help most of it."

"Very funny."

"Look, you're super clear how much you hate me. I get to be an asshole back to you if you're gonna be an asshole to me." She shrugged and smiled at Merlin. "It's only fair."

Merlin rolled his good eye before turning to keep walking down the road. "The town isn't far."

"What do we do when we get there?"

"I told you. Steal supplies, burn the place down, then keep going."

"Maybe we could just *ask* them for help?" She didn't like the idea of stealing, let alone burning the place down. Eod was trotting beside her with a stick in his mouth, the issue of the weird man entirely forgotten.

"No."

She sighed.

When they reached the town, the sun was just starting to set, lighting up the clouds with an array of purples, pinks, reds, and golds. Avalon was *gorgeous*, no way around it. She smiled. It was peaceful.

Right until someone saw them. It was a young woman with long, multi-colored hair the tones of a peacock. And if Gwen wasn't mistaken, her hair was actually made of feathers. The basket of vegetables she was carrying fell to the ground at her feet, scattering its contents. Her eyes flew wide and then ran screaming into the town. "Guards! *Guards!*"

"Oh, great." She slapped a hand over her eyes.

Merlin snarled. "Yes! Run in terror, puny mortal! Run from the elementals, for we have returned to ruin you all!"

Gwen slapped a hand over her eyes. And only had one thing she could say.

"Fuck."

* * *

Mordred landed with a deafening *ka-thud.*

The grass in the clearing blew over with the force of his dragon's wings. "Tiny" was now his name, for better or worse. Likely worse. *Only one person would name my great and fearsome beast something so entirely insulting.*

With a quiet sigh, he looked out at the landscape. It was lush and green, with flowers blooming in every color. Birds were chirping and singing their songs of spring, reveling in the return of the seasons. He turned his attention to the clearing next to the glade where he knew he would find the elemental he had come looking for.

It was undeniably breathtaking.

And it meant chaos, war, and death.

Soon enough, the warmongering elementals would start their bids for power once more, not caring for those who were slaughtered or the destruction of homes and villages. But that was the least of his concern. Because amongst them, hiding somewhere on the isle, was Grinn—the demon and so-called Ash King.

Finding and stopping him was Mordred's first motive—all the rest had to wait.

It gave him a good reason to allow the elementals to choose

their paths forward. Would they seek to war with each other once more? Would they rally against him, unified against a common enemy? Or would they sensibly choose peace? Simply pick up the pieces of their ragged lives and appreciate the freedom he had granted them by smashing open the Crystal?

It had not been much of his choice at all, he had to admit. It had been in a fit of rage and pain that he had destroyed the Crystal. But now that the deed was done, and the magic had been freed, it would be dishonorable for him to immediately seek its return to a new prison.

No, he would have to give the elementals a *chance.* A chance to either prove their newfound wisdom or to flaunt this opportunity back in his face and seek war.

He would not be the one to start the bloodshed.

While he would never live up to the legend of his uncle, Mordred was not that much of a tyrant.

Though many would choose to argue.

He dismounted his dragon, patting the creature on the neck. He knew the elemental he had come to see would not harm him. Even if she was not notoriously peaceful, always choosing to play the diplomat, the simple fact remained that while he was in his iron armor, she *could not* harm him. None of the elementals could. It was his "unnatural state of being" that spurned the elementals to hate and distrust him, to turn against him.

Heading into the glade, his mind returned to the topic at hand. The Gossamer Lady was respected and nearly revered by all the others—she was ancient and powerful, though one would hardly guess at first blush. It felt wrong to storm her doorstep, so soon after she had returned to it.

Yet, if there was anyone in Avalon who would be able to help him locate the demon, it would be her.

But there was another reason why he felt more than a little guilty for barging in on the Gossamer Lady. For while she might be pleased to see a knight enter her home, he was not the one she would be wishing for.

No, it would be the Knight in Gold that she would far prefer.

They were wed, after all. Perhaps not in name—but in all other ways that mattered.

Mordred stopped at the edge of a pond that was covered with flowering lily pads. He could see the flash of brightly colored fish, some spotted in orange and red, some white, some blue. Dragonflies flitted about from reed to reed, flower to flower. Sitting on a rock in the center of the pond was the woman he had come to see.

She seemed to shimmer and glow with the world around her. She was running a brush along her straight black hair, humming quietly as she did. Long, delicate wings like a butterfly's were folded at her back, the ends just barely touching the water.

She wore a sheer dress of pale blue that gathered and folded around her.

He rested his hand on the hilt of his sword.

"Hello, Zoe. Galahad sends his love."

THREE

"Do you come to injure me, Prince in Iron?"

Mordred frowned, though he was not surprised. "No."

"Then stay your blade. I shall do you no harm." The Gossamer Lady finally turned to look at him, her eyes a brilliant magenta that shimmered and changed colors as he watched to a pale blue that matched her dress. "How fares my love?"

"He is well. He misses you deeply." It was against his better instinct to remove his hand from his hilt, but he did so anyway.

"Why is it that he is not the one who has come to visit?"

"Because I have not allowed it."

She sighed. "You still hold him prisoner."

"Yes." This was not going well. "I have come to request your aid, Gossamer Lady."

That made her laugh. Not cruelly, perhaps—but not precisely jovially either. "Oh? When last we met, you were dragging me to that terrible prison of your making."

"When last we met, the demon had been captured, and the others attempted to murder me. Including you." He kept his expression calm, and his voice flat. He had not come here to argue. "Out of pity for your connection to Galahad, I imprisoned you last."

"Yes! Such pity, such *kindness*,' she scoffed. "To see all my brethren, my friends, my world—fade away and be trapped, piece by piece. To see the beauty of Avalon drained away by a cruel prince fueled by revenge."

He shook his head. "I have not come here to reminisce, Zoe."

"Then, allow me to guess at your reason." She stood from the stone, her wings unfurling as she flitted from the rock to the shore. She was short and small of frame—he towered over her. But it did not trouble her. "You seek the demon once more."

"He will destroy this world if left to his own devices. He will turn Avalon into a ring of hell if we allow him. No matter what you think of me and my *kindness*, surely you do not wish to see this world put to the torch." He watched her carefully, attempting to keep the resentment out of his voice. He failed. Rather miserably, he might add.

"And what do you wish for me to do? Find him for you?" She floated from the ground, hovering in mid-air effortlessly, her wings gently swaying as she did. It at least put them at equal height.

"Yes. You have a connection to this land that is stronger than any other. If he has returned, if he is setting the world ablaze, certainly you must know."

"And why would I help you? Why would I aid you, dark prince?" She chuckled, floating away from him a few feet.

"To protect Avalon."

"You say that as if your method is the only one worth pursuing. Have you not considered another way forward that does not involve iron blades and iron cages?"

"I am allowing you all to remain free for—"

"Allowing!" Her expression turned cold. "Mordred, Prince in Iron? You have been alone in this world for too long. You have forgotten your place in all this, usurper. You stole our lives away to reign supreme."

"I imprisoned you all to save this world."

"And it is for that reason that I know it was not out of the kindness of your heart that you *allowed* us our freedom. No. Your heart has not changed."

It has. More than you know. But he did not say the words. They were not for her. "Will you aid me in locating the demon?"

"No."

"You will choose to let the world burn?"

"No." She flitted closer to him. "There is another way."

"Do tell."

She chuckled. "Oh, prince. I have tried to sway you before. I shall not waste my breath again."

His jaw ticked. "Zoe—"

Her eyes flashed to black from lid to lid, as a terrible darkness came over her. The pond and all the life around it was no longer a serene oasis, but a rancid swamp. "*Begone.*" She blinked. And like that, the darkness was gone, and the world returned to the way it was before.

She was Avalon, through and through.

For better or worse.

Turning and leaving without another word, Mordred steeled himself against the task that lay before him. He would have to hunt the demon himself.

And if any other elementals stood in his way?

So be it.

Let them dig their own graves.

* * *

It was a solid day of riding before Lancelot found a town large enough to perhaps know something of what had happened.

And large enough that not every single peasant hid from him. For no matter how he called after them to say that he was no longer a servant of the prince, it seemed nobody believed him.

Not that Lancelot much blamed them for their fear.

Seeking out an inn, he pushed open the door to the tavern to see what information he could find. Barmen were usually the best gossips, even if they had to be paid for their trouble. That was no trouble for him.

There were some benefits to being an elemental of silver.

Letting his helm melt back into him, he walked up to the bar. The man behind it was big, gruff, older, and had a decent number of scars that told Lancelot quite quickly that the big man had been in his share of brawls. Likely inside his own establishment.

"I mean no trouble." Summoning several silver coins, Lancelot placed them down onto the wood surface. "Only information and a pint."

"That'll buy you the information." The barman sniffed dismissively. "What's it to you to double that for a pint, since you can just make more?"

"If I were to flood the town with silver, it would hardly have value anymore, now would it?" Still, Lancelot summoned more of the coins and put them down next to the others. "There. For the pint."

The man did not hesitate to slide the currency off the surface and pocket it. He poured Lancelot a pint, as requested, before standing in front of him, eyeing the knight warily. "What do you want?"

"I found myself in the Crystal at the hands of the Prince in Iron. And now, I find myself strangely freed and the world's magic restored. I want to know what year it is and who paid the price for our freedom." He chugged half the pint before letting out a grunt. It was warm and terrible. But it was beer. And that was all that mattered at the moment.

Though he would not be buying a second.

"I expect not much time has passed at all. His knights"—the gruff man scoffed—"his *other* knights have all been called back to his keep. Likely preparing for war."

That was a safe bet. Lancelot nodded. "And the other elementals?"

"Haven't seen them. I'm sure they're all lying low, licking their wounds. Nobody's come in here, at any rate. Not until you." The man narrowed his eyes. "What'd you do to wind up in the Crystal?"

"Tried to betray him. Well, I couldn't. Not on account of the spell that kept me enslaved to him." Lancelot snorted. "So I tried to convince his new love to do it for me."

The barman raised a thick brown eyebrow in disbelief. "Love? The prince?"

"A human girl from Earth, turned into a fire elemental by some unknown magic." Lancelot shrugged. "Matters not. I suspect she's dead now. She must be the one who shattered the Crystal. Do you know if she lives?"

"Haven't heard anything about her. I suspect the same as you—that she's a goner. May she rest in peace." The barman shook his head. "Messy lot, you bastards. Always causing more mayhem than you're worth. Do me a favor and get out before trouble follows you here."

"You will not have an argument from me, friend." Lancelot downed the rest of his beer and placed the empty mug back down on the wood surface with a quiet *thunk*. "I find myself with a new mission, regardless." Smirking, he pushed up from the stool and headed to the door. "I have a prince to kill and a young lady to avenge."

Lancelot heard the barman mutter something along the lines of *fucking elementals*, but Lancelot neither cared enough to retort nor was he in a bad enough of a mood to want to pick a fight over it.

In fact, he was in quite a good mood, all things considered. Summoning his silver steed again, he climbed atop the elegant creature, all made of smooth lines and careful craftsmanship—not like the twisted, hideous amalgams that Mordred created—and rode for the direction of the keep.

It would take him some time to arrive there, as he suspected he was on the far side of the island from the Prince in Iron's stronghold.

That would serve him nicely, however—it took time to build an army.

Time and charisma.

Two things that he considered himself to have in abundance. There was only one problem—the army he needed to raise would be of other elementals.

And he could not imagine that was going to go well.

There was one woman he could seek out that might not kill him at first sight—one who might be sympathetic enough to lend her assistance. But there was a chance that she would consider herself too stuck in the middle between the factions to truly choose, as had been the case so long ago. But if Lancelot *could* convince her to join him... then others would fall in line behind her.

Because the Gossamer Lady was beloved by all. And that included, chief amongst all—Galahad.

* * *

"I'm not gonna burn down the village, you asswipe!"

Gwen couldn't believe that somehow Merlin was even worse as a person than he was as a cat.

"Useless child!" Merlin huffed and bared his teeth at her, several missing from what must have been years of fighting. "Teach them to fear us!"

"No." She folded her arms across her chest. "I won't. They haven't done anything wrong."

"If you wait for others to strike the first blow, you will not live long." He turned his back to her, stalking off. "Stupid—"

Cutting him off, she shoved her finger in his face, angrily pointing at him. He had to pull up abruptly to keep from crashing into her. She glowered. "You know what? I'm sick of you being such an asshole to me. It's not productive. And it certainly doesn't make me want to help you."

"Helping me is helping *you*, don't forget." He glared right back. "Or else you're stuck here until you get us both killed."

Sighing, she shook her head. He didn't get it. "Whatever."

"I will speak slower for you. We need supplies. I am going to take them. With or without your help. That is simply the way of it." He stepped around her, clearly done arguing.

Throwing up her hands, she opted to follow him.

They made it about fifty feet before a regiment of armed soldiers trotted up to them. They pulled their shields close as a man on horseback took up the rear.

"Stop!" The mounted man held up his hand. "Elementals, begone from here."

"I told you." Merlin shot her a look.

"Shut up. They're just scared, and you're not helping." Gwen took a step forward and smiled at the man. "I apologize for my... uh... angry friend here, we mean you no harm."

Merlin snorted.

She continued, ignoring him. "We're just traveling through. We're headed—"

"Do not tell them where we are going," Merlin snapped.

"We would appreciate any help you could give us."

"Help?" The man blinked, clearly not having expected that. His horse shifted nervously from one side to the other, eyeing Merlin warily. Honestly, Gwen didn't blame the animal in the slightest. Merlin gave off a *weird vibe.* A weird and very not-human vibe, despite his current appearance. She wondered what he really was. But that was a conversation for another time.

"Right. Like, a horse, or supplies, or whatever you might be willing to spare." She was tempted to ask for a cart, but they'd probably be doing a lot of camping, so it would just end up being a pain in the ass. She hadn't ever gone camping in a medieval-esque world before. "A tent, food, supplies for sleeping in the woods. That kind of stuff."

"We are elementals. We take what we need. We don't *ask,*" her "friend" grumbled to her.

Glaring at him, she planted her hands on her hips. "And that's probably why everybody fucking hates elementals. So, maybe you should try shutting up and having an ounce of empathy for once."

Merlin muttered something under his breath but didn't interject any further.

Turning back to the soldiers, she did her best to smile. "Sorry about that."

"If we provide you with supplies, will you leave without trouble?" The man on horseback patted the creature's neck, trying to calm his steed. "We do not wish to see our homes razed."

"Y—yeah. Sure. That works." How bad were the elementals before the Iron Crystal that everybody was terrified of them? Well, Gwen *did* have scary burny superpowers and was walking along with a guy threatening their whole town. She supposed that would make her a major threat to people who had limited or no magic of their own.

Her brain skipped like a record on that sentence. It was amazing how normal it was all becoming to her in such a short period of time. But she supposed that was to be expected when she had to adjust to so much all at once. Dragons, fire powers, living armor, demons, and Arthurian knights.

"I ask that you stay here under guard." The man clicked his tongue, turning his horse around. He didn't wait for her to reply as he rode off into the village, likely to gather up what she had listed.

The soldiers were all staring at them in various shades of fear. It was strange having people afraid of her—she wasn't sure she liked it. She consoled herself by scratching Eod on the head between the ears. He sat down at her side and leaned up against her thigh.

Dogs made everything better.

Merlin was getting antsy, pacing around behind her, making the soldiers more nervous by the second. When minutes stretched by, she sat on a nearby wooden fence to wait. It was maybe a half hour later that the first man returned, holding the reins of a mare. Saddlebags, and rolled-up stuff that was probably a tent and some blankets, were all tied to the animal.

"Here," the soldier said. He stayed a few steps away from them, clearly not wanting to get too close.

"Wow, thank you." Gwen smiled. It was nice not to have the soldiers turn on them and attack them. Or betray their trust. She patted the neck of the mare, who snorted and nudged her, wondering if she had food. "Soon, honey."

"Please, go." The soldiers stood aside, clearing the road out of the village.

"We should set them ablaze now," Merlin commented to her quietly. "Teach them a lesson for their rudeness."

"They aren't being rude, they're terrified." She rolled her eyes and climbed onto the horse's back. She didn't even bother offering Merlin the horse instead. Screw him. He could walk.

Clicking her tongue, she pulled on the reins of the mare to turn her around. As they passed the soldiers, she smiled again. "Thank you all again. I'm sorry for any hardship this has caused."

They all stared at her blankly, as if the words were foreign to them.

Merlin walked beside the horse, mumbling to himself as they headed out of the little collection of homes and back into the woods. It felt nice to be out of the open, and without men with spears and swords staring them down.

Eod was happily running ahead of them, sniffing at every blade of grass. Gwen realized that the dog had probably never smelled spring before in his entire life. How many people had been born on Avalon, only knowing gray skies and eternal fall?

She'd ask Merlin why everybody hated elementals, but she was pretty damn sure she knew. He'd just proven it to her. First, they seemed to think of themselves as gods and conducted themselves accordingly. They likely rampaged through people's homes and villages without any thought for the people they were hurting.

And two, if Mordred had been telling her the truth, elementals were always fighting and probably making more of a mess of things in the process.

She wondered if Lancelot was okay, wherever he was. She assumed the Crystal had released him when it had cracked and released all the magic. She could use a friendly face and a smile. Well, okay, besides Eod's. A friendly face and a smile that understood English.

Merlin was terrible company. Though at least he had gone silent and stopped berating her and complaining.

Suddenly... she was thinking of Mordred again. Part of her wished he was there, even though she knew how very, very poorly that would go. Her heart ached as she replayed in her mind the look of betrayal on his face. She hadn't wanted to do it.

But the Crystal was *wrong*. There had to be another way to let the magic of Avalon stay free without the elementals ruining everything. And that looped her back to Grinn, who wanted his power back in large part so he could try to conquer the island again.

Could she really go home, knowing she was responsible for suffering and death? Once she got back, this would all turn into a strange dream. Part of her might always wonder what had become of everyone, but she'd be safe. It wouldn't be her problem. Avalon wasn't her responsibility. Right?

Why did it feel like she was just trying to convince herself and failing?

"So, who are you?" She decided she had to break the silence. She was just getting sucked into sad thoughts. "Clearly, you're not Merlin. So, what's your real name?"

"No."

"Your real name is *no*?" She blinked.

He let out a long-suffering sigh. "I am not going to tell you my name. It still isn't safe for you to know."

"Who the fuck am I gonna tell? The dog?"

"Everyone we meet." He grunted. "It will make things complicated. So, no. You can keep calling me by that idiotic name for now."

"You suck."

"I'm aware."

They fell into silence for a long stretch of time again. She tried another tactic. "How old are you?"

"Why do you care?"

"I'm trying to make conversation. To learn something about you."

"Please don't."

"Well, it's either that or I start singing 'Ninety-Nine Bottles of Beer on the Wall' again."

He groaned. "Fine. I remember watching the humans scratch their first markings on cave walls. However long that was." It was clear he hated talking about himself.

"Wow. That explains all the scars and stuff. No offense, you look like you've seen some shit."

"That was all since coming here." His lips peeled back in another grimace. It reminded her of a cat about to snarl. "I *despise* Avalon."

"What happened?"

"The other elementals." He was rigid, once more fuming, the memory of his past triggering his rage. "They are greedy, jealous, capricious, treacherous, power-mad *fools*. They took my eye as a warning. The rest was from my fight to survive."

The other elementals took *his eye* as a warning.

Gwen's shoulders drooped. She had hoped to meet some more of them, to see what they were really like. They couldn't be *all* bad. Nobody was *all* bad, right? She looked at Merlin. Maybe she'd have to amend that belief.

Maybe Mordred was right. Maybe elementals shouldn't be free. It brought her thoughts back to the Prince in Iron like a trainwreck. God, she missed him.

Night began to fall in earnest, and it was time to set up camp. Surprisingly, Merlin didn't protest as she led the mare off into the woods, following a small creek, and found a clearing where they could safely set up.

The villagers had given them *tons* of stuff. A tent, two bedrolls, plenty of dried goods, some fishing supplies, canteens for water. She smiled. They might have been generous out of fear, but at least they were generous.

Taking everything off the mare, she set it all aside to give the poor animal a break. She tied a rope to the horse's bridle and attached the other end to a tree, giving the creature access to the creek and some space to lie down and sleep.

Merlin was sitting by the edge of the clearing, staring off into the darkness.

"I'll see if I can catch us some fish. Do you think we can risk having a fire?" She set out the bedrolls. Eod had no problem claiming one as his own, happily chewing on a stick. She supposed that would be hers.

Merlin squinted up at the sky. "Probably. A small fire, though."

That was fine by her. Taking out the fishing supplies, she sat by the shore and began putting a hook on a line.

"What are you doing?"

Glancing at him, it was her turn to play disgruntled. "What does it look like? Catching us some fish, like I said."

"With *that*?" He sighed. "You are an elemental."

"Yeah, a fire elemental, it's not like I can just—" She paused, and then looked at the creek. She decided to try something. Sticking her hand into the water, she tried to set the water itself on fire. It hissed and steamed. And then began to boil.

A few fish floated to the surface. Cackling, she quickly rushed to grab them with a net. The water was quickly renewed with more from the creek. Wading into the stream, she decided to repeat that a few more times. When she had collected enough to feed her, Merlin, and Eod, she headed back to the shore.

"It's like those people who fish with dynamite."

"Humans." Merlin lowered himself down until his head was resting atop his crossed arms.

Getting a small campfire going was even easier. After gutting the fish, she put them on sticks and propped them up over the campfire to cook. "I used to love camping with my dad. His family is from Oregon, so every summer we'd go out there and spend a week in the woods. I guess that'll come in handy."

Merlin simply grunted. They ate their dinner in relative silence, with Eod happily devouring everything she gave him. After chucking the remains back into the creek, she lay down on her bedroll. She had it to herself for precisely two minutes before Eod was flopped down beside her, curled up by her legs.

Smiling, she scratched his head and gazed up at the starry

sky. It was beautiful, even if she didn't recognize any of the constellations.

She had wanted an adventure.

And here it was. Going to see a sorcerer. She'd try to ignore the rest of the impending doom and gloom until she had more facts to go on. No point in having a panic attack over things she couldn't predict.

Huh.

Now that she thought about it, she hadn't had a panic attack that day at all. Which was damn good, considering all the shit that kept happening to her. She should feel proud of herself, but something kept needling at her. It took her a long time staring up at the sky to realize what it was.

Mordred.

It was hard to feel pride when she also felt guilty. She wished she could go ask for his help or his advice. Or just sit and laugh with him. Maybe play a game to pass the time. She wanted to feel his arms around her, to hear him say that everything was going to be okay. To have him kiss her and say he forgave her. But that wasn't going to happen. She had gone and fucked all that up.

Time would tell if it had all been a mistake or not.

She rolled onto her side and kept a hand on Eod's fur as she shut her eyes and tried to fall asleep. Maybe she had made a mistake. Maybe she hadn't. Maybe the world was better now. Maybe it wasn't.

But one thing was undeniable now.

She cared about the Prince in Iron.

She cared about him a great deal.

And she just wished she could tell him that.

I'm sorry, Mordred.

FOUR

Mordred was brooding.

He knew he was. He was no fool. He had no misgivings about who and what he was. But it was either brood or fly into a rage and take his anger and frustrations out on those who had done nothing to deserve it.

The knights had all returned from patrolling the island, flying their dragons high above the forests and villages. But there was no sign of chaos—no burned homes, no fields left in cinders.

The demon was lying low. The bastard was a schemer and was likely licking his wounds and gaining strength in order to wage a full-scale assault. Mordred suspected he was likely gathering other elementals to stand against him. It would be the smart thing to do—what Mordred himself would do, in the demon's position.

Grinn would use the desire for bloody vengeance to create allies where there formerly were none. And Mordred had no allies, save for his knights who had little choice in the matter. No one—he doubted even Gwendolyn—might stand with him against Grinn.

Gwendolyn.

He sighed drearily at the thought of the young woman and put a gauntleted hand over his eyes. He was furious with her. He wanted to shake her like an impudent child. But damn him to the void, he *missed* her. Her laughter, her bright smile—her kiss. He had slept better with her at his side than he had in centuries.

He truly was a miserable, empty, pathetic, lonely shell of a man, wasn't he?

His uncle would be so very proud of him.

Laughing quietly at himself, he rested his head against the high-backed chair and shut his eyes. Mordred supposed he would be able to ask his uncle in person soon enough, as the others would come for him and see his head parted from his neck for his crimes.

Who was he kidding?

He was not bound for the same destination as the True King of the Britons. If there was a place where the righteous went to rest, Mordred was not destined for those shores. No matter how hard he had tried to be an honorable ruler—he would never be king.

When there was a tap on the jamb of his door, Mordred did not bother to look over. It was likely Galahad come to scold him for not attempting to sleep. Why bother?

Something rested down on the table next to him with a clink. Looking over, he furrowed his brow. It was a plate of food. When he saw who had come in, he understood. Shutting his eyes again, he braced himself for a lecture of a very different kind. "Hello, Maewenn."

"I see the plates the servants bring back—you haven't eaten properly in days."

"I fear I have not had much of an appetite." By the Ancients, he willed this conversation to be over with quickly.

"Considering recent events, I suppose I'm not surprised.

You have a penchant for punishing yourself." Maewenn rearranged the items on the plate, as if the presentation alone would change his mind.

"Do I, now?" He fought the urge to roll his eyes. "I had not noticed."

"Aye, be as sarcastic as you like, prince. The simple fact of the matter is that you'll need your strength. You know what'll follow now that you set them all free." She poured him a glass of wine.

"The thought had not crossed my mind." He finally shot a glance at the cook who was still fussing over the tray of food. "Do tell."

"Your tone won't work on me. Eat, prince. For those of us who still rely on you." She nudged the food closer to him. "Don't make me stand here and watch, like you're a child."

He sighed. There was no arguing with Maewenn once the cook had put her mind to something. Picking up the tray, he placed it on his lap and began with some of the grapes. He had not felt hungry until the taste hit his tongue.

His traitorous stomach growled.

"Not a word, cook," he warned the woman with the point of a claw.

She lifted her hands as if in surrender, showing he would get no comments out of her. "Only here to make sure you don't faint on us."

He muttered to himself, something not terribly flattering toward her, but decided to keep his grousing to himself. She was simply trying to look after him.

Clearly having accomplished her goal, the cook turned to leave. But after a few steps, the metal shoes of her armored form stopped thumping on the wood floor.

"Speak your mind, cook. It is not like you to withhold your opinion." Mordred tore off a hunk of bread and ate it. Now that he had begun, he knew he was likely to finish the plate.

"You did the right thing, letting them all go." Maewenn wrung her hands. "Especially Gwendolyn."

Yes, especially Gwendolyn. The thought of the firefly hit him with an unexpected pang. It had not been a calculated decision to destroy the Crystal. It had been from pain and anger that he had done it. Such rash decisions never ended well.

"I suspect I will die for it. They will wage war upon me, and my head will be on a pike on the garrison walls before the season is out." He sneered.

"I never said it was smart."

That made him laugh. Tired and half-hearted, but a laugh all the same. "Noted."

She turned to leave again.

After a pause, he said what he knew he should have said a long time ago. "Thank you."

"It's simply my job to feed you." She shrugged with a clank.

"I am not thanking you for the food."

Maewenn watched him silently for a moment, as if caught in shock. It was hard to tell, since the armor had no expression that could change. After a long pause, she curtsied, and left the room.

Silently, left alone with his thoughts once more, he made sure to empty his plate.

* * *

Lancelot slowed his horse to a walk as he followed the road closer to the stream. He was seeking out Zoe, the Gossamer Lady—Galahad's lady love. She was one of the most powerful, and one of the most widely respected of the elementals. If he could secure her assistance, his attempts to raise an army of individuals prone to violent infighting *might* succeed.

Might.

Or it might fail spectacularly. That, to be honest, was where he would put his coins on the table if he were forced to place a bet. But Mordred had to be stopped. And Lancelot could not call himself a knight if he allowed Gwendolyn's sacrifice to go unavenged.

Now if only—

Something wrapped around his ankle, and dragged him from his horse unceremoniously and without warning, dropping him onto the packed dirt with a heavy *thud* of armor.

He groaned.

Whatever had grabbed him was now pulling him backwards. Scrambling for his sword, he slashed at whatever it was. His blade cleaved through it without much trouble. It took a moment for him to realize what it was.

A branch, about as thick around as his thumb, and covered in jagged, horrid thorns that were now stained with his blood. One would not think that a vine would stand much of a chance against his armor—but it had woven its way in between the plates.

The moment it took him to register what had attacked him was all the time his assailant needed to make another attempt. A second vine slashed around Lancelot's throat, squeezing hard enough to restrict his air, several of the thorns piercing through the gaps in his chainmail.

Grabbing the vine with one hand, he slashed at it with his sword, chopping himself loose. Staggering to his feet, he yanked the thorny branch away from him and quickly worked to regain his footing.

Though he suspected that if his attacker wanted him dead... he would be so already.

For he knew the woman standing some twenty feet away from him, her hands tight into fists. She looked like a street urchin—her clothing was ragged and torn; her skin was smudged with dirt. A tangled mess of dark hair shrouded her features. She might have been as tall as a pony on a good day, and easy to mistake for just some abandoned young woman.

But he knew better.

He coughed and wiped at the blood that was oozing down his chainmail. "Lady Thorn. How nice to see you." Unlike many others, this elemental chose to keep her original name to herself. Or, perhaps, she did not recall it. She was simply Thorn.

She spat on the ground in front of her. "Scum. I want you to bring a message to your master."

"He is no longer my master." Lancelot kept his sword at the ready.

Thorn tilted her head to the side. "Liar."

"I will prove it to you, if you promise not to strike when I am vulnerable." He slowly, carefully, sheathed his sword.

"I could have ripped you apart before you even felt the first sting, lapdog." Thorn sneered.

"Trust me. I know." Lancelot vanished his armor, deciding that a show of trust here might earn him a powerful, if unpredictable, ally. Or at least let him escape with his life. Thorn kept her dark eyes locked on him the whole time as he pulled aside the fabric of his shirt, revealing the spot on his chest where the shard of magic had kept him enslaved for so many years.

The scar was there from its presence—but the magic itself was gone. "I was put into the Crystal for scheming against him. When it shattered, I was freed of his influence."

Thorn watched him curiously in silence for a moment. "What is your mission now, then, knight?"

"To kill the rusted bastard and throw his fetid corpse over the cliff into the ocean." Lancelot did not bother to try to hide his hatred. He knew he would not be able to—and in this instance, it might prove useful.

"Then we have the same goal." Thorn looked off into the

woods thoughtfully. "I am planning on marching on the keep and killing him myself. Perhaps two of us would fare better."

"We will need many more than two to succeed, Lady Thorn." He let his shoulders loosen and relaxed his posture just a bit. He did not trust her—he never would—but he would not question any allies he could garner. The adage was as old as he was, but an enemy of an enemy was indeed a friend.

She swore, and spat on the ground. "I can handle him."

"I… do not wish to discount your penchant for violence, nor your skill, my lady—but this is Mordred. We cannot let our mutual anger get the best of us. We must raise a larger force of elementals."

"I have no patience for this. I want him dead *now*." She stomped her foot like a child.

Amongst her many traits, Thorn was also a tiny bit insane.

"And I sympathize, believe me I do. I was that man's slave for over a millennium and a half. Do you not think I wish to see him suffer?" Lancelot grimaced. "But I also wish to survive this fight."

Thorn sighed. "Very well. You have seven days. I will meet you at the keep."

"I—"

Thorn turned and walked into the underbrush, cutting him off. She became *part* of the tangled thicket and disappeared.

Lancelot rubbed a hand over his face. *Elementals.*

But at least he had the start of his army.

At least there was that.

* * *

Mordred found the Knight in Gold standing upon the ramparts, watching the forest that was now in full spring bloom. Between the keep and the forest, a field of grass swayed, green and fresh, in the setting sunlight. It was beautiful—even if it was a sign of the mayhem and the death that was certain to come.

Galahad was on watch, waiting for the inevitable army to come and lay siege to their home.

And perhaps he was on watch for someone else as well.

Mordred stood beside him, his black hood over his head, choosing to shield his eyes from the glare of the setting sun as it slipped closer to the horizon. He did not ask what troubled the knight. He knew quite well what it was.

Ages ago, with the formation of the Iron Crystal, Galahad was forced to part ways with the woman he loved. He was forced to watch as Mordred trapped Zoe in the Crystal. Mordred had done it last out of respect to his companion and closest excuse for a friend. But perhaps saving her for last was crueler than it had been kind.

Now, both of their hearts belonged to those who were doomed for imprisonment or worse.

Out there was the soul Galahad had not seen in over three hundred years. One who Mordred was certain he would give anything to hold in his arms once more. One who Mordred had gone to see instead, knowing that if he let Galahad free, he would never see the Knight in Gold again. He and Zoe would go into hiding, far away from all the strife and troubles of the world. Somewhere they could simply go to be together.

For Mordred had the same desire, if far more fledgling, for Gwendolyn.

"I cannot spare your presence," Mordred broke the silence. "You are my strongest knight."

"I know," Galahad responded, his voice quiet and doing little to hide the knight's clear grief. "I have not asked."

"You needn't speak the words."

"Nor you to explain yourself." Galahad's eyes were sorrowful and tired as he kept his gaze locked upon the trees—likely wishing and dreading for the glowing form of his lady love to appear. Wishing to see her once more while dreading what he knew would have to follow. "Tell me, is she well?"

Mordred nodded once before turning his attention back to the same woods. "Perhaps I have not come to deliver an explanation, but instead an apology." At Galahad's silence, he continued. "For I find myself in the rather unusual and unpleasant situation of being a hypocrite. And if there is any shred of dignity or honor left in my blackened soul, I hope it is to recognize when I am being quite distinctly inequitable."

"You have always known when you are being unjust, my prince." Galahad straightened his shoulders, easily adding to his already considerable height when he was not slouching. "It is simply that you believe that the success of your mission outweighs all cost to those around you."

"I believed so, until Gwendolyn."

"Yes, I suppose." Galahad smirked, just barely, with a curl to that gray mustache. "I will confess to some guilty satisfaction at your recent struggles. That you might know what it is like to lose the one you love."

Mordred did not bother to pretend that he did not love Gwendolyn. It must be brutally obvious to the Knight in Gold. Especially since his rash decision to let the young fire elemental go free. Something he had not allowed Zoe.

"Tell me, Galahad, do you despise me?"

The Knight in Gold stood there silently for a long moment, clearly debating his answer. After careful consideration, he answered with a single word. "No."

Mordred would always value the knight for his honesty and his integrity. "I will not rebuild the Iron Crystal. Not until I am given no other choice."

"Oh?" Galahad sounded surprised.

"I would hardly be a just ruler if I seek to imprison those guilty of no crime. I will wait for the elementals to seek the ruination of this world once more. If—*when*—they repeat their actions? Then, I shall rebuild the Crystal. But for now, I shall not hunt them down. Not until given cause. There is only one who I will seek to destroy." He needn't name the bastard.

Galahad smiled, full of tentative hope. Hope that he might have a future of peace ahead of him. But his smile quickly faded as the likely reality set in.

For asking elementals to keep peace was like asking a cow to fly.

You might be able to hurl it from a trebuchet and replicate the intent, but it would not be long until it came crashing down.

But hope was insidious and hard to root out. Galahad nodded once, in thanks, and went back to his silent watch of the forest.

Mordred left the knight to his post and decided he was, for once, quite weary.

He simply hoped his dreams were not plagued with the sound of laughter and the taste of woodsmoke and spices against his lips. How sad had he become that he could not stand to be apart from a woman he had only known for a flicker of a single candle in all his long years?

How pathetic.

But it was unavoidable. Letting out a wavering breath, he headed down to the chamber where the shattered remains of the Iron Crystal still sat like a monument to his own foolishness. Most of the shards in the pit had gone dark, the magic leaking out and returning to the world. But a few remained shimmering in their strange opalescence. Finding one that was the proper size and strength, he plucked it from the ruins and went to fetch the second half of what he needed.

Walking into Gwen's chambers made him flinch. He was glad there was no one to witness his brokenhearted malaise. Finding a hairbrush on a table, he was happy to see plenty of her multi-colored, fiery strands on the pillow. Gathering them up, he returned to his own quarters, shutting and locking the door behind him.

Sitting in front of his fire, he straightened the strands of her hair until they were all aligned in the same direction. He wound them around the crystal slowly, thoughts of her heavy on his mind.

Was she safe?

Was she with Lancelot?

Did she regret what she had done?

Had their time together meant anything to her?

Or was it all part of her lie?

Holding the crystal perched between the points of his claws on one hand, he breathed a slow exhale onto the shard as though it were an ember of a dying flame. It flickered, glowed brighter and, like the fire in his hearth, changed from its array of colors to oranges and reds and yellows.

The hair he had wound around it had become part of it. Changing the magic to be linked to her. Carefully, so as not to damage the spell he had just cast, he created a delicate iron cage for the shard, suspending it from a thin chain that he placed around his neck.

It was a simple spell. One made for lovers who were parted and could not stand not to see each other. His mother had taught him how to use it to spy on his enemies. He supposed he was not entirely certain which Gwendolyn was at the moment.

Toying with the gem, he stood and readied himself for bed. Now he was both eager for sleep and yet dreaded it in the same breath.

Shedding his armor and his clothes, he climbed beneath the sheets and shut his eyes.

Do you feel my absence as I feel yours, Gwendolyn?

FIVE

Gwen was dreaming of home.

She was standing on the bottom rung of a wood fence that had been backed with chicken wire. Otherwise, they'd have to fetch their goats from the neighbor's parcel again. She wasn't sure why they always wandered off into Mr. Belcher's yard, but goats generally defied explanations.

She threw a fistful of the feed into the grass, watching as they all came charging out from deeper in the field, bleating in greeting and excitement.

It was a beautiful sunny day. A gentle wind was pushing her hair—which was brown, not blazing red—into her eyes. One of the billy goats came up to her and tried to steal the bag out of her hands. "Hey! Jerk." She scratched his head. "There's plenty for everybody."

The goat bleated and bonked his head into her arm. Not roughly—just insistently.

"Yeah, yeah, *fine*. You're so spoiled." She lowered the bag a bit so he could shove his head in there and gobble up a few eager mouthfuls before she took the bag back away. "Now eat out of the grass like the rest of the peasants, huh?"

After she was done throwing out enough for their breakfast, she rolled up the top of the bag and turned to head back to the barn.

And in that moment, the world around her snapped. Like the flick of a switch, she was no longer on her farm in Kansas. She wasn't even standing in Mordred's keep. She had no clue where she was—but it was like something out of a nightmare.

The walls around her were immense, soaring high up overhead into arches and peaks that reminded her of a gothic church. But everything was made from iron—some rusted, some not. Chandeliers hung from the ceiling and cast eerie flickering shadows. Where there should have been beautiful wood carvings, there were twisted, arching and tangled vines made from metal. She recognized the style—it was like the patterns that covered Mordred's armor.

Mordred.

And as if thinking his name was all it took, the candles flickered in a sudden gust of wind. In one of those brief moments of darkness, he appeared in front of her.

She took a staggering step back.

He was a thing of nightmares. He wore his plate armor, save for the helm, but his face was obscured by the heavy black hood of his cloak. It was like the first time she saw him—more of a terrifying force of nature than a man.

Trying to burst into flames to protect herself, she realized she couldn't. It seemed in her dreams she was still human.

Mordred took a step toward her.

Gwen did the only sensible thing.

She turned and ran for her life.

The hallways were twisted and warped, and seemed to make no sense in their pattern or layout as she ran as fast as she could. She took a wrong turn, however, and wound up standing in a version of Mordred's study—the one with the huge metal table that had the map of Avalon etched into its surface.

There was only one way in or out, and she had just barreled through it. Jumping out the window was probably a *terrible* idea. Turning to head back to the hallway and try again, she almost tripped over her own feet.

He was standing there in the jamb, nearly taking up the whole of the door. He was once more walking toward her, clearly not in any hurry. It demonstrated exactly how little her running had mattered.

"I—um—Mordred—I—" She put up her hands in front of her, pathetically trying to slow him down. "I—I—" She wanted to say she could explain. But she couldn't. There was nothing to tell him. She had lied to him and betrayed him.

The words died on her tongue.

And she doubted this nightmare version of Mordred cared. He was just a product of her guilty mind. She kept retreating from him as he stalked toward her. "I—I'm sorry, I really am, I—I didn't—" She squeaked as she backed into the table. She glanced down at it to see what she had hit and, in that moment, he closed the distance between them.

He didn't say a word.

A clawed gauntlet snapped around her throat, pressing her down to the table, firmly and without any room for argument. He didn't slam her down—it wasn't violent—but there was nothing she could do to stop him. She quickly found herself on her back on the table, his massive form looming over her as he kept one hand around her throat and the other, with those wicked and sharp talons, pressed to the table next to her head. He wasn't hurting her. But she knew there wasn't any point in struggling.

His face was lost in the darkness of his hood as he leaned down over her. She was shivering. Both from fear, and... from something else, entirely.

God above, she had problems.

Because the sight of him over her did confusing and terrible things to her.

"Mordred, I..." She didn't know what to say.

He lowered his head down closer to hers, strands of his iron-gray hair brushing against her cheek. His breath was hot as it washed against her, his voice little more than a low rumble near her ear. "Run and hide, Gwendolyn. Run and stay hidden for as long as you can. Because when I find you, I will never let you escape."

All the air rushed out of her lungs at his words. And she didn't know when she'd get the chance to fill them again as he crashed his lips against hers in a fiery, needy, demanding kiss that she was certain was trying to suck the soul out of her body.

One of her hands was twisted in the fabric of his cloak. The other was pressed to the side of his throat, feeling the race of his pulse beneath her hand. She wasn't trying to push him away. God help her, she was trying to pull him closer.

He broke the kiss, leaving her breathless, as he trailed his lips to her ear once more.

"*You belong to me.*"

With those words from him, her dream shattered. It was still dark, and now she was covered in a cold sweat.

Stupid dreams. Stupid goddamn dreams. Gwen rolled onto her side, and fell back into a restless, but at least dreamless, sleep. It'd be time to get on the road soon, and she'd need as much sleep as she could get.

Dawn came and they set about packing up their camp without much fuss or conversation. It was easy to be distracted by the tasks at hand, let alone all the beautiful colors and wonderful sights of Avalon.

And she also had a new game. It was called "Annoy the Shit Out of Merlin." It was a really easy game, to be fair. But it was super fun all the same. Today, it was by singing as she rode atop the mare—who she had named Sunshine, which *also* annoyed Merlin.

She knew she didn't have a bad singing voice. And she was just amusing herself as they spent yet another day walking along the dirt road through the woods. "How far are we from the sorcerer?"

"Another day or two," the old man replied. "Thankfully."

Old. To be fair, he didn't look that old. Maybe in his late forties? But late forties, sailor-style, that was to say he looked far more weathered than his years. Besides, he said he was as old as humanity anyway. Old still counted.

Gwen shook her head. It was weird to think that in just a few days, she probably wouldn't have fire powers anymore. She had barely started getting used to them. Even *enjoying* them a little. She still hadn't even answered the question of whether or not she wanted to go home.

She pictured a life, living in the keep with Mordred, playing with the dogs and raising new puppies as the years went by. They could have been happy together. They could have had a life—hundreds of years, maybe—spent in each other's company. It was a fantasy. A fairytale.

But nothing was ever that easy, was it?

Mordred had to be a cruel tyrant, keeping everyone and everything a prisoner or under his iron thumb. Without Merlin, Gwen would have no power. She'd be just another stupid human lost in a world of magic that was going to kill her someday sooner rather than later.

She had gone from a cast-iron frying pan into the elemental fire. It was becoming more and more clear that she probably had no business being in Avalon. Which sucked. She had wanted an adventure. And for a few moments now and then, as she was riding along in the woods watching magical critters scurry through the underbrush, it felt... nice.

And then she remembered the asshole not-cat walking next

to her. She wanted to go home. She wanted to stay. She missed Mordred *immensely*. But she knew there wouldn't be a fairytale ending for them.

She figured there were a few ways this could play out. The first thing they had to discover was what happened when Merlin managed to pry them apart. There was no question that she didn't want to spend the rest of eternity dealing with the grumpy jerk.

If this wizard that Merlin thought was so great could separate their life forces, Gwen would have a choice to make. The first option would be to have Merlin send her home. In which case, she'd go back to Earth, and all this would be no more real than last night's strange dream. She'd have to live the rest of her life questioning her sanity and wondering what had become of Mordred, Galahad, Lancelot, and all the others when war inevitably broke out. Would they go back to being trapped in the Crystal? Or would Mordred lose, and die?

She would never know.

If she stayed in Avalon, she would be a mortal. Weak and easily murdered. Assuming she lived any sort of length of time... she'd, what? Try to make amends with Mordred? That wasn't likely. He probably despised her now.

No, all it would do was give her a front-row seat for the mayhem and the war between the elementals. As a squishy human prone to easily dying.

Either way?

Everybody probably died. Or were worse off for her having come to Avalon.

Her mood failed, and she stopped singing.

"Thank *fuck*, as you like to say." Merlin shuddered dramatically. "I thought perhaps you were trying to drive me insane."

She pulled on the reins of the horse, stopping the mare. "I don't think I want to split our life forces, Merlin."

"What?" He stopped and turned to her. "Are you insane?"

"No. Avalon is fucked and I'm the reason for a massive war. If I give you your power back, I won't be able to help."

"You have already done enough. Because of you, the Iron Crystal is broken. You've already started a massive war." He sneered. "It's too late to save your conscience."

"No, it isn't. I can talk to Mordred. I can talk to the elementals. Maybe—"

"Maybe *what*, you idiot child?" He laughed. "You can talk some *sense* into them? Please! Don't be a fool. Elementals cannot agree on anything. Ever. They are a danger to everyone and everything around them. Do you think they'll just forgive him and move on?" He snorted. "Come on. Let's go."

"No." She squared her shoulders.

Merlin put his hand over his face. "Listen to me very carefully, child." He took a step toward her. Sunshine began to step side to side nervously, not liking his nearness. "I am going to separate our life forces. One way or another. I will *not* suffer through an eternity tethered to you. If I have to drag you there, kicking and screaming, I will,' he snarled.

Eod began to bark at him, getting in between them to protect her.

Merlin reared back his hand as if to strike the dog.

"Don't you *dare*!" Gwen hopped off the mare and stormed up to him. Grabbing him by his beard, she yanked his head down roughly. "You touch that dog and I swear to fuck I will rip your limbs off!"

Merlin blinked his one good eye, shocked, and took a step back.

"You leave the animals *out* of this, do you understand?" She kept screaming at him, her hands balled into fists. Oh. Hey. She was on fire again. Apparently, she burst into flames when scared or angry. Fun.

Well, she burst into flames for now anyway. Taking a deep breath, she forced herself to breathe and put out her fire.

Walking over to Eod, she crouched and petted the dog, trying to calm him down. He was still growling at Merlin, his tail tucked between his legs and his fur standing up on his back.

"Good boy, Eod. You're good. You did it." She chuckled. "You did a mighty protect."

The praise seemed to do the trick. Eod almost instantly simmered down and began to lick her cheek.

"I will not hurt the dog," Merlin said after a pause. "But you are coming with me to see the wizard. I will have us split apart, regardless of your petty qualms."

"And if I refuse? Would you really drag me there?"

"We have no choice, Gwendolyn. The way we are linked is unnatural. It cannot last. Think of me what you will, think of this world what you will—you aren't meant to have this power." He stared off down the road. "We don't even know if the wizard *can* separate us. At least let us go there to find out." His voice fell, growing almost vulnerable for the first time. "I wish to be free. I wish to be whole. I wish to be alone."

Frowning, she couldn't help but feel bad for him, even just a little. She had his power, and because of that, he was suffering. She couldn't do that to him forever. It was cruel. "I'll go with you. I'll let the wizard split us up if he can. But if he can, we get to talk through the details first, okay?" She stuck her hand out to him.

He looked down at her hand, and then took it with one of his enormous ones. His fingernails were all jagged and broken. They reminded Gwen of her old cat's claws. "Deal."

"Great." She walked up to the mare and climbed back into the saddle and nudged Sunshine in the sides, urging her to start down the road again.

"Have you decided if you wish to stay or go home?" Merlin resumed walking beside her.

"No." She frowned. "Still figuring that out."

"Hm." He said nothing else on the matter. And she was happy to let it go.

They rode for another hour in silence before they passed a farm. It made her smile and made her feel just a tiny bit homesick at the same time. "I think I want to stay, honestly. This world is full of adventure and magic. It'd be hard to go home, knowing what I was missing out on. I just hope my family is all right, now that they're homeless and all."

"The house is fine."

"*What?*"

Birds took off from the field at her shout.

Merlin shrugged. "You can create fire without burning material. So could I. It was easier to fake the inferno. I'm sure there was some light charring, but it didn't last long enough to do actual dam—"

"You lying sack of shit!" Gwen threw a fireball at him. It hit his shoulder and might as well have been a snowball for all the damage it did. "You made me think—you—agghh!"

Merlin was snickering.

"It isn't funny!" She threw another fireball at him. "I thought my family was homeless and they thought I died!"

"I'm sure they still think you're dead, if it's any consolation."

"It isn't!" A third fireball. She let out a long, ragged sigh and gave up. "You're such an asshole. Why didn't you tell me that sooner?"

"You didn't ask."

"I fucking *hate* you."

"Yes, yes, I know." He was still quietly laughing.

"Still isn't funny."

"Yes, it is."

She gave up again. Shaking her head, she looked over at the small, squat medieval-looking farmhouse sitting by the edge of the road. It was haphazard and crooked, like most of the buildings she had seen. And the fence that surrounded it once more looked as though it had been grown rather than built.

Magic.

"I wonder if they'd lend us some more supplies." She checked the contents of the saddlebags. They had enough for the trip to the sorcerer, she suspected—but the trip back was questionable. *Back where? Does it even really matter?* "Couldn't hurt to have some more food in stock, even though we're doing all right catching fish."

"I, for one, am incredibly sick of fish." Merlin shuddered. "Ask if they have any real meat. And if they don't offer any, burn their house down."

"No, I will not, you goddamn psychopath." Pulling up in front of the house, she hopped off the horse. The wood shutters that were the only coverings for the windows were open. "Hello? Is anyone home?" She smiled in as friendly a way as she could. "We're just traveling by, and wondered if—"

Someone appeared in the window. It was an older woman. Her expression was a glower as she grabbed the wood shutters and slammed them shut. "Go away, demons!"

Gwen frowned. "I'm not a—"

The woman slammed the other window shutters closed.

"—demon." She sighed. "So much for that." She decided to walk for a bit to give Sunshine a break from having to carry her weight. Taking up the reins, she started off.

"Burn the house down. Burn the whole damn field, I say," Merlin growled. "Teach them a lesson."

"For the last time, no. I won't. They're scared. They have every right to be scared of you. Of both of us." She shook her head. The sun was starting to set, and the sky was a beautiful array of wonderful colors. Oranges, reds, purples, yellows, and pinks filled the sky as the clouds glowed.

There were birds circling high above. They were the size of condors—and one of them was bright turquoise, like a parrot.

Avalon was beautiful. Absolutely beautiful.

Maybe I will stay here. Maybe it won't be so bad, after all.

The universe took that exact moment to teach her a lesson for being hopeful about her future.

For a few seconds, she didn't understand what had happened. She just felt a splitting pain. Like someone had pinched her back extremely hard. It reminded her of that one time she caught herself on a rusty nail in the barn.

"Ow—" She looked down.

She stared at her stomach.

Suddenly, the world became very complicated.

Right before her eyes, Merlin changed. His form shifted from that of a human to one that was very much... not.

It was a demon. There was no other word for the thing standing in front of her. Easily twelve feet tall, it resembled a black panther if it had been crossbred with a gorilla. Its front arms were much longer than its back haunches. Claws the length of her forearm looked like those of a tiger, if it hadn't scratched at a tree for far too long.

Curling, twisted and jagged horns jutted up from its head. One was broken off, and a thick slash of a scar obscured one eye, the orb itself being glassy white. Its other eye was glowing a wicked, fiery red. Its sharp, dangerous fangs were damaged as well. One was missing.

The demon roared and charged in the direction of the farmhouse.

Holy shit, Merlin is a demon.

Ow. Why do I hurt so much?

Eod was barking. Sunshine had reared up and was running toward the woods.

It didn't really matter to Gwen at the moment. Pulling up the edge of the chainmail, she watched as blood began to ooze down her stomach. That was a little more important than the demon, all things considered.

What she was staring at was an arrowhead. Right where an arrowhead had no business being.

Three inches to the left of her belly button. It must have punched through the chainmail in the back.

Her head began to spin.

Her knees gave out.

The world went black.

SIX

When Gwen came to, everything was kind of a blur. She was lying on her side on something soft. Well, soft-ish. Softer than the ground, at any rate. Groaning, she placed a hand to her side where something hurt like a motherfucker.

Oh right. Arrow. That whole thing.

"Don't poke at it."

The gruff voice of Merlin jarred her out of whatever hazy place she had been in—that weird spot between sleeping and awake. Or in her case, unconscious. She had plenty of experience with passing out, after all.

"And don't let the damn dog lick it."

She lifted her head. It was a bad idea. "Where—" She groaned again and put her head back down. Rubbing at her eyes, she tried to blink back into focus. It was dark, wherever they were. It took her a hot minute to realize that they weren't outside. They were in a small, one-room home that looked as though it had been made out of whatever the owners could find and slap up. Timbers, barely hewn down from trees, made up the framing. The walls were plaster, clay, bits of rough-cut lumber, whatever else it seemed they could find. A fire was burning in a shoddy hearth, the mantle tilted to one side at an odd angle.

The whole place looked like it would come down with a good sneeze. But it was shelter, she supposed. The wood shutters that covered the holes in the walls that served as windows were all closed.

Wait. "Are we...?" She rubbed her eyes again.

"Seemed a shame to waste it." Merlin was sitting by the fire, glaring at it like he was somehow mad at the flames. "Luckily, it was a hunting arrow. The damage was minimal," he explained.

He had wrapped cloth around her stomach. A deep red splotch covered where the arrow had protruded. She couldn't see her back, but she assumed she had another matching blotch where the arrow had gone in.

"Thanks for taking it out and dressing the wound." She laid her head back down. She felt gross when she tried to keep it upright. Her stomach lurched and she hoped she wasn't going to be sick. "Do I remember you turning into a giant freaky cat-demon?"

Merlin was silent for a long time.

"Merlin?"

"That isn't my name."

"Then tell me your real one."

He continued to glower at the fire. "You can figure it out on your own now."

She furrowed her brow, trying to put it together. And then it hit her, all at once. Demon. Merlin was a *demon.* "Mordred told me a story about..."

"About the demon who wanted to destroy the world? You mean you actually *listened* to something someone said to you? I'm impressed." The demon rolled his eyes. "Yes, girl."

Merlin was Grinn.

The Ash King.

The one who started a war to burn all of Avalon.

And she was responsible for setting him free.

"Oh, no..." *I fucked up*, was the first thought she had. *I fucked up big time*, was the second. "Oh, fuck. No, no, no—this can't be right."

Merlin—Grinn—huffed a laugh. "Oh, trust me, it is. I am he, the one and only. I am Grinn, the dread Ash King. And you have my power."

"I'm really not going to give it back to you now."

"Do you think you have a choice?" He sneered. "I told you. I will drag you there kicking and screaming. And now that you're injured, it'll be even easier."

Her only hope was that the mage wasn't an idiot and wouldn't split them up. It wasn't worth arguing about. They wouldn't get anywhere. She groaned and put her hands over her face. Eod, thinking she was in pain—well, she was, but that wasn't why—began to lick her cheek.

"Hey buddy, it's all right, I'm okay." She petted the animal reassuringly. "I'm just trying to grapple with the fact that our traveling companion who just patched me together, who I'm sharing a life force with, is a madman out to destroy the world, is all."

"I didn't do it for you." Grinn huffed. "Remember that what hurts you, hurts me. I wanted that thing out of you as fast as I could. Besides, I didn't need you going into a panic attack while I tried to deal with everything. And as for destroying the world? I can't do anything right now. A problem for another day."

She sighed. And here she thought he was actually trying to be a friend. "You could just pretend you were doing something nice for me."

"Nobody ever does anything nice for anyone. Not without having a self-serving inspiration behind it." He jabbed at the fire again. "Not humans, not demons, nobody."

"That's not true. There are plenty of examples of random acts of kindness."

"Which they do to get that little happy glow in their hearts," he said, laying his contempt on thick. "It's just to make yourselves feel better about being generally shit."

Shutting her eyes, Gwen kept gently scratching Eod's head. She was glad for the hound's presence. Deciding she didn't want to get into an argument with a literal demon about the value of humanity, she changed the subject. "What happened?"

"The bitch's husband came out of the hut and shot you with an arrow. Your mutt charged the dumb bastard and ripped his throat out before I could get to him." Grinn laughed once. "He isn't as useless as I had thought."

She blinked her eyes open again and turned her attention to Eod. "He did?" It was hard to believe that this doofus watching her with his tongue hanging out of the side of his mouth had ripped out a man's throat.

"You think Mordred keeps dogs for fun or companionship? They're hunters, bred to kill." Grinn leaned back in the chair he was sitting on in front of the fire. "And think what I like, he's bonded to you."

She didn't like the idea of the man dying. "And then what?"

"After I made sure the bastard was good and dead, I murdered the old woman. We're in their house for the night. Seemed a waste of decent shelter and food. We'll burn this place down once we leave."

"Why did you kill her? She wasn't the one who shot me." Gwen frowned. She didn't like that either of them was dead. Eod going attack dog was one thing—the old woman had been killed in cold blood.

"And let her run off and warn everyone else about us? Use your head, girl." Grinn got up from the chair and went to a shelf, rustling about in baskets. Eod's ears perked up, sensing the opportunity for food, and he ran up to the demon to sit by his side, waiting for whatever scraps Grinn felt like offering up.

Which, apparently, was a collection of cured sausages and

cheese. Grinn threw some into a basket and brought it over to her. Without asking, he grabbed her by the shoulders and hefted her up to sitting.

"*Ow!*" She cringed as her side lit up in pain. "Wait a second, you—"

"Eat." Grinn dropped the basket into her lap. "Then sleep."

She would almost thank him again for taking care of her, except that it was clearly for his own ends. Eod was now sitting beside her again, his head on her lap, looking up at her with soulful, begging doggy eyes. Tearing off some cheese, she fed it to the dog.

"Where're their bodies now? Don't tell me you ate them." Gwen figured she'd probably end up eating half of what he gave her, and the other half would go to Eod.

"Humans taste disgusting." Grinn wrinkled his nose. "No. They have enough stores that I didn't resort to that. They're behind the house. We'll drag them inside and burn them with the building in the morning. Make it look like an accident."

"I... am really disturbed that you know what humans taste like." The sausages were good at least. Not too salty.

"Demon," he reminded her. Like he had to.

They ate in silence for a while. "Will I have a scar?" She peered under the wrapping around her stomach. The wound was red, raw, and angry. But it looked like it had already stopped bleeding.

"Probably."

"Not exactly the souvenir I'd ask for, but at least if I go home, I'll have some proof this wasn't all just a weird fever dream." She leaned her head back against the wall, shutting her eyes. She felt kind of woozy. But the food was helping settle her stomach.

Eod dropped a paw in her lap, reminding her that there was still food and it was not currently in his face. Smiling, she patted him on the head and fed him a bit of bread.

Avalon was magical. But it was violent. She supposed the scar would be a fitting reminder. She wanted to ask why Grinn thought the man had tried to kill her, but she already knew the answer.

Elemental.

It was hard to wrap her head around being hated so much for no reason. After finishing her food, she patted Eod on the head. "All gone, good boy."

Eod lay down on the floor beside the cot, clearly not wanting to leave her side. She smiled. Dogs really did make everything better. Even if he had gone Cujo on that guy. She was glad she hadn't seen it. Shuffling back down to horizontal, she did her best to fluff up the hard lump of a pillow, and tried not to think about the fact that it was supposed to be owned by an old married couple who were now a pair of corpses rotting behind the house.

She wanted an adventure, didn't she?

This is what real adventures were apparently like.

Death, and pain, and violence.

Grinn was back in the shape of a black cat, curled up on the chair by the fire. She tried to let the crackle of the logs and the warmth of the room comfort her. Keyword there was try. She was also trying very hard not to cry.

Don't cry in front of the asshole cat-demon.

Don't cry in front of the asshole cat-demon.

Don't cry in front of the asshole cat-demon.

Unfortunately, the more she tried not to, the more inevitable it became. She sniffed and wiped at her eyes. Eod picked his head up and licked at her cheek again before climbing up on the cot and curling up next to her. She hugged him and buried her face into his fur.

"This is the way of things in Avalon, Gwendolyn." Any hope of Grinn not having heard her crying was dashed as he spoke up. "The elementals do not trust each other. And the peasants do not trust the elementals. A brawl between two elementals has left entire cities in ruins. This is the kind of welcome you should come to expect. They would rather see you dead than help you. You would have better odds of survival as a mortal than as an elemental who wishes to think the best of those around her."

It was shitty advice. No, that wasn't quite true. It was probably really good advice, it just *felt* shitty. It was hard for her to believe that everybody in Avalon would rather put an arrow through her heart than simply let her walk by without trouble.

"Not everybody is the same."

Eod kicked his legs and rolled onto his back beside her, already stealing some of her pillow.

"Better to stay bonded to animals, Gwendolyn. Mordred is wrong about most things—but in that, he's correct. Dogs do not betray their masters." Grinn laid his head back down. "Get some sleep. We leave at first light."

"But I'm—" She had been shot with an arrow, goddamn it.

"We leave at first light."

With a sigh, Gwen realized there was no point in arguing with him. If she weren't already exhausted and wounded, she probably would have stayed up all night, lost in thought. But the slow, heavy breaths of the dog and the warmth of the room dragged her off to sleep whether she liked it or not.

That seemed to be the theme of the day.

Whether she liked it or not.

That might be why she wasn't exactly surprised when she found herself standing in Mordred's study, warped and twisted as it was in her dreams. Great. That was all she needed—her guilty mind torturing her with visions of Mordred, likely about to lecture her for her stupidity.

Clawed hands, heavy and broad, settled on her shoulders from behind her. She shut her eyes, resisting the urge to lean against him. Damn it all if she just didn't seriously need a hug today. She sniffled.

Who cared if she cried in front of dream Mordred? He wasn't really there. "Take it easy on me tonight, will you? I've had a really shitty day."

He turned her to face him, but she kept her eyes shut. She didn't want to see his disapproving, angry glower. When the backs of his knuckles traced over her cheek, she was so surprised at their tenderness that she blinked and looked up at him.

Those rust-colored, molten eyes of his were filled with concern. His hood was gone, and so was all his armor save for what covered his arms. She decided she was going to call the look *Business Casual for Supernatural Tyrants.* She wanted to crack a joke about it, but there was something so arresting in the way he was staring at her that she just couldn't.

"You are hurt." His eyes flicked between hers, as if searching for more. "What has happened? Are you all right?"

At least her dream version of Mordred was concerned about her. "I'll be all right." She let out a wavering breath. "I got shot with an arrow."

"*What?*"

She jolted at his angry shout.

His hands were on her shoulders again, squeezing them insistently. "Who? Who has done this to you?"

"A farmer." Dreams were weird. Wouldn't her dream version of Mordred already know about this? Whatever. It was just her sleeping mind trying to logic through what had happened and process the trauma. "He was just scared and trying to protect his home. I don't blame him."

"Tell me he is dead." His expression darkened in rage. "Or I shall quickly see it done."

"Eod beat you to it." She wrinkled her nose. "I'm glad I didn't see it. Hard to imagine that cute puppo ripping someone's throat out."

"Then I trained him well." He stroked a gauntlet over her hair soothingly. "Are you safe?"

"I think so. I don't really know." She shut her eyes again, loving the feeling of his touch. "I'm scared and I don't know what to do."

"I should not have sent you away. I... was angry."

"Understatement," she murmured. "But I deserved it."

He tilted her head up toward him. "Come back to me, firefly. I will keep you safe."

She studied his face for a moment. There was concern and worry etched deep into his handsome features. But there was something else there too. Something she didn't dare give a name to. Something that was almost as terrifying as when he was glaring at her.

"You told me to run and hide. You said next time you saw me that I'd be your prisoner forever." She felt a tear escape the corner of her eye.

Deftly, he wiped it from her cheek with the back of one of his claws. His voice was soft, achingly tender, as he pulled her closer to him. "Would that be so very unpleasant, in the end?"

"I..." Would it?

Would it *really?*

She didn't know. It was all too much. She sniffled again, trying to hold back more tears. "I don't want to be a prisoner."

"You would be safe with me." He picked her up, easily lifting her in his arms. The world around them melted and changed. He placed her onto the soft surface of his bed. Not even a moment passed before he was kissing her. It was lacking the angry passion of the previous dream. This was gentler, but no less needy. No less desperate for her.

She returned the embrace, needing to feel him there beside her. Needing to have some semblance of hope that everything was going to be okay. That he might forgive her, that they might have a future together.

Is that what I want?

To be with Mordred?

Even if it means I'll be his prisoner?

Wouldn't it be worth it?

It was just a dream. He wasn't really there. He was likely still furious with her in reality and wanting to pull her head off her shoulders. But here, in her fantasy, she could pretend like he was there.

That he wanted her back.

That he loved her.

God. Was that what she really wanted?

For Mordred to love her? Why?

Was it because of how she felt for him?

She didn't love him...

Did she?

In his arms was the safest she had ever felt in her life. Somewhere the fear that plagued her life was far away and meaningless.

Love.

And she knew it wasn't a matter of whether or not she was destined to love Mordred.

It was simply about how long it would take for her to accept that she already did.

When she could feel the dream fading away, his lips pressed against her cheek. It already felt so far away. "Come back to me, firefly."

But it was only a dream.

He wasn't the real Mordred.

No matter how much she wished he was.

* * *

Lancelot kept his sword sheathed and his helm off as he headed deeper into the glade. He knew he was going in the right direction, as the small, glowing, flitting insects that dashed about in the twilight were growing more numerous.

The grass around his boots was thick and lush, almost blue-green in color as he sought out the Gossamer Lady. The trees went from their normal collection to entirely birch, the white paper-like bark almost seeming to glow. The air had an ephemeral quality to it.

It was the kind of place that would lure any man deeper—and certainly, the Gossamer Lady had done that plenty of times to unsuspecting folk. She might not have been born fae, like Galahad, but she certainly had adopted their mannerisms upon being gifted with magic by the isle.

He came to a clearing with a small crystal-clear pond in the middle of it. A rock jutted up from the water in the center. And sitting atop it was the lady in question. She was singing to herself, brushing out her long, pure midnight hair that seemed to shimmer and glint like the stars at night. It flowed about her as if caught adrift in water, as did the sheer dress that she wore. The layers did little to hide her, and seemed to only accentuate what was poorly hidden beneath.

She was, quite simply, astonishing.

"Come closer, knight." Her voice was melodic and soft. But Lancelot knew the truth—she was just as dangerous as any other. Her threat may not come with sword and shield. But Lancelot knew many men had drowned themselves in that pond after one look upon her.

He was not surprised that she had sensed his approach. "I come in peace, my lady."

She laughed quietly. "Do you, now?" She turned to him, her eyes shining like purple gems. Some part of Lancelot had always been jealous of Galahad having won the Gossamer Lady's heart. But Galahad was a good friend and honorable knight. Lancelot would not meddle.

He bowed in greeting. "I am no longer a slave to the Prince in Iron's magic."

"So I see." She pondered him for a moment. "I do not smell the stink of it upon you."

Lancelot frowned. "Galahad has not forgotten you. Nor your vows."

She shut her eyes for a moment. "Why have you come, Silver Knight?"

He straightened his posture and placed his hand upon the hilt of his sword. "I seek to build an army."

"Whatever for?" She ran the brush through her hair again. The tendrils of it curled and swayed around her, caught in that invisible drift. It was hypnotic.

Tightening his grip on his blade, he felt as though he were upon a precipice. With each action, his course was becoming more and more irreversible. But for some reason, this felt more serious than before, though he could not say why. "I seek to destroy the Prince in Iron. And I need your help."

SEVEN

Gwen was fairly convinced she was going to throw up or pass out as she climbed onto Sunshine's back and into the saddle. She broke out in a cold sweat as pain arced through her, making her head spin. She had to double over and focus all her effort on breathing as she clung to the mare's mane. It was a struggle to keep herself upright.

Grinn, in human form, had been doing all the heavy lifting that morning. Literally and figuratively. He had packed up everything that was salvageable for supplies from the old couple's home.

She was still processing the fact that the guy she had been traveling with, and her *stupid asshole cat,* was actually Grinn, the world-ending demon bent on destroying the world. His current task—dealing with the corpses—seemed perfect for him, all things considered.

She had tried not to watch as he dragged the couple's bodies into the small house. Tried, and failed. They were dead largely because of her. The least she could do for them was to see the result of her simply passing by their house.

Grinn took his demonic form once he'd finished and shuddered as if being stuck in human shape was disgusting to him. It probably was. "Burn it down, Gwendolyn."

She wasn't in the mood to argue. And he was right anyway. With a sigh, she did her best to sit up straight. It hurt. A lot. And riding was going to hurt even worse, she knew. But they couldn't stay here. Lifting up a hand, she snapped her fingers, lighting them on fire. It was still such a cool trick.

It'd be a shame when it was gone. Throwing a fireball into the open door of the home, she watched as it easily set the structure ablaze. It was basically held together with straw and hope, so it didn't take long before the thatched roof was smoking.

"We should go before the neighbors come to investigate." Grinn was already walking down the road ahead of her. Sunshine followed him reflexively. "Or worse, the knights."

Gwen groaned in pain and once more tried not to retch. She held her hand to her side and tried to keep pressure on the wound—if only because it helped distract her from the agony—and just did her best to stay conscious. "This sucks."

"Try not to get shot next time then." The demon glanced at her over his shoulder. "If you'd just killed them when I told you to, you wouldn't be in this situation."

Letting out a ragged sigh, she shut her eyes. "Whatever."

"You know I'm right."

"You're technically right. But I'm not going to go around slaughtering people just because they *might* hurt me." Trying to straighten up, she grunted in pain before finding a position that didn't hurt so much. It was better than walking, she supposed. But barely. "Because that's how you get into this situation in the first place where everybody is trying to kill everybody else. Somebody has to break the pattern."

"It isn't going to be you."

"No, you're right. It probably isn't. But I have to try. Because otherwise, I become a rampaging, bitchy, cruel, friendless demagogue bent on world destruction for no other reason than *waaah, nobody likes me.*"

"And here I thought you liked Mordred." Grinn huffed.

"I wasn't talking about—" She sighed. "Never mind." They proceeded along in silence for a long time. Grinn was back in his demon form, apparently deciding it was more comfortable to travel that way than as a human. She couldn't help but stare at the enormous, twelve-foot-tall, cat-gorilla-demon walking along next to her. He had claws the size of her forearms, many of them broken and jagged. She could see one fang sticking out of his maw, the other missing. He was a demon—an actual *fucking* demon.

That would be cool if it weren't for the elephant in the room. "Why do you want to burn the whole world to ashes?"

Grinn turned his head to glance at her for a moment before facing the road ahead again. "Neither of us belong here. We have that in common."

"What do you mean?"

"I am the only demon to ever be abducted by Avalon's twisted magic. I *hate* this place, Gwendolyn. I despise it and all those who live here. All I have ever desired, all these years, is to simply go home." He grimaced, baring his one good fang. "To be free."

"And... you can't?" She frowned. That sounded tragic.

"No. No power, no magic, nothing—has ever been able to unbind me from this forsaken place. I am trapped. If I cannot make hell my home, I will make my home into hell." He shrugged. "I will reign over my own circle of destruction, if I cannot return to where I belong."

Okay, less tragic. She sighed. "You'd kill everyone just to feel like you were home again?"

"Yes. Soon, none of this will be your problem when you return to Earth."

"I don't know if I can go through with that, Grinn. I don't

know if I can go home knowing you're going to be killing everyone here."

"I see being attacked has not knocked some sense into you."

"One scared person who acted out of what they felt was self-defense doesn't mean the whole world should burn."

"Mm-hm."

They fell into silence again as they traveled down the path for a stretch. "What's hell like?"

"Simple. The fallen rule, each over their own circle, and we serve them in ranks. I was once the right hand to Astaroth, the Grand Duke." He almost sounded wistful, talking about it. As if he really missed his home.

"Fallen? Like, *the* fallen?" She blinked. "Have you ever met them?"

"Don't ask stupid questions."

"Well, I don't *know*, maybe they're recluses, or some shit." She rolled her eyes. "Cut me some slack, will you? My whole reality got turned upside down." She gestured at the world around her. "I've just learned that demons, and hell, and fallen angels are *real*, okay?"

He grunted, as if conceding her point. Almost. "I have met them. I was third-ranked to the fallen themselves."

"What're they like?"

"They are older than you can imagine. There is a particular... strangeness that forms in a creature that has existed longer than many universes." He shrugged. "No two are alike. Some might be kinder to you than an archangel. Some might pick their teeth with your bones on a lark."

That made sense. After pondering over the confirmation that demons and hell really existed, Gwen made it another ten minutes before she had to keep asking questions. "I don't get it."

"You'll have to narrow that down," Grinn replied.

She sighed. "I got shot with an arrow. Can you be nice to me, please?"

"No."

Whatever. Stupid demon. At least he was predictable. "I don't get how this magic works. The 'shared life force' thing."

"I've yet to hear an actual question."

Putting both her hands over her face, she fought the urge to scream. The demon was so incredibly infuriating. She understood why nobody liked him; she really did. Sob story or not. Dropping her hands to her sides in exasperation, she stared up at the sky and begged for patience. "Would this arrow have killed me if we weren't linked?"

"Probably. I don't know human anatomy. But you certainly wouldn't be yapping on and annoying me, even with the fact that elementals heal quickly."

"What does it feel like for you?"

"I obviously have no physical wound, but I feel the pain. Half of it, to be precise."

"Shit, this is only *half* the pain?" She frowned.

"I doubt you would be on a horse otherwise."

That was a good point. She sighed. "So, if somebody stabs you, I'll feel half of it."

He glanced at her with his one red eye. It kind of glowed. Which would be cool if he wasn't usually using it to glare at her. "Planning on stabbing me?"

"No, just predicting other people stabbing you." She paused to think over the different scenarios. "What happens if somebody chucks you into a volcano?"

"Gwen." He stared at her like she was stupid.

Right. Fire elemental. "Whatever. You know what I mean. What if somebody chops off your head?"

His furry brow lowered in thought. "I'm unsure. I've never seen that tested before. I wouldn't recommend trying it."

"What's this generally used for? Like, why do demons have this spell?"

He muttered something under his breath.

"What?"

"Mated pairs," he said with no small amount of disgust. "If a demon mates with a mortal, it shares its immortality with the other."

"Eeewwuuhh—" She made a face. "I'm not your—"

"Of course you aren't!" he snarled. "Don't be vile. I was desperate. It was the only resource I had at my disposal that would keep me alive and apart from Avalon for so long."

"What'll happen to me when our life force is separated?" She was looking forward to that more and more, even if it was dangerous. Even if it meant he was going to start a war. Because she certainly didn't want to be stuck with a demon for the rest of... apparently forever.

"You will lose your elemental abilities. I will be restored to my rightful power."

"I'm not going to die from it, am I?" She narrowed her eyes at him. She didn't trust Grinn. Even if he told her the truth, she wasn't sure she was going to believe him anyway. But it didn't hurt to ask.

"It might. I honestly don't care if it does. This situation is untenable, no matter how you feel about the risks."

Well, at least he was being honest. "You're such an ass."

"So you've said."

They fell into silence, leaving her to think over the logistics of the plan for the rest of the day. Finding another stream to camp at, she settled in for another night of cuddling with the dog. At least Eod had stopped barking at Grinn every time the demon walked into the clearing.

Not like she really blamed the pup.

It was just after dinner when it began to rain. Sighing, Gwen got the thick cotton sailcloth that the villagers had given them and began making a bit of a lean-to by tying it to trees at various angles.

Being shot hurt. Like, a lot. And every time she moved, the

wound was happy to remind her that it was still there. But Grinn was clearly uninterested in helping, so she was on her own. She really had always loved camping with her dad, and now it all came in handy. With the spare canvas, she did the same for the mare. She didn't want the poor horse to get cold, even if it probably wasn't really necessary. She had to take a second to breathe and not throw up from the pain every now and then. But knowing it wasn't going to be fatal took a lot of the oomph out of it.

"I see how it is," Grinn complained from where he was hunkered down by the sputtering fire. "A hovel for the horse, but not for me."

"First of all, you're making me do this all by myself *while I'm wounded*, so fuck you. Second of all, you're too big, dude." She shook her head. "You wouldn't fit under either of these. Go back to cat form, and just sit under here with us if you want. That would require, y'know, proximity."

He grunted. "I prefer the rain. And you are managing just fine on your own. Time you learned how to endure real suffering for once."

"Whatever. The point is, it's a you problem, not a me problem." She settled down on the bedroll with a collection of meat, bread, and cheese from the villagers. Eod was already lying on the bedroll, enjoying the shelter from the rain that was starting to pick up in intensity. The patter of water droplets on the leaves and a full day of traveling while in pain knocked her out pretty quickly after she lay down.

Halfway through the night she woke up to shift, and nearly kicked a small, black, furry object by her foot.

Grinn.

She smiled faintly. The demon had finally given in, it seemed. He was as far away from her and Eod as possible, curled into a ball at the end of the bedroll. But at least he was out of the rain.

Some small part of her almost felt bad for him.

Almost.

* * *

Mordred did have to admit to himself that he missed the sight of the starry sky. The moon was full and beautiful, turning the field of swaying grass into an ocean that rippled with the wind like waves.

How he wished to take his dragon—*Tiny*—and go find Gwendolyn. She was injured. She had been harmed by a villager, and perhaps nearly killed.

How he wished to catch her in his arms and demand she never, ever do anything so foolish as betray him again. Their dreams together had only proven to him how much life she had injected into his days—how much joy.

But the question of the demon's whereabouts was still his primary concern. He had to locate Grinn and take the creature's head as a trophy before he could worry about what to do next. Or else, there would be little world for her to enjoy when all was said and done.

Footsteps approached. Heavy, but not with the gait of Galahad. Mordred felt the corner of his eye twitch. "What do you want, Percival?"

He had lived with his knights for sixteen hundred years. He knew what they sounded like.

"I think I should take a contingent of our forces and go into the city. Round up all the elementals we can find." The Knight in Copper kept his distance from Mordred. It was probably wise.

"Oh?" Mordred kept his gaze out on the forest beyond. "And why should we declare war?"

"Because you declared war three hundred years ago when you formed the Crystal. Do you think they will just let us be?"

Mordred would almost be amused by Percival's desire to see Mordred's reign resume, if it weren't for the fact that it was entirely based on the Knight in Copper's desire to stay alive and in power. Cracking his neck from one side to the other loudly, he decided he was in no mood to talk to Percival. "No."

"Then allow me to take your soldiers and—"

"You misunderstand me. My answer to your request is *no*." He pulled his clawed hand into a fist where it rested on the stone balustrade, the points audibly scratching on the surface. "We search for the demon. Nothing more."

"But—"

Mordred shut his eyes. "If you do not wish to be thrown from this ledge, Percival, I suggest you leave me be."

The Knight in Copper was not a fool. He turned and left. Mordred understood his desire to start the fight before it came to them. It would be the wise choice, were victory Mordred's sole concern.

It should be.

And perhaps a month ago, it would have been.

But there was a chance—slim and hopeless as it may be—that the world would find another way. That the elementals would see the past three hundred years as a warning of what would follow if they began their violent squabbling again.

Even if it meant that they were united against him, at least the world would know peace.

That had been his goal, after all... hadn't it?

And if all the elementals required were a common enemy, he had certainly given them one, though he would argue they already had one in Grinn. But when was the last time anyone ever listened to him?

Turning from the balustrade, he headed inside. His other knights would return from their patrols soon, and he would have to listen to more questions and wary looks, wondering if he had lost either his mind or the will to live.

No, it was neither.

He was simply heartbroken.

The questions from his knights would have to wait until the morning.

Mordred decided he needed to get well and truly drunk.

Priorities are priorities.

Percival's concerns were not invalid. One month ago, before that little firefly had come into his life, he would never have broken the Crystal of his own volition. He certainly would not have let her walk free. Nor would he be hunting the demon alone, letting his former prisoners gather their wits and their forces and ready for what was most certainly going to be a war against him.

But she had given him *hope.*

And damn her to the pits, it would be the death of him.

EIGHT

"I just realized something."

"Oh, good."

Gwen ignored Grinn's sarcastic response. She was atop Sunshine again, still feeling lousy from the wound. It was getting better quickly, but it still ached like a *bitch.* "Sorry for trying to make conversation."

"I'd accept your apology, but I don't think you intend on stopping."

"I just realized I've been having fewer panic attacks since coming here. Which you'd think would be backwards, seeing as Avalon is actively trying to murder me."

Grinn grunted but didn't provide any reply.

"I'm just wondering why that is. It seems strange. Maybe it's the magic of the place?"

"Or maybe you now understand real fear and have simply learned that casual panic is useless."

She stared at him flatly, wishing she could just kick him. Whatever. She'd enjoy freaking out less, either way. Even if it was because of the life link between them, or Avalon's magic, or Grinn's more jaded reason. She'd take it.

An hour passed in silence before she couldn't take it anymore. This was their pattern—she'd talk, he'd grump, she'd go silent. Lather, rinse, repeat. But she couldn't *help* it. There were so many things she wanted to understand. "So, I have a question."

"I wait with bated breath."

Gwen shot a glare at Grinn for his snarky tone, even if he wasn't looking at her. Jerk. "Do, like, demons have families in hell?" She rubbed at her side as she rode. "Or are demons all solo creatures?"

"What a bigoted assumption. You should be ashamed." His tone was flat, and she honestly couldn't tell if he was joking or not.

"Well, how am I supposed to know? You're demons. For all I know, you just get blorped into existence and spend the rest of eternity torturing human souls." She resisted the urge to huck a fireball at the back of his head.

He sighed with the tone of a creature who had given the same speech a thousand times. "First, we do not torture human souls."

"You don't?" She blinked.

"No."

"Huh." That was surprising. She almost asked him what the point of being a demon was, then, but she figured that was *maybe* racist. Toward demons. Which she hadn't even known was a thing until right then and there. "Where do people go then?"

"Nobody knows."

"Seriously?"

"Yes, *seriously*." He mumbled something under his breath about having to deal with children and babysitting. Gwen let it slide.

"But demons and angels exist."

"Yes."

"And, so, heaven exists."

"Yes."

"How'd the whole myth start?"

"Humans have the need to control each other. The need to subjugate. The easiest way to do that, they discovered, is through your species' unerring need to have an *answer* to everything, coupled with your idiotic insistence that all of you, no matter how small and worthless, has to matter." Grinn clearly had strong feelings on the subject. "That makes religion the perfect way to manipulate your kind. The myth is one *you* created, not us."

"I..." She wanted to argue. She really did. But she pulled up a blank. "Huh."

"And to answer your other question, yes. We have families. We are not 'blorped' into existence. We are born. Raised. Same as you. The only ones who simply exist are the archangels and archdemons. They have been around since the dawn of time." He shook like a dog, raining bits of gray ash as he did. She supposed that was probably where he got the moniker of Ash King.

"Neat." She sat in silence for a second. "Do you have a family?"

"What did I just say?"

"I know, but maybe they're all dead or something!" She threw up her hands in frustration. "I'm trying to get to *know* you, Grinn."

"Why?" He turned his red eye toward her.

"Because we're stuck together, and nobody gets born into the world being this much of a colossal asswipe without having a reason for it." Now she was the one getting annoyed. "So excuse me if I'm trying to understand you."

"Don't bother. We will not be attached for much longer and then you will not have to worry about fulfilling this strange need of yours for idle conversation." He turned his focus back to the road.

Shutting her eyes, she shook her head, biting back the rant she wanted to deliver about how maybe, just maybe, if he weren't such a bastard, people might not hate him so much. But she figured it was probably a chicken-and-egg scenario—no way of knowing which came first. His bad attitude or his bad reputation.

It was minutes later when Grinn finally answered the question. Long enough that she had entirely forgotten what they were talking about. "I had a wife."

That caught Gwen so much by surprise that she didn't know what to say. She just stared at the demon. Grinn offered up no more explanation than that. Just simply, *I had a wife.*

And she supposed he didn't really need any more.

Those four words spoke volumes. Frowning, she knew her reply was probably going to earn her another lecture about how he didn't need her pity, yadda, yadda. "I know it doesn't mean anything, but... I'm sorry."

He grunted and said nothing.

She decided it was best to just let it go. They rode in silence for the rest of the day, with Eod trotting ahead and scouting the path. When they came to the next field, she looked up and whistled.

The mountain at the middle of the island had looked a lot smaller from the back of Mordred's iron dragon. Now that she saw it in full, it really was something. It looked like one of the mountains in the center of a tropical island—jagged but covered in greenery. A white cloud ringed the top. To say it was picturesque was to put it mildly. Something was swooping around the top—large enough to be seen, even at their distance. Two smaller creatures seemed to be chasing it off, like sparrows attacking a hawk. "What's that?"

"Griffin," Grinn replied like it was no big deal. "Probably getting into the roc nests."

"Whoa." She laughed. It was still wondrous to her, even if it was no skin off the demon's back. "What's a roc?"

"A giant eagle."

"*Cool.*"

"Yes, until they come down and eat you. Let's try not to stay out in the open for long. We can reach the wizard by sundown if we don't stop."

It was such a strange thought. If everything went the way Grinn wanted it to go, Gwen would be powerless and home before the morning. Or powerless and still in Avalon.

Her shoulders slumped. She suddenly wasn't excited about the prospect. But she kept up with the demon all the same.

Maybe I can learn magic from the wizard. Become a sorceress or something. She smiled at the notion. That'd be fun. She could learn magic, try to apologize to Mordred and... probably wind up murdered.

She sighed.

"What now?" Grinn glanced at her.

"Nothing."

"It is never 'nothing' with you. What?"

"I don't know where I belong. I want to stay here, mortal or not, but I don't know where I fit in. I should just go home, that would be safer, but..." Gwen kept watching the griffins chasing after the roc. "Griffins. Dragons."

"Then stay in Avalon. Get eaten by some flying magical predator. I don't care."

"I know you don't." And she supposed that was part of the problem. "I don't think anybody does." And there was the other half. Would Mordred want her to stay? Could he possibly ever forgive her for betraying him? Did he even *miss* her?

Did she even matter to him at all?

Eod would miss her.

But he was a dog. That was their job.

It was her turn to sulk in silence. The path on the other side of the field turned into a climb as they made their way up the base of the mountain. "Is he far up the side?"

"No."

Simple question, simple answer. She supposed that was fair. It was just as Grinn said—the sun was just starting to set as they came across a house in the middle of the woods. She wasn't sure what she was expecting—a castle, a mud hut, a shack covered with bits and pieces and odds and ends. The house was an old, Tudor-style antique, with its distinctive brown beams and spackled plaster exterior. Smoke was curling up from the fireplace, giving her some hope that they hadn't walked all that way for nothing. Someone was home.

The weirdest part about the whole thing was that the house looked—like King Arthur's castle—as though it had just been dropped onto the mountain out of nowhere. Part of a huge boulder next to the home was sheared clean in half, as if the whole house had just *appeared* where it had no business being.

Maybe it had.

Sorcerer and all.

"You sure he isn't Merlin?" Climbing off the back of Sunshine, Gwen tied the horse to a tree with a long stretch of rope to make sure the mare didn't wander off. Eod was sniffing at the door, his tail idly wagging.

"Don't know. Don't care." Grinn suddenly seemed nervous, staring at the building with his red eye warily. "Knock. Let's get this over with."

"What's the problem?"

"Mages are... unpredictable. Dealing with them is always messy." He curled his lips back in a half-snarl. "And I doubt he has any reason to do me any favors. The last time we met I may have set him on fire."

"And you're just mentioning this *now*?" She slapped a hand

over her eyes. "Jesus fuck, Grinn. Try leading with that next time."

"It doesn't matter. It's your job to convince him."

"Mine? How the hell am I supposed to convince him of anything? I don't know him!" She threw her hands up in frustration. Sometimes, she wanted to just grab the demon and shake him. "But, fine. Fine. We came all this way." She walked up to the door. Eod was now sitting there, tail thumping on the sorcerer's front steps. The door was solid wood, with a hatch in the middle covered with a metal grate.

Raising her hand to knock, she jumped as the little hatch opened inward.

"Go away!" a man shouted from inside.

The hatch swung back shut with a *thwack*.

Gwen glanced back at Grinn. The demon was just glaring at her with a grimace. He wasn't going to be any help.

Sighing, she turned back to the door. "I'm sorry, but we're really in need of your help." She paused. No answer. "Mr. Wizard, sir? I know this probably isn't a good time, but—"

The little hatch opened again. "*No!*"

The hatch swung back shut with another loud slap.

Rubbing her temples, Gwen decided Avalon might have lessened her issue with panic attacks, but it sure as shit seemed intent on replacing them with headaches.

Great.

This was just *great*.

"Look, I get it. I do. But we have a serious problem that only you can help us with."

The hatch opened. "*No!*" The hatch slapped shut.

All right. Now she was getting annoyed. Balling her hands into fists, she glared at the wood surface. "All I want is for you to hear me out. Just listen to me. If you can't help me, or don't want to help me, we'll leave."

Grinn started to say something. Without turning to him, she

flipped him off. That seemed to be enough to shut him up for the time being.

"Just hear me out, please. I'm not here to cause problems."

"That's all you people do!" The mage didn't even bother opening the hatch that time. Just shouted through the door. "Go! Away!"

Now what? She took a deep breath and tried again. "Listen, buddy. I have had a *shit* month. My house was set on fire by my asshole cat who turned out to be a giant demon bent on world destruction. I have been chased, drugged, and lied to. I was the prisoner of the Prince in Iron. I'm the reason he destroyed the Crystal. I'm now apparently in the middle of some giant impending three-way war, and I don't know what to do. But one thing I do know, is that I'm stuck tethered to this big crotchety asswipe—"

Grinn growled. She ignored him.

"—and I'd really like to figure out what to do about that. Oh! I almost forgot. I also got shot by some chucklefuck with a bow. So I would really, *really* appreciate it if you would listen to me for ten minutes."

The hatch opened. "Let me say it in words you'll understand. *Fuck off!*" Thwack went the hatch.

That was it.

That was absolutely it.

She was done. Stick a fork in her, she was done. "Open this door and listen to me or I swear to *fuck* I will burn your goddamn house down!" She burst into flame.

The door swung open. The man on the other side was not what she was expecting. She had figured he would be some old man with long white hair and a long white beard. Not a dude in his early forties, with unkempt, dirty blond hair and day-old stubble. He was wearing linen britches, no shirt, and an open dark blue velvet robe that had seen better days. He scratched his stubble. "Well, you could have just started with that, you know."

Narrowing her eyes at the wizard, she put out her fire. Great. Another smartass. That's all she needed.

Eod barked at the man once in greeting, his tongue hanging out of the side of his mouth.

"Nice to meet you too, young man," the mage replied to the dog. "And yes, I'm sure I have something for you to eat inside. At least *you* have manners." He shot Gwen a glare.

"Me? I tried to be nice!"

"Mm-hm." The sorcerer looked over her shoulder at the demon. "I'll talk to you. He stays outside."

"But—" Grinn stepped forward.

"Nope. I'm allergic to demons." The wizard stepped aside. Eod took that as his cue to run in, nails scrabbling on the wood floor as he made himself perfectly at home, sniffing everything interesting.

"Come in, Gwendolyn Wright." The wizard held his arm out to gesture for her to go in. He smiled at her as if everything leading up to that point had been a game. "I've been waiting for you."

Yeah. Avalon was going to give her a serious headache.

NINE

"We will need assistance, dear Lancelot, lest you think we can battle the prince on our own." Zoe had invited Lancelot back to her home as her guest, and he had not hesitated at the idea of sleeping indoors for a few nights.

The Gossamer Lady had asked for time to think through her decision, and now it seemed she had come to a conclusion. Lancelot looked up from where he had been sitting outdoors, sharpening his blade.

Not that it needed it.

But it gave him something to do.

"Oh?" He stood. "Have you decided to join me?"

"It is... difficult for me, you must understand." Her delicate wings draped from her back like a cape. "To stand against the prince is to stand against my beloved. I do not wish to join the fray directly."

Lancelot nodded once. He could not say he blamed her. He had never had to do battle against someone he cared for. "But...?"

"But I will aid you in finding those who will. However, our kind is still scattered to the winds—confused and picking up the pieces of their former lives. I suspect it will be challenging to gather the elementals until more time has passed."

"The longer we wait to attack him, the more time he has to resurrect his own legions." Lancelot grimaced. He had only ever fought beside Mordred's iron army—and that had been horrifying enough.

"I agree. Therefore, I recommend we divide our strengths. You should work on gathering up more mundane forces while I work to convince the strongest of our kind." Zoe gazed out at the woods beyond her home.

It was a simple, two-room house that was modest by most standards, but Lancelot found it perfectly suited for the butterfly. Fresh and drying flowers filled the air with the constant sweet smell of the ground in full bloom. She was like life itself—so far away from the cold, dreadful keep and its overbearing master to which he had been enslaved.

It was no wonder that Galahad loved her so.

"But I feel you will need assistance. More than simply what I can provide." She hesitated. "You know who I am referencing."

Lancelot sighed. "Please, anyone but *him*."

"You really must learn to forgive him for what he did to you. That was hundreds of years ago—and it was only a childish prank." Zoe chuckled. "It was quite amusing."

"For everyone *but* me."

"That is the point of a prank, yes."

Lancelot rubbed a hand over his face. "Why do we need to speak to *him*?"

Zoe looked off into the distance again thoughtfully. As if listening to the world around her. Lancelot did not fully understand the depths of her power, he suspected she did not either. But Zoe was the kind who simply accepted the way of things and did not question them.

And so, he followed her lead.

"He has guests. Important guests. Ones I think you will wish to intercept."

Lancelot fought the urge to groan. He also knew better than to ask who it was specifically. "Well, then. No time like the present."

* * *

Gwen walked into the wizard's home and fought to keep her mouth from hitting the floor. Unlike the man himself the inside of the home was precisely what she expected from a wizard. There was *stuff* everywhere. Bookshelves were cluttered with objects, crammed floor to ceiling with stacks of things. Some books, scrolls, stacks of paper, either loose or bound into bundles. Jars and bits and pieces. Swords, knives, crystal balls, jars of sticks and leaves. Some things were actually glowing.

And one jar of eyes was distinctly watching her.

She decided at exactly that moment she wasn't going to touch anything.

The sorcerer brushed past her into the room. Eod was sniffing a plant, tail wagging. The strange man hummed. "Yes, good nose. That does come from the eastern region by the big green lake."

"Wait. Can you talk to him?" Gwen blinked.

"Of course. What kind of mage would I be if I couldn't talk to animals?" He sat down on a stool in front of a desk, his back to her, and picked up a pencil.

"That's awesome." She chuckled. "I wish I could talk to animals."

"No, you don't. Do you know how very loud the world is when you can understand bird songs?" He huffed. "Loud and extremely horny things, birds are."

That made her laugh. "How long have you been on Avalon? You talk like someone from modern-day Earth."

"I honestly couldn't tell you. I don't know. I don't know where I came from, when, or..." He paused, looking up from his work briefly. "Literally anything about myself. It's quite inconvenient at parties."

"Wait. What?"

"I could have arrived here thirty thousand years ago, or thirty seconds ago." He shrugged and ran a hand over his unkempt hair. "So don't bother asking for details."

"Do you even know your name?"

"Nope."

That sounded depressing. "I'm sorry."

"Eh. It's not so bad. He doesn't have a real name, doesn't seem to bother him any." He stuck a thumb out at the dog who was now sitting there and scratching his chin with his back paw.

So much for him being Merlin. Or maybe he was, and just didn't remember. He kind of reminded her of Doc Brown from *Back to the Future.* Not in looks, but certainly in vibe. Or, hell, *Doctor Who.* "Can I call you Doc?"

"Sure. Call me whatever you like." He kept sketching away at whatever he was doodling. It looked like an airplane—but not a modern one. More like a Da Vinci drawing. "Just not Tiny. What a terrible thing to name a dragon."

"I thought it was cute." Apparently, the wizard knew everything. That at least saved her time. She walked up to one of his bookcases, unable to help from peering at the strange things in jars. "Do you know why I'm here?"

"You want a way to split yourself from the demon outside. Or rather, he wants you to find a way to split. You're not so sure about it." He tapped the back of his pencil on the desk for a moment. He gestured at a puffy leather chair that looked distinctly way too modern for Avalon by the wall. "Sit."

She did so, feeling like she was being ordered around by her schoolteacher and she was back in second grade. The chair was overstuffed, and definitely modern. Weird. "Where'd this come from?" She poked at it.

"Mordred is not the all-knowing hotshot he thinks he is. There are still ways in and out—little ones—and damn it all, I wanted some comfy furniture." Doc sketched away at the paper in front of him.

She supposed that made sense. "Can you send me home?"

"Do you want to go home?"

Gwen's thoughts went to Mordred yet again. "I don't know. I want to stay; I just don't think it's the smart choice."

"Well, then figure it out first. Then ask again." He picked up a pair of thin-framed glasses from the desk and put them on before swiveling on his stool to face her. Leaning over, he grabbed her by the chin without warning, and turned her head left, then right, then left again. "Hm. Yep." He let her go and pushed his glasses to the top of his head before going back to the paper.

"What?"

"You and that demon. Right mess he's made of you. For shame. You seem like a nice girl."

She sat up straight. "What does that mean? Why do you make it sound like I'm gonna die?"

"Because you probably will." He snickered.

"Thanks." She slumped back into the chair and crossed her arms over her chest. "You really aren't helping."

"I'm not here to make you feel better about your life, sorry." He turned the pencil over and tapped it against the desk again. He seemed to always be moving—fidgeting his leg or twirling the hair on the back of his head. "I'm here to... actually, I don't honestly know." He snorted in laughter like it was a private joke and went back to drawing.

"Can you separate Grinn and me?"

"Do you want me to?"

"Damn it, I don't know!" She groaned.

"Well, there's problem number one to solve." He sniffed dismissively. Glancing over at Eod, who was now lying on the floor watching the exchange, he sighed. "I know, I know. You really are so very patient with her."

"Don't tell me the dog is on my case too." That's all Gwen would need: the dog lecturing her too.

"Oh, hardly. He loves you. That's extremely clear. That pup'll follow you to the ends of the world to keep you out of trouble." Doc smiled down at the dog. "That's the beauty of animals. But you already know that. That's your real gift, you know."

"What is?" She furrowed her brow. "Animals?"

"No. Yes. Sort of. You see the simple truths in people. We all just want to love and be loved in return. Animals are just more obvious about it." He pondered her for a second. "And on the other end of the spectrum, we have your dear Prince in Iron. Same need. *Veeeery* different approach."

"I... he doesn't..." She felt her cheeks go warm. Damn it, was she blushing? Why was she blushing?

"Mm-hm." It was clear the sorcerer did not believe her in the slightest. He went back to his drawing.

"Can we get back to the demon thing?"

"Sure."

"Great." She sighed. "I don't want to stay tethered to Grinn. I just..."

"Don't want to unleash him, triggering a world-ending fiery apocalyptic war the likes of which could tear this whole dimension apart at the seams, starting an endless chain reaction of death and chaos that might devour reality as we know it?" Doc grinned. "That?"

Gwen blinked. And stared. "Holy shit, man."

He tapped his finger against his temple. "They say I'm not right up here. I'm starting to believe them."

"Who're *they*?"

"I don't know!" He laughed sharply and turned back to his work. "Anyway."

Yep. He was insane. An insane wizard who didn't remember his own name. Just when her life couldn't get more complicated.

"I was also just getting used to having fire powers. That was terrifying at first, but now it's kinda cool."

"Fire is a pretty cool power. At least you aren't the elemental of mayonnaise."

She made a face. "There's an elemental of mayo?"

"No. Wouldn't it be gross if there was?" He snorted. "I had you *going* there for a second, didn't I?"

"I hate this. So much." Putting her head in her hands, she placed her elbows on her knees and tried not to scream or cry. Or both. She counted backwards from ten. Not to keep herself from having a panic attack, but to keep herself from burning this guy's house down anyway.

Doc was quietly snickering. "I also don't get visitors much."

"I can't imagine why." She ran her hands over her hair, tugging on the strands, using the sting to center her thoughts. "Is there a way to split us up and not have Grinn go on some terrible rampage?"

"Hm. Probably not. But I'm a wizard, not a psychologist."

"I don't think I can spend the rest of my life tethered to that demon." She chewed her lip. "I just don't know what else to do."

"Mordred could stop him. Stopped him once before." The wizard pushed up from his desk and walked to a cabinet. Sorting through it, he found a bottle and uncorked it. Sniffing it, he coughed, made a *blechk* sound, recorked it, and placed it back on the shelf before trying it a second time. "You could always beg the bastard for forgiveness."

Looking down at her hands, she sighed. "He won't. I betrayed him. That's his thing."

"I know. And you'll probably do it again. But that's what people do." He walked back with two small glasses and poured the oddly greenish liquid from the bottle into them.

"Betray each other?" She arched an eyebrow. "Not you too. I can barely deal with one grumpy, jaded bastard. I don't need two."

"No, well, yes. But—" He picked up a glass and handed it to her. "What I meant was, people make choices. And regret most of them. That's what they do."

Looking down into the glass, she sniffed the liquid. It tasted like the worst kind of Easter candy. "What is this?"

"Absinthe. Sip it."

Deciding to take his advice, she did just that. "Oh, gross." She coughed.

"Yeah, but it hits the spot." He downed his glass in one go and refilled it. Something told Gwen he drank a lot of the stuff. He offered her more.

"I'm good, thanks." She put the glass back down in front of her. "And I don't know if I regret my choice. I mean, Avalon couldn't stay the way that it was."

"I agree. Quite boring, it was. Imagine me, a sorcerer with no magic to use. I took up a lot of hobbies. I was garbage at knitting to begin with, but if you have a *lot* of time on your hands, you can get good at anything. Would you like a scarf? I have about twenty thousand of them."

"Sure, maybe later." She laughed. He was weird. Definitely insane. But she kind of liked him anyway. "I just don't know how to fix this. Or what I'm supposed to *do.* I just wish I had a plan."

"Plans are funny things." He scratched his head. "They make you think you're on solid ground, when you're really on a bridge to nowhere. Overrated things. Your problem is that you don't know what you *want.*"

"I know I don't want Avalon to be sucked back into the

Crystal *or* thrown into a terrible war. I just don't know if I have any power to keep either of those things from happening."

"Hm. I don't know either, to be frank." Doc downed his second glass of absinthe and poured himself a third. "But you don't have to figure all that out just yet."

"I don't?"

"You've got some time to figure out what you want to do. Because *fortunately*"—he dragged the last word out—"I can't separate you and the demon anyway."

She honestly didn't know if she was relieved or not. "You could've started with that, you know."

"Could have. Didn't wanna." He snickered. "This was more fun." Taking the bottle to go, he headed for the door. Feeling like she was chasing the back end of a runaway train, she followed him. "Let's go break the news to your angry friend, and then we can settle in for dinner, eh? I'm starving. Oh!" He stopped and turned to face her so suddenly she nearly slammed into him. "Have they invented hamburgers and fries yet?"

"Uh... yes?"

"Fantastic! That's what we'll have! Table for five and a dog." He cackled and then went out the front door, skipping a few steps, whistling the whole way.

"Five? What do you mean, five? There are three of us." Pressing the heels of her hands into her cheekbones, she let out a low groan. She was now stuck with a demon *and* a lunatic. "Fuck my life. Seriously."

Eod barked.

She pointed at him. "Don't you start too."

"*What*?" Grinn roared from outside. "You *liar*!"

"Great. Just. Just great." Gwen wasn't shocked that the demon didn't take the news well, but she hadn't expected him to fly off the handle. Walking outside, she yelped. Grinn had the wizard grasped tight in his hand, holding him off the ground by his neck.

Doc was gagging and kicking uselessly.

Grinn was already ranting. "You will separate us, you *useless* pile of dust, or I will dash your brains out all over the cliffs! You—"

"Put him down, asshole." Gwen stormed up to Grinn and kicked him, rather uselessly she suspected, in the shin. She wasn't even wearing shoes. "He hasn't done anything wrong."

"Oh, but he has." Grinn dropped the wizard all the same. Doc fell the several feet he had been suspended and landed hard on his ass with a grunt. The demon snarled down at the man. "He has wasted my time."

"Get over yourself for once, will you?" She glared up at the demon.

"I'd listen to her." Doc coughed, rubbing his throat. "And if you'd give me a second to explain—"

"Talk. Quickly." Grinn's lips were peeled back in a silent snarl. "I can still murder you, power or no."

The sorcerer climbed back to his feet and brushed himself off. Not like it really mattered, he still looked like he had just fallen out of bed. "You went and used demonic magic and didn't think Avalon's influence would screw it up? It's not my fault."

"I had no choice. I was desperate. Do you think I *want* to be stuck with her?" Grinn was pacing back and forth now along the edge of the wizard's front lawn, looking like a caged tiger.

"I deeply dislike you," Gwen said. She felt the need to interject that, not like it would be a surprise to the demon.

"I think she does wonders for your charming personality, honestly," said Doc. "But! I digress. Here's the issue, in *short*, demon—you two aren't so much two bowls of spaghetti tangled together—you're two different bowls of mashed potatoes put together. Or sand. Sand! Let's use that metaphor instead, eh?"

Grinn was grumbling something about a skull full of moths. Gwen tried not to laugh.

"Picture this. You have two jars of sand. One of you, one of her. You poured them into one bowl, mixed it all up, and you're asking me to sit there and separate them again with a snap of my fingers. It's going to take a lot more magic than I have on hand." The wizard shrugged matter-of-factly. "You're going to need someone or something with way more power."

"Is there anyone on Avalon with more magic than you?" Gwen didn't like the idea of being stuck on the road with Grinn for another who-knew-how-long, but it at least bought her some more time to sort out what she wanted to do.

"Nope!" Doc cackled and held out his arms to his sides. "I'm the best this place has got, kid."

Grinn was doing that low, feral growl that meant danger.

She knew this was going to get ugly, fast. "Wait. You said some*thing*. What did you mean?"

Doc scratched his chin. "Did I? I did. Well, I suppose an artifact of great power could have enough in it to use it almost like a lightning rod. Think about it this way—you can kill someone with your bare hands, right? But killing someone with a hand grenade is a hell of a lot easier. It's a tool." He hummed. "It'd probably destroy the object in the process, which is a shame." He stopped as if he was going to say something else.

Gwen waited for him to start talking again. When he didn't, she sighed. "Are there any artifacts like that on Avalon?"

"Only one that I can think of, and you aren't going to like it." He smiled with a weird hint of glee. He was enjoying this way too much.

"I don't like any of this. What else is new?" She rubbed her temples. She wanted a nap and a stiff drink. This place really was going to give her a headache.

"Yeah, but you really-really-*really* aren't going to like this."

"Just say it, you idiot!" Grinn snapped.

"Well. The one thing I could think of that would have

enough power to separate the two of you, is... well..." He paused. "Caliburn."

Grinn and Gwen agreed on one thing.

And they voiced it exactly the same way and in unison.

"*Fuck.*"

TEN

"Take my hand, knight." Zoe held out her palm to Lancelot. He trusted her. It was not like the Gossamer Lady to play such overt tricks. She was one of the good ones. It was part of the reason why it had been such a tragedy to see her committed to the Iron Crystal.

Not the only reason, of course.

But part of it.

Lancelot placed his hand in hers. Her fingers were so small and delicate compared to his. She gestured her hand, and he watched in awe as a portal opened in the space before them. That was true magic—not like what he could muster. He was always impressed by those who could wield the chaotic forces of the island. For better or worse.

She pulled him through the split in space, and Lancelot felt the world around him simply shift.

* * *

It was Gwen's turn to pace around as she threaded her hands into her hair and tried to grapple with the news Doc had given them.

Caliburn. They had to take and destroy Caliburn. Mordred's goddamn sword. King Arthur's relic. Her mind raced through the possible ways this could all play out, and every single one of them ended with him ripping her head off and using it as a door knocker.

Ask for it nicely? Nope, dead.

Steal it? Nope, dead.

Trick him out of it? Nope, dead.

Bargain for it? With *what* exactly? Sexual favors? Nope, dead.

Grinn wasn't handling it much better than she was. He was sitting by the edge of the lawn, a large, long-clawed hand over his face, looking for all the world like someone had just told him he had terminal cancer.

Not exactly. Just possibly a terminal case of Gwen.

"We steal it." Grinn stood and turned toward the woods. "That is the only option we have."

"Sorry, won't work that way." Doc was cleaning his fingernails with a toothpick he had pulled out of his robe pocket. "Caliburn is bonded to whomever it was given to. It's passed down. He'd have to give it to you."

Grinn laughed in that "how can my day possibly get any worse?" kind of way. Unfortunately for him, it seemed the universe had one more trick to play on him that day.

"And three, two, one..." The sorcerer took five steps to his left, very pointedly. "And here we go."

"What?" Gwen blinked.

A hole opened up in space, right where the wizard had been standing. She recognized it as the same kind of swirly, weird, drawn-on kind of portal that she had jumped through at the very beginning of this whole debacle.

A woman drifted through. Her bare feet were touching the ground, but she looked like she floated more than she walked. A sheer, transparent dress in every shade of pink and purple curled around her as though caught in an invisible pool of water. So did her jet-black hair. She was easily the most beautiful woman Gwen had ever seen.

And she recognized her almost instantly. Even though the version of her that she had seen had been ghostly and made of threads of pure gold. This was Galahad's lover—Zoe. A pair of butterfly wings were folded at her back, draping from her shoulder blades like a cape.

The woman held the hand of a man who stepped out of the portal shortly after her. Someone else Gwen recognized. She couldn't believe what she was seeing. "*Lancelot?*"

The knight looked equally shocked, his silver eyes going wide. "Gwen?"

"Lance!" She ran at him, unable to contain herself, and threw her arms around his neck in a leaping hug. She winced at the pang in her side, having forgotten about her wound. "You're okay, oh my God you're okay!"

Lancelot chuckled and hugged her, clearly being careful not to squeeze too hard in his full plate armor. "Gwen, by all that is holy, you are all right." It seemed he was just as relieved as she was. "I thought for certain you must be dead. Mordred—"

"He destroyed the Crystal. Not me. I couldn't take what happened to you, so I betrayed him, and he went off the handle, and now—" She was blathering, like she always did when she was freaking out. "And now I learned that the guy I've been stuck to the whole time is—"

Grinn interrupted. "Hello, knight."

The next few seconds were complete chaos.

Lancelot pushed her out of the way, sending her staggering toward the mage, who didn't do anything to catch her and simply stepped out of the way. Jerk.

It took Gwen a second to get the right way around, and by the time she had, Lancelot had his sword drawn and was already charging at Grinn.

"Demon! Begone from here!"

Grinn laughed, cruel and mocking, and stood up on his hind legs, rearing up so his height was even more considerable, maybe close to twenty feet. "You wish to fight me, little knight? Come then. See how you fare."

"Knock it off, both of you!" Gwen burst into flame and ran in between the two of them, holding her hands out as if she could actually keep them physically separate. "It's a long story, Lance. He's not here to start a fight."

"But I will gladly end one." Grinn sneered.

"And you, you shut the fuck up and let me explain." She glared at the demon. "Before you get stabbed and we both have to deal with *that*."

Grinn sighed and dropped back down to all fours with a thump, his long, tufted tail swishing annoyedly behind him. He turned his attention to Zoe and, baring his teeth, hissed at her like an angry tiger. There was clearly no love lost between them. Zoe had chosen to hide behind Lancelot, which was likely wise.

Lancelot looked unconvinced, still holding his sword and glowering at the demon. "What is he doing here, Gwen?"

"Okay, so..." She sighed, and stared up at the sky, begging for patience from whoever would listen. This was going to suck. "Grinn is the one who tricked me into coming here. He joined our life forces together using some sort of wacky demonic magic, like, ten years ago, and now we're trying to figure out how to split ourselves up again. This"—she gestured with her fiery hands—"is his magic, not mine."

"Damn right it is." Grinn's toothy smile was gloating and cruel.

"I said shut up." Gwen pointed at the demon. Extinguishing

her fire, she went back to her explanation. "That's why we're here with the mage, trying to figure this all out."

"You two are... bound together?" Lancelot grimaced. "Which means that I cannot harm him without harming you."

"You got it." Doc looked utterly bored. "And I can't split them apart. Even I don't have enough magic to separate those two. We need Caliburn to do it."

Lancelot quickly caught up with what was happening and joined the general vibe. "*Fuck.*"

"Yep." Gwen sighed. "Welcome to the party."

"I'm gonna go get dinner started." Doc headed indoors.

Oh. He had said *five* people were coming to dinner. "How'd you know?"

The wizard only laughed as he disappeared through his front door. Shaking her head, she decided to stop asking the man questions about *how* or *why* anything he said or did made any sense at all. It'd just be a waste of breath.

Letting out a long-suffering sigh, Lancelot sheathed his sword, not taking his angry glare away from Grinn. "Can I expect you to attack me when I turn my back?"

"We have a common enemy at the moment. And so, for the time being, no." Grinn curled his tail around his feet. "Once Mordred is defeated, however..."

Gwen cringed. She didn't like where this conversation was going.

"I plan to see him dead in the ground before my work is done." Lancelot's expression grew dark. "Once that is done, I look forward to facing you in battle."

Grinn chuckled. "We shall see." Standing, he padded toward Doc's house. He shifted into his cat form before reaching the threshold, as otherwise he wouldn't fit through as a demon. Why he didn't pick his human form, she didn't know. She decided she didn't care.

Gwen's shoulders slumped. What was she doing? Could

she really stand against Mordred knowing that the people around her wanted him dead? A delicate hand rested on her shoulder.

"Fret not, dear child. The dice have not yet stilled their roll. We know not how this shall yet unfold." It was Zoe. Her voice was as smooth as silk, gentle and kind. Gwen turned to her and was instantly fascinated by her purple eyes, which looked so much like amethysts it was astonishing.

No wonder Galahad had fallen in love with her.

"I am the Gossamer Lady. It is an honor to meet you, our savior." Zoe leaned forward and kissed her cheek.

"I—uh—I heard about you from Galahad." Gwen felt her cheeks go warm in response—she must be blushing.

"How is my knight?"

"Misses you terribly, but otherwise fine. He was a good friend to me." Gwen smiled at her.

Zoe let out a quiet breath. "All I wish for is one more chance to hold him. I hope the fates are so kind."

"I hope so too." Gwen couldn't imagine what it was like to be apart from someone she loved for so long. Or maybe she could. *Damn it, you idiot. You can't be in love with Mordred.*

As if hearing her thoughts, Zoe's expression turned sad and sympathetic. She pulled Gwen into a hug. It felt like being hugged by a cloud. "Be true to your heart, child. All else leads to madness."

Gwen nodded, knowing that was extremely true. But with no idea what she could do about it. Nothing at the moment, at any rate. Her stomach grumbled loudly, and she laughed quietly. "Sorry. Apparently, I miss hamburgers."

"I do hope he has not only made meat." Zoe sighed. She must be a vegetarian. That tracked.

"I'm sure he made you something." Gwen glanced over at the home. "He seems to know everything."

"That is the way of that wizard." Zoe shook her head. "A

strange creature, even amongst those of us who are truly bizarre. Tell me, my dear child." She took Gwen's hands in hers. "How fare you?"

"I'm holding up, I guess... I don't really have a choice." It was weird to have somebody care after listening to Grinn bitching at her for the, well, whole time he'd started speaking to her. "I'm confused and don't know what to do. Oh, and I got shot by an arrow, that still sucks."

Chuckling, Zoe leaned in and kissed Gwen's forehead. In that moment, a strange warmth filled her. Like standing in bright, wonderful sunlight. The ache in her side slowly faded and then was gone.

Zoe smiled in that way that only ancient, wise creatures could smile. It reminded Gwen of her grandmother, even if Zoe looked no older than Gwen. "I can only remedy one of those things, I fear."

"Thank you." She peeked down at the wound. Sure enough, it was healed, and a pink scar was left behind. "I don't know how to repay you."

"You will in time, I am more than certain." Zoe turned from Gwen and began to walk inside, her wings almost seeming to glitter in the evening sun.

Gwen smiled at Lancelot. "Food?"

He nodded once. "I have had nothing but greenery these past two days. I adore the Gossamer Lady and am endlessly grateful for her hospitality. But I think I am about to die from hunger."

She laughed. "Not much of a salad guy, huh?" It was so good to see him. So good to know he was okay. At least for now.

"If by that you mean a bowl of dry lettuce, carrots, and raw potatoes, then yes." He made a quiet *bleh* sound.

"Ew, please tell me you didn't eat the raw potatoes." She began walking inside with the knight.

"I am not *that* foolish." Lancelot's armor melted back into him, much like Mordred's could do, leaving him in britches and a white shirt tucked into gray pants. Before they went inside, he caught her hand and turned her back to face him. "Gwendolyn Wright, I cannot thank you enough for what you have done. I..." His expression turned strange and fearful. "I cannot describe what being trapped inside that Crystal was like."

It was clear he would have nightmares about it for a very long time. Hugging him again, she rested her head on his chest. She felt terrible for betraying Mordred. She really did. And she missed the Prince in Iron. To say she had complex feelings about him would be to put it mildly. But she decided she did not, under any circumstances, regret the Crystal being destroyed.

At least not yet.

Lancelot returned the hug again, this time resting his cheek on the top of her head. "I do not know what will come of all this. But you are a kind, righteous, and honorable young woman. Thank you. From the bottom of my soul, *thank you*."

She squeezed him tighter. "He blew it up, you know. Not me."

"But you were the catalyst. And for that, I owe you my undying fealty. I will protect you, Lady Gwendolyn Wright."

"Let's hope it doesn't come to that." She smiled up at him but couldn't put much weight behind her words.

"Let's." He smiled back. It was his stomach's turn to remind them that dinner was waiting for them. He chuckled. "Come, before I faint from starvation."

Shaking her head at his melodrama, she followed him inside. She didn't know what was waiting for them. She was certain it wasn't going to be a smooth ride.

But at least, for now, she could sit down and have hamburgers and fries with a pack of friends.

Well, a pack of friends, and one crotchety demon.

Life certainly got interesting, didn't it?

ELEVEN

Dinner had been exactly as uncomfortable as Gwen would have expected, sitting down with a wackjob wizard, a literal fairy, a knight bent on revenge, and a demon in cat form who very clearly despised everyone else at the table but was super into the hamburgers. The sound of an angry cat eating was always one of the funniest things for Gwen, but she tried not to provoke the demon any more than was necessary.

After the incredibly awkward dinner of stilted conversations, she was relieved that she would be sleeping indoors on an actual bed. She liked camping as much as a human possibly could, but there was a point where the joke ran thin. And besides, she'd be back on the road sleeping under the stars the following night.

Because it was clear that wherever the answer to her dilemma was, it wasn't here. Eod curled up by her feet and let out the telltale heavy sigh of a dog settling in for the night. Scratching him between the ears, she lay down and shut her eyes.

In order to split up her and Grinn, they would need to destroy Caliburn—something Mordred had to give up *willingly*.

Not only did that seem impossible, she didn't even know if she wanted it to happen in the first place.

Destroying Caliburn seemed like a big fucking deal. And her being attached to Grinn and having his power was the only thing keeping him from unleashing another bloody rampage. Maybe she was supposed to stay like this—tethered to the asshole "cat" for the rest of her life.

But that raised a whole new level of complications. Namely, she knew Grinn wasn't going to put up with it. And while he couldn't set shit on fire, it was clear there was a whole mess of other ways he could cause problems.

Hugging the pillow to herself, she wished she had someone she could talk to. Really talk to. Zoe seemed nice and all, but Gwen wasn't sure she'd have any advice past a patient smile and a gentle pat on the head.

No, she needed somebody who would *get* it. Lancelot certainly wasn't it. Doc was too insane to keep on track with a conversation for longer than a minute or two. Besides, he had pointed out the fundamental issue that she didn't know what she wanted.

And damn it all, she didn't.

She didn't want to split from Grinn and start a war, but she didn't want to stay tethered to him. She wanted to be with Mordred, but she disagreed with how he wanted to rule the world. She wanted to go home, but she wanted to stay.

I hate everything about all of this.

With her own heavy sigh, she clutched the pillow and tried her best to fall asleep. After an hour of her mind spinning in circles, she finally nodded off.

And promptly found herself standing ankle-deep in mud. The sound of clashing metal and the shouts of men surrounded her. She froze, trying to understand what she was looking at.

It was a battle. The field around her had been turned into a mud pit by the boots of a thousand men. Bodies were strewn everywhere—some dead, some dying. Weapons were abandoned where they had fallen.

The sound of cries for violence and cries for mercy filled the air. She had seen all the movies—she'd watched enough documentaries about medieval warfare. But they did a poor job of showing what it would be like to stand in the middle of it.

The soldiers who were still standing looked exhausted, trudging through the muck that was equal parts dirt and blood, swinging their weapons with all the energy they had left. She watched as a man in full armor and a dark gray cape knocked another man to his knees before ramming the point of his sword into the gap in the man's breastplate and helm. The man screamed, then slumped to the ground lifelessly as the first soldier ripped his sword back out from his victim.

Gwen fought the urge to be sick. The soldier in the gray cape walked away from his dead foe, clearly exhausted but stalwart. He stopped a few feet away from her, seemingly not noticing her, and pulled his helm off to push his hair from his face.

It was Mordred.

She blinked, staring. It was *human* Mordred. His hair was long and blond, soaked with sweat and covered in dirt. He had a blotch of an angry bruise forming along the side of his throat and his jaw where he must have been hit hard by someone or something. His eyes were a deep green.

For one moment, he looked so *tired.* As if for all the world he wished he could stop. There, with the backdrop of violence and war, was a man who was weary beyond all words. But he took a breath, placed the helm back over his head, and turning, began to wade through the mud to find his next foe.

When had she started to cry? She wiped her hands across her cheeks and sniffled.

"Do not waste your tears on me."

The world around her changed with the flick of a light switch again. No longer on the battlefield, she was in the strange, nightmarish version of Mordred's study. She turned to face the sound of the voice, and found him standing in front of his fireplace, staring into the flames. He was once more as she knew him—the elemental, not the mortal. He wasn't in his full armor, but, like usual, his arms were still covered in the iron that was a part of him.

He looked down at his clawed, gauntleted hands. "Such is the way of soldiering. You fight, you kill, and you go on to do it again." He sighed. "Yet you are surprised that I seek to prevent war."

"No, I just don't agree with the way you want to go about doing it." When Gwen finished drying her tears, she walked up to him. She knew he wasn't really there—this was all just a dream—but maybe she could talk things through with the fictional version of Mordred, if she couldn't ask for guidance from the real one.

The subconscious was weird.

"It was my last resort. And it will continue to be so. But I will not see this world destroyed, Gwendolyn." He turned to her; his green eyes were once more molten rust. "You are healed."

"Zoe." She shrugged. "Apparently, she can heal people."

"Ah." He winced at the Gossamer Lady's name. "How is she?"

"I mean, she's a goddamn fairy, so that's cool." She sighed. "She has *wings*. That isn't fair. I want wings."

He chuckled. "Then have them."

"What?"

"You are an elemental and a shapeshifter, firefly." He held up his hand as proof. "We shape our bodies as we wish. Do you think she was born with those wings?"

"I don't know, I mean, Galahad is from, like, Tir... somewhere. He's not human." She shrugged.

"Tir n'Aill. And yes, I suppose I see your point. No, she was from Earth, same as you." He held out his hand to her. "I am glad she healed you."

She gave him her hand, always amazed at how glaring the difference was between her small, normal fingers, and his metal gauntlet with its jagged, rusted talons. But he was no less gentle with her as he grasped her hand and pulled her closer to him. "Are you safe?"

"Yeah. I'm at the wizard's house, and—"

"Oh, no." Mordred sighed and shut his eyes. "Not *him*."

"Is he actually Merlin?"

"If so, he is not the one I knew. But perhaps he has changed his face. I cannot stomach speaking to him long enough to discern the truth." He traced his other hand over her hair, stroking back the strands. "You are troubled."

"I don't know what to do." She leaned into his touch. She couldn't help it. "I don't know whose side I'm on. I don't know where I'm supposed to be. I don't know what people want from me. I don't feel like I'm in control of anything, I'm just being dragged along for the ride. And I hate not having a say in anything."

"I certainly have not helped your dilemma, I fear." He smirked slightly. "Forgive me for casting you out. I..."

"I know. And I'm sorry." She stepped into him and wrapped her arms around his waist. It was still funny to her that she could barely reach all the way around him. Bulky bastard. "I just... the Crystal is just so wrong."

"I hoped you would come to understand. That perhaps, out in the wilds of Avalon, you might experience the same treachery and violence that forced me to act." He rested his cheek atop her head and wrapped his arms around her. "But I did not know how much it would grieve me to see you hurt."

"I'm all right. I'm not alone."

"You are with the one who brought you here, aren't you?" His arms tightened around her just slightly.

"Yeah."

"Will you tell me their name?"

She hesitated. It was just a dream. She knew it was. But she didn't want to take the risk. "I... can't." That was all she'd need. Mordred flying off the fucking handle because of Grinn. She had no idea what kind of chaos that'd cause. She couldn't take even a fake version of Mordred shouting at her. "I'm sorry."

"You do not trust me." He didn't sound hurt or disappointed. It was just a statement of truth.

"Can you blame me?"

"No." He chuckled. He kissed the top of her head. "In your position, I would trust no one. And that is the advice I give you now. To some, you will merely be expendable. To others, an amusing novelty. And to a dangerous few, a means to an end."

No kidding. "Yeah. I get that sense."

"Come back to me. Return to the keep. Forgive me for my anger." He tilted her head up to him. "Please, firefly. Let us find a new way forward together."

"A way forward as your prisoner?"

"Yes. But the chains that will bind you are nothing compared to those that bind me to you." His voice was soft.

That was the most tragically romantic thing anyone had ever said to her. It made her want to cry and beg him to take her back. Was that really what she wanted? To be with him? If this was really her subconscious playing Mordred for her, then... yeah. Apparently, that *was* what she wanted. "You promise you aren't going to rip my head off?"

He smiled. "I promise. Though I expect I will wish to lecture you at length for your foolish decision to poison and betray me." His smile became just a little wicked, a playful devilishness pulling at the edges. "Perhaps I will even find a creative way to punish you."

Her face bloomed in warmth. "Damn it, Mordred." She laughed and ducked her head.

Catching her chin in his gauntlet, he turned her face back up to him and kissed her before she could say another word. It was a gesture so full of emotion that it took her breath away. She almost began to cry again.

It was a gesture full of *love*.

With all her heart, with everything in her, she realized she wished it was real. She wished Mordred loved her. And she wished she could make it up to him for what she had done. He broke away from the kiss and simply held her to him, letting her rest her cheek against his chest and feel his strength and his warmth.

"I have decided to allow the elementals to be free, for now," he explained, his voice a rumble. "I only hunt one—the demon Grinn—to keep him from his inevitable warpath. The rest will be able to choose to repeat their former mistakes or to seek a new path forward. I will not rebuild the Iron Crystal if they do. But should they resort to their squabbles and warmongering, I will have no choice."

Gwen was glad he didn't see her wince at Grinn's name. Shit, shit, shit. Just... shit.

This isn't real. This is just your stupid brain telling you stories to help you parse through your stupid situation. She shut her eyes. "I understand."

"Come back to me, Gwendolyn Wright."

"I don't know if I can. But..." She paused and made up her mind. "But I'll try."

"That is all I could ask for. Now, rest, my firefly." He kissed the top of her head. "And tell the Gossamer Lady that she is welcome in my home. Her husband misses her terribly."

Wouldn't that be lovely.

Too bad it was just a dream.

"I will," she promised him anyway, knowing she wouldn't.

The dream faded away a few moments later, and she slept without any other disturbances. That was until she was woken up by Eod kicking her in the face. "Ow!"

The dog barked. The way a dog barks when it really, really has to go out. With a sigh, she climbed out of bed. It was barely past dawn. "You suck, dog." She felt like she hadn't slept at all. Pulling on her chainmail clothes, she headed outside and watched as the dog ran off to go do his business somewhere in the woods. Or to chase squirrels. Or both.

Sitting down on the front steps to Doc's home, she folded her arms across her knees and rested her chin on them.

She was a little surprised when the sorcerer himself came out and sat down beside her. "Morning."

"I hate mornings," he grumbled in reply. He looked like he had slept worse than she did, and that was saying something. "Rough night?"

"Yeah. I guess you could say that." She shut her eyes. "Weird dreams."

"Hm." It didn't seem like he believed her, though she wasn't sure why. "Have you made up your mind on what you want yet?"

"I think... I think I need to go back to the keep and talk to Mordred. One way or the other, he's the way out of this mess. And I..." She trailed off. She didn't know how to put her feelings into words just yet.

"I know. I understand." Doc patted her on the back. "Relationships are fucked up, am I right?"

She laughed. "I think this goes well past fucked up."

"Not for Avalon." He snorted. "Trust me. Well, I'm going to go get a pot of coffee going. I think we're in for a long walk." Shoving himself up to his feet, he grunted.

"We?"

"Do you think I'm going to miss out on all the fun? *Please.* I want a front-row seat to this shit show. It's gonna be spectacular."

"Do you know that because of your weird psychic powers?"

"Nope." He laughed once. "I just have a brain. Who knows? Maybe I'm wrong about this one." He went back indoors, finishing his thought as he went. "But I don't think I am."

No, she didn't think he was either.

TWELVE

It was after breakfast that Gwen sought out Grinn. The demon was on the edge of the wizard's front lawn, avoiding all conversation with anybody, and sitting in that "angry loaf" position that cats did when they wanted to sit down but also wanted to make sure they could nope out or attack at any point.

He glanced at her with his red eye and then turned his attention back to the woods. "What?"

She sighed. Great. Already off to a great start that day. "I think we should head back to the keep. It feels stupid to have walked all the way here only to walk all the way back, but..." She shrugged. "I don't know a better way."

"Why?" He sneered. "Eager to go back to your lover?"

Yes. "No." She folded her arms across her chest as Grinn snorted in disbelief. "The fact of the matter is, we need Caliburn to fix this. He wants you dead or whatever, and I don't want to go down with you."

"I will not lose to him."

"I don't wanna take that chance. The only way I get out from the middle of you two is if I'm no longer attached to you. And the only way to do that is with Caliburn." She was rolling the dice that the Prince in Iron wouldn't just decide to kill her alongside the demon, but that was a risk she was going to have to take.

It was clear from her dreams that she desperately wanted to apologize to him and see if there was a way forward for their sorry excuse for a relationship. If that's even what it was. She had no idea how Mordred really felt about her—whether or not she was just a distraction or if she meant anything.

She supposed she should start with that. Because if he didn't care about her, he'd probably use her to get to Grinn. Bait, or whatever. If he did care about her, maybe he'd help her out of her situation.

Step one—get back to Mordred.

Step two—figure out how Mordred felt about her. If he cared, tell him about Grinn and that whole messy situation. If he didn't care about her, or didn't care about her enough, well...

Her options there were either to help Grinn get Caliburn or not. She'd cross that bridge when she got to it.

At least I have a plan. It's a terrible plan, but it's a plan.

"Either way," she continued. "We need Caliburn. And the only way to get to it is through Mordred. So it makes sense."

"And what is your plan? To ask for the most powerful relic in Avalon?" Grinn huffed, clearly thinking she was an idiot.

"Maybe, yeah. If I explain to him—"

"Explain?" He laughed. "You truly are a fool. He is more likely to use you to weaken me. If he learns you have my power *and* we are linked, do you think he would hesitate to impale you on iron spikes? You do not understand how much hatred he holds in his black heart for me."

"I wouldn't talk about black hearts." She rolled her eyes.

"And it is for that reason that I know him. We share the affliction." He sat up, curling his tail around his front legs. "No. He will use and manipulate you in the name of the greater good. He will sacrifice everything to see me defeated."

He was probably right, but damn it, she wanted to have a plan. "So, what do we do?"

Grinn went silent for a long moment, staring off into the woods. The gears were clearly spinning. "We go toward the iron keep."

"I just said—"

"For very different reasons," he cut her off. "We will need to join Lancelot in his war against Mordred. You and I will join the fray. We will go as near to the keep as we dare and wait for the right time to strike. We will take Caliburn from his corpse."

At least they had agreed to go in the right direction. She would have to sneak off to see Mordred or to send him a message of some kind.

Doc walked out of his house, smiling broadly. "Are we ready to go? Where is my cart?"

Gwen was happy for the interruption. "Your cart?" She arched an eyebrow. "We have a horse."

"Oh, no no no. That just won't do." He rubbed his nose. "I refuse to walk the whole way and I am deathly allergic to horses."

"Can't you, like"—she wiggled her fingers in the air toward him—"summon yourself something?"

"No, that's not how"—he wiggled his fingers back at her—"it works."

Grinn muttered something about how much he hated wizards.

Gwen shook her head. "Whatever. Well, can you deal with walking to the nearest town? We can try to get a cart there. If Lancelot is trying to raise an army, he'll probably need some supplies from the town, or... something. I don't know. I don't know what it takes to raise an army." This felt so strange. Joining forces with Mordred's enemies when she cared about him and helping them rally an army when she didn't want a war.

Stick to the shitty plan, Gwen. Just stick to the shitty plan.

The wizard wrinkled his nose in disgust. "I will ask Lancelot for his silver horse."

In the end, by the time the five of them—and Eod—got onto the road, it worked out that Grinn, Gwen, and Lancelot were walking. Zoe was atop Sunshine and the wizard was riding Lancelot's silver horse.

Lancelot walked up ahead with Zoe. Eod was off scouting the road, and Gwen was walking beside the wizard. Grinn was fifty or so feet behind them, clearly wanting nothing to do with any of them or their conversations.

She glanced behind them now and then to make sure he was still there. And he was—a scrawny, ancient, battered-up demon that walked like a gorilla but looked like a panther with horns, padding along and *sulking*.

She frowned.

"You're right to feel some pity for him," the wizard said, keeping his voice low.

"I know he misses home, but..." She sighed. "I don't get why he has to be so terrible to everybody."

"It's more than simply missing his home, dear." Doc was cleaning his fingernails with a toothpick again. "Has he told you the whole story?"

"No. He doesn't like to talk. Especially not to me."

He chuckled, and then let out a sad sigh. "Well. It was about a thousand years ago now, or more, after Mordred and his knights came to us, but not by long. Hell suffered some strange manner of cataclysm. You see, it is not meant to touch Avalon. No demons had come here before and none since. I do not know what caused it, but, for a fraction of time, our two worlds collided."

"That... sounds bad."

"Avalon, for all its chaos, adapts to new states of being very quickly. When one does not worry about the order of things, new information isn't troublesome at all." He shrugged. "Avalon simply changed to have a little bit of hell in it."

"Weird."

"That it was. But as quickly as the cataclysm had come, it passed. The alignment fell away, and the part of hell that was here went with it. But it left behind some of its denizens." He flicked the toothpick away into the shrubbery.

"That's how Grinn came here?"

"Mm-hm. And about a hundred of his kind. Including his wife and his children."

Dread gnawed at her. "Oh no." Gwen remembered Grinn's words. *I had a wife.*

"Oh yes, I'm afraid." Doc's expression, usually jovial or perhaps borderline insane, fell to one that showed the weight of the centuries. He looked *tired.* "The elementals did not take kindly to the demons who were trying to scratch out a corner of the world for themselves. Demons, not knowing how to exist outside their own nature, thought to build their own kingdom here. They were exterminated. All except one."

"He kept saying he was the only demon who had ever been here." Her heart sank. Poor Grinn—no wonder he was so angry. He had watched his wife, his children, all his fellow demons... They had all been wiped out except him. The thought of it made her sick. She wanted to turn around and hug the angry cat monster, but she knew Grinn would just smack her aside and yell at her about it.

But she just couldn't imagine what it was like to go through that. No wonder he hated everybody. No wonder he hated Avalon.

"He is the only one that remains. It likely pains him too much to admit otherwise. He was gifted the power of fire by the island as he watched his people and his family die. He is an elemental, same as any of the others—and that afforded him protection under the law that says that unless all other elementals vote for it, he could not be killed. They put him on trial, and he almost joined his family. There was one dissenter who wished to spare him."

"Who?"

Doc smirked. "Mordred."

That made no sense to her. They hated each other. "Why?"

"You would have to ask him. I think the prince took pity on the demon, and thought perhaps, with a show of empathy, Grinn could help Mordred in his quest to calm the warmongering of the others. He wanted an ally." He snorted. "You see how well *that* worked out."

She shook her head. Poor Mordred seemed to go from one betrayal to the next, over and over again. And here she was, potentially setting him up for another.

"I think you're doing the right thing, for what it's worth." The sorcerer scratched his stubble. "But I don't envy you for being stuck in the middle of all these idiots."

She chuckled. "Yeah. All I really want is to avoid a massive war. But I don't know if it's possible."

"Probably not, I'm afraid to say. But by trying to prevent it, you may save many lives in the process."

"Don't you know how it's going to play out? Like, how the future is going to go?" She watched him, hoping he might give up something with his expression even if he didn't tell her the truth. Was everything going to go to shit? Was Avalon doomed?

"I only know everything that *is*. I know what was, and what is, but not what will be." He gestured aimlessly in the air as he tried to explain. "But think of it like a lighthouse. I can use the *now*—which is the flame in the lens—to see out into the *what will be.* Because I can see what was, which... uh... I guess the tower in this metaphor—I can predict what is to come. But the farther away I go from the source, the fuzzier things get. Does that make sense?"

"Um. Kind of?"

"All right, think of it this way. Say you knew that I was having a fight with Lancelot. The two of us were screaming, shouting, absolutely furious at each other. Say you knew that I had picked up a rock. Say you knew that I was rearing my arm back. What do you think might follow next?"

She furrowed her brow. "You throw the rock at Lancelot?"

"Precisely. I know what is, what got us there, for every single thing in the history of *ever*, and so I can use that to tell you what might follow next. But maybe, instead of throwing the rock, I choose to swallow it whole. It's possible. It's unlikely, but it's possible."

She supposed that made sense. "Huh. That sounds complicated. How do you keep it all straight?"

"My head is a crowded place, we'll put it that way." He laughed. "And I think that's probably why I'm a bit insane and don't remember a damn thing about myself. I'm too full of everybody else's details."

"I guess I don't blame you." She smirked. "I'd be loopy too." After a small pause in the conversation, she had to ask. "Do you think you might be Merlin?"

"It's possible. But the knights you've met, including that hothead up there," he said, as he gestured at Lancelot. "Have all met the real Merlin. Unless I somehow managed to change my entire self, or... reverse age, or something, I don't see how they wouldn't recognize me and clue me in by now."

"Do you know where he went? Merlin?"

"No. Which is strange, seeing as I know everything else. So perhaps I am him, since I can't see any of my own details." He shrugged. "Or maybe it's a wizard thing. I don't know. Why?"

Gwen sighed. "I guess I just hoped that somebody like him would be able to just... get me out of this whole mess. That he'd know what I should do."

"Life isn't that easy, no matter how much magic you throw at it. Sometimes, there's nothing that magic can do to fix the situation." The wizard shifted in the saddle and grimaced. "My ass is going to be so bruised later."

She laughed. "Not a rider?"

"Allergic to horses, remember? And I can't just *make* myself one like the elementals can. I'd have you make me one, but I prefer not to be immolated before lunch."

"Wait. I can make horses?" She blinked. "Like Lancelot and Mordred?"

"Hon, you can do whatever you want with fire. Want to make a giant dragon made out of flame? You could. The only thing stopping you is, well, you." He shifted again, grunting in pain.

"I guess I haven't tried."

"There's your problem."

"It won't matter for long anyway." She frowned and folded her arms. "I won't be an elemental forever."

"How do you figure?"

"Well, either Grinn gets his way, and he splits us up, and takes his power back, in which case there's a giant fucking war and I'll probably die, or Mordred decides I'm too much trouble and kills me when he kills Grinn." She shook her head. "Either way, I'm probably dead."

"Probably."

She glared at him.

"You said it, not me!" He threw up his hands in frustration. "You're *probably* dead. But like I said, maybe instead of throwing the rock, I swallow it whole. Nothing's decided. So, here's my advice—be unpredictable."

Rubbing her hands over her face, she decided that while talking to the wizard was fun and all, it was also going to give her a headache.

"Are we there yet?" Doc shouted up to Lancelot. "My ass is cramping up!"

Yeah. Definitely going to give her a headache.

* * *

Mordred was pacing in his study when Galahad found him. Glancing over at the tall knight, he accepted the inevitability of what would follow. "Zoe sends her love. She and Gwendolyn have met."

Galahad paused, his wizened face caught in a look of surprise. "How do you know this?"

Pulling the necklace out from under his linen shirt, Mordred showed it to the Knight in Gold before putting it back.

"Ah." The knight sighed. "You are spying on her in her dreams."

"Hardly spying, I have made myself very well known." He smirked.

"Have you told her that you are invading her mind?"

"Not in so many words. She must know." Mordred shrugged.

"I would not assume that," Galahad replied. "She is not of this world, remember."

"I suppose you are right." But part of Mordred was enjoying the game—the fantasy of it all. That in their dreams, at least, they could be together without the weight of the real world crushing down upon them. He stopped by a window to look out at the field of grass and the forest beyond. Like Galahad, he now had another reason to watch for the arrival of others. Part of him expected an army to step from the glade at any point.

Part of him hoped for a young woman to emerge instead.

"How is the Gossamer Lady?" Galahad was clearly fighting back the hope in his heart, though it escaped into his tone regardless. "It seems many have been to visit her, yet I cannot."

"She healed Gwendolyn of a wound. I have told Gwen that Zoe is welcome here as my guest whenever she likes—though, as you said, Gwen might not believe I was anything more than a figment of her mind." Sadly, Mordred figured he should likely explain to his firefly what was truly happening. Galahad was right that he should not have assumed she would know—she was from a realm without magic and mystery, after all. "I will explain it to her next time we sleep, in hopes she can convince Zoe to come here."

"Thank you, my prince."

"It is not for you." He smiled teasingly over at the knight. "I cannot deal with you moping about the keep like the ghost of some lonely sailor lost at sea."

Galahad chuckled. "Yes. I suppose that is fair."

"Perhaps—" Mordred was about to say *all will be well.* He should have known not to let hope claw its way into his heart. He should have known better. The world had taught him that lesson again and again. Yet it seemed he would never learn.

The necklace began to burn. Hissing in pain, he tore it from his neck. He watched as the heat from the crystal caused his gauntlets to glow as though he had put them into a forge.

"What is it?" Galahad stepped closer.

"Something is wrong. Something has happened." Mordred felt a sudden terror and helplessness grip him. "Gwendolyn is in danger."

THIRTEEN

Gwen fell back in the line to walk beside the demon. For several minutes, he did his best to ignore her existence. She waited, not really knowing how to start what she wanted to say anyway.

Finally, Grinn gave up and let out an exhausted sigh. "What do you want, human?"

She stared down at the ground in front of her. "I don't know. I just wanted to say I'm sorry for what happened to you."

He grunted. "I hate that wizard."

"Why? He was just trying to provide some context, is all."

"It is not his story to tell. If I wanted you to know, I would have told you myself." The demon grimaced. "And it does not *matter,* Gwendolyn. I am the way I am. And there is nothing you or anyone can do to change it. Understanding the *why* is a foolish waste of time."

"To you." She shook her head. She didn't know why she bothered. "Well, all I wanted to say was that I was sorry for what happened to you and your family. And if that makes me stupid, then fine. I'm an idiot."

"Finally, she admits it."

"I swear to fuck—" She put her hands over her face. "You know what? Never mind. I give up."

"Good."

God on high, she wanted to scream. She sped up to get away from Grinn, and spent the rest of the early afternoon walking in silence between him and Doc. Luckily, the nearest town wasn't far.

Aercester was what the sign said as they passed it. It meant literally nothing to her, except for the fact that it sounded incredibly British. As they stepped within the city limits, the group circled up to create a plan.

Lancelot was keeping an eye on the streets. "I do not think we should stay here long."

"I agree," Zoe added. She looked nervous. "I do not think we will be terribly welcome. Especially not with..." She glanced at Grinn. "Him."

"Can you take your cat form?" Gwen suggested to the demon.

"I will not hide from peasants—they should fear us." He bared his remaining fang, the fur on his shoulders standing up.

"Great. Awesome. Sure. So, let's make it quick." Gwen desperately wanted to scream again or throw something large and heavy at the demon. Whatever. "We need to buy a cart for Doc's delicate feet."

"Don't take your mood out on me, missy." Doc waggled a finger at her. "And we could very much use a cart. I'm not the only one who's complaining about it."

"Yeah? Who?" She called his bluff.

"The dog." Doc looked so proud of himself.

She rubbed her hands over her face. This was all seriously giving her a headache. "Fine. Great. A cart for you *and* the dog. What else?"

Lancelot was holding onto the hilt of his sword. "I will stop by the taverns and see if there are any other elementals in the area that we could approach for aid. We will not have long to build an army before Mordred goes on the offensive, I fear."

"So... it sounds like we're splitting up." Gwen sighed. They had just found each other again, and it meant she was going to be left alone with Grinn and the sorcerer. One of whom she didn't mind most of the time, but the other one grated on her nerves on a good day.

"It seems so." Zoe clearly didn't like the idea either, judging by the frown etched on her face. "Mordred will hunt the demon relentlessly. And if we seek to stand against him, this would be our opportunity to gather without his notice."

Grinn was mumbling something under his breath, but she ignored him.

"Great. I love being bait." But she couldn't argue it was a good plan. Between Mordred's desire to stop Grinn and his likely overwhelming need to rip Gwen's head off, it meant that they were the perfect distraction.

Zoe walked up to her and hugged her without warning. "You must be brave, young one. You must follow your heart. Do not let the coldness of others wither it away."

It was good advice, but Gwen shook her head. "I feel like every option I have is a bad one. I'm caught in the middle of shit I didn't start."

"Such is the way for so many of us." Zoe stroked her knuckles along Gwen's cheek. Her touch was warm and soft. "Victims of the revenge that others seek." She looked so very sad. "But I would like to give you a gift before we part ways. I do not know when next we will meet."

"I—"

Zoe caught Gwen's face between her hands and kissed her. Gwen's eyes flew wide, not knowing what to do except to freeze up as the fairy literally *kissed* her.

When the Gossamer Lady spread her wings behind her, unfurling the beautiful, massive, translucent butterfly wings,

Gwen *felt* it. She felt it like they were her own. She could feel the afternoon sun warming them. Like an extra set of arms, it was like she had limbs that had been asleep the whole time and were only now waking up.

It felt so natural.

Zoe broke away, a smile on her beautiful features. "There we are."

Gwen blinked, astonished. Something shifted at her back.

Wings!

"Holy—" She whirled, trying to see all of them, but it was stupid as they were attached to her back. She laughed and gaped at the parts of them she could see. She certainly had wings, but they were *nothing* like Zoe's. The Gossamer Lady's were beautiful butterfly wings.

Gwen's were leathery, like a dragon's. Or a bat's. The peaks of the wings had two talons. She wiggled them, and they felt so much like fingers it was surreal. "Holy *shit*." She laughed. Reaching out, she touched the skin of the new limbs. She wished they were graceful and beautiful like Zoe's—or at least maybe feathery like a phoenix. Phoenixes were fiery animals, weren't they?

But it seemed that wasn't going to be the case for her. The wings were a brighter red at the top and turned to a dark, nearly black crimson at the ends. She supposed beggars shouldn't be choosers.

"Thank you." She smiled at Zoe, who was beaming with pride.

"They suit you." The fairy leaned in and kissed her cheek again. "I hope they are yours forever. I hope you are able to learn to use them. Flying is like no other experience you will ever have."

"I fear the locals have noticed us," Lancelot broke into the moment. "Though however tempted I am to ask you to kiss again." He grinned.

"Oh, shut up." Gwen glared at him, though half-heartedly. "Men. I swear."

Zoe chuckled. "Wise beyond your years. But he has a valid point. We should go about our business before we are under siege."

Gwen would try to argue the point that they hadn't done anything wrong, so why would the townsfolk try to hurt them... but the two new scars from her arrow wound were proof that they should very much be concerned.

The wizard climbed off the back of Lancelot's metal steed, and they prepared to split up. She walked up to Lancelot and hugged him. "Please be careful."

He smiled down at her and hugged her back, careful not to crush her new wings. It was such a weird feeling to have extra limbs. "I will do my best, my lady. And we will see each other again, when Mordred is defeated and Avalon is free of *two* tyrants." He shot a glare toward Grinn. "Beware of him. You are useful to him as a shield until the moment you are not."

Nodding, she didn't disagree. She'd like to think that Grinn had some sort of fondness for her after she took care of him for ten years as a cat and now had spent almost two weeks trying to help him, but she knew she was probably kidding herself. "I won't trust him."

"Good." Lancelot kissed her forehead. "The wizard's desire to follow you means that you are important to the future of this world. Be careful with your choices."

"I don't want to be."

"We do not get to choose when fate places us in its focus. I wish that we could." He took a step back from her, his silver helm melding over his face. She had seen Mordred do the same trick a hundred times, but it never ceased to amaze her. "I will see you soon, my lady—when Mordred is dead, and I sever that demon's head from his shoulders."

"I am eager for the moment you get your chance to try,

knight." Grinn huffed a laugh. "I have decorated my home with the bones of men greater than you."

"Guys. Not right now." Gwen was tempted to burst into flames to make her point, but they were trying to look harmless to the locals who were now peering out of their homes through cracked windows and doors.

"You are right. We will gather our supplies and go. I tire of this. I tire of all of you." Grinn walked away on his own, heading down a side street.

"Wait—" Gwen sighed and threw her hands up in frustration. "Whatever." She took the reins of Sunshine. "I guess this is goodbye for now."

"For now," Lancelot assured her.

She smiled at him and waved goodbye as Lancelot and Zoe went the other way, deeper toward the center of the town, leaving her, Doc, and Eod with no other choice than to follow after Grinn.

The streets had gone eerily quiet since their arrival. It was making her nervous. "How stupid are we being right now?" she asked the wizard. "On a scale of one to ten."

"Eleven. But I suspect that is by design." His expression was firm and unusually dour.

"What do you m—" She never got a chance to finish her question. And she didn't get a chance to hear his answer.

The sound of gunfire echoed through the street. Somewhere up ahead, she heard Grinn roar in rage. Pain lanced through Gwen, and she looked down at herself, expecting to see more holes. But she wasn't the one who had been shot.

Grinn had.

Her knees felt weak as the link between them went into effect. Somehow, deep down inside, she knew Grinn would be dead if it weren't for their shared life force. Which meant that if she got hurt next, it was over for both of them.

And sure enough, a small brigade of soldiers rounded the

corner. They were dressed in colonial garb, and four of them had old-school muskets, fitted with bayonets. Two were already covered in a black liquid that she assumed was Grinn's blood.

The wizard pushed her aside. "Gwen—*run!*" Electricity began to crackle around his hands as the soldiers finished reloading the muskets and raised them to fire in their direction.

She didn't hesitate. Turning on her heel, feeling like she was about to faint at any moment from the drain of keeping Grinn "alive," she ran down an alley to the sound of the boom of gunfire, of lightning, and a dog furiously barking.

Sadly, she didn't make it far.

Dead end.

"Fuck!" She turned to run and try another way.

"Halt!" A soldier was blocking her path. He had a musket in his hand. He stepped forward, pointing it at her. "Die, *fiend*."

He was going to shoot her.

If he shot her, she'd die. For real.

Panic hit her, fast and hard, like she hadn't experienced in a very, very long time. Tears streamed down her cheeks, turning to liquid fire that hissed as it touched the cobblestones by her feet. "Please don't—don't make me—" She was ablaze. She hadn't even noticed when it happened. "I don't want to hurt you."

"Your kind are a plague!" He pulled back the hammer on the lock of the musket. He wasn't going to listen to her.

With a scream, she held out her hands in front of her. A blast of fire erupted from her and enveloped the soldier. He screamed. His gun went off. The musket ball hit a wood door beside her with a *crunch* into the surface. But it had missed her.

But she hadn't missed the soldier.

He was lying on the ground, still burning... and not moving. His flesh was blackened and charred, already cracked, blistered, and flaking. The smell of cooking flesh filled the air.

Dead.

She had killed a man.

The smell was too much. Weeping, she turned and lost her breakfast, her stomach heaving in disgust at what she had done.

She had to run. She had to run away. She had killed a man. She was trapped. She couldn't breathe. Everything was too close. Too warm. Too real. She had killed a man.

Her head spun. The world suddenly felt blissfully far away.

She fainted.

* * *

It was a risky ploy. Mordred knew the magic he had spun into the crystal necklace was not meant to be wielded in such a way. But he did not know what else to do. Standing in his study, he clutched the necklace tight in his metal hand, not caring for how hot it burned. It did not hurt him.

Gwendolyn was in danger. Real danger.

And he was helpless to aid her if he did not know where she was. Shutting his eyes, he focused all his will into the magic he wove. He tightened his fist, shattering the jewel. The power of it crashed into him like a wave, instantly dragging him under.

He collapsed to the ground, the world going dark around him.

Hear me, Avalon—you shall not take her from me.

FOURTEEN

Someone was holding her. Gwen instantly knew who, just by the feel of the arms that circled her, clutching her tight. The slight metallic smell was also a giveaway. She was still crying, even though she knew she had passed out and was unconscious.

After what had happened, she figured she was going to cry for a very long time.

Clinging to the dream version of Mordred, she buried her head against his chest and wept. Through her tears and her heaving attempts to breathe, she couldn't help but blather. "I didn't want to—I told him to stop—but he wouldn't listen—I killed him, oh God I killed him." The smell of cooking human flesh was still thick in her throat. She didn't know if she'd ever forget it. "But I—I—I didn't want to die."

"Shush, firefly... shush. It will be all right." He stroked her hair.

"No, I—I don't think it will." She curled her hands into the fabric of his shirt. She was already staining it dark with her tears. At least she wasn't on fire in her sleep, that was all she'd need. "Grinn's been shot which means—"

"*What?*" He grabbed her by the shoulders, his mood changing in a blink.

She froze. Dread settled on her like a dark cloud. "This isn't a normal dream, is it?"

"What of Grinn, where is he? Where are you?" Mordred's expression was a mask of equal parts worry and rage. "Tell me the name of this town!"

"I—I—" Oh no. Oh, she had fucked up and fucked up hard.

"How long have you been traveling with him?" His mood darkened, his rage turning to *hate*. "He is the one who brought you here, isn't he?"

"I didn't—I didn't know. He didn't tell me his name until after the Crystal was destroyed." She felt so very small. Like she'd been caught doing something terrible by her school principal. "I didn't mean to—"

He swore, so loudly and harshly that she jolted in his grasp. He shut his eyes, took a breath, and slowly let it out. When he turned his attention back to her, it was clear he was on a razor's edge. One wrong move from her, and she had no idea how he would react. "Where are you, firefly?"

This was going to spell disaster. She knew it. But she couldn't help it. "Aercester." She sniffled. "We're in—"

The dream shattered. She was being shaken by someone. She yelped and pushed them away with one of her wings. She was still shaking and covered in a cold sweat. It was Doc.

He offered her a hand up. "Time to go, kid."

She took his offer and let him heft her up to her feet. She found herself staring at the smoldering corpse of the soldier.

"No, no. Don't." Doc turned her away from the body toward the entrance to the alley she had run down. "Lancelot and Zoe are probably already gone. Grinn is awake and hurt but able to move. Eod is fine. I'm fine. It's time to leave."

"I—" Gwen didn't know how to explain Mordred and the dreams that were suddenly not dreams.

"Yeah. I know." He smirked. "C'mon." He took her hand and led her away. The street was littered with the bodies of the soldiers—each one with a large black burn mark on their chests. Dead from electricity, she assumed. She had seen the wizard shooting lightning. Eod ran up to her, ears flat but tail wagging in happy concern.

"I'm all right, baby." She ruffled his head. She was so relieved he hadn't been shot or wounded. "Thanks for protecting him, Doc."

"Naturally. What kind of hero would I be if I let the dog die?" He straightened his tattered blue robe.

She wanted to ask him why he thought he was the hero, but whatever. She didn't care. They had to go before Mordred arrived. She didn't know how long it would take him to get there on the back of his dragon, but she was certain he was already on his way.

And when he did show up…?

All hell would break loose.

He had begged her to go back to him for safety. But he had also vowed that the moment she was in his grasp, he'd never let her go again. She'd be his prisoner—for better or worse—for the rest of her life.

However long it ended up being. She didn't know how to explain to Mordred the situation between her and Grinn. But she knew it wasn't going to go well in the slightest. Would he use her to get to the demon? Or did he care about her enough to give up his quest for revenge?

Don't ask stupid questions. She knew the answer to that one, she just didn't want to admit it.

It was easy to steal a cart and supplies when all the soldiers were dead. They hooked Sunshine to the wooden tongues alongside another horse who eyed them warily but didn't seem like he was going to fuss too much about being horse-napped.

Grinn limped up to them, still bleeding from several large wounds in his chest.

"Oh, God." She covered her mouth with her hands. He looked awful, and clearly in agony. "Do you—"

He shifted to the shape of a cat without a word, clearly intending to jump onto the back of the cart. But he collapsed before he could, his legs giving out.

Carefully, she gathered him up in a blanket. He was awake, and said nothing as she made him a spot to rest in the corner of the cart. At least he didn't bite her. Eod jumped in a second later, sniffed the cat, and then lay down beside him.

She patted the dog. "You really are the best, y'know."

"He knows," Doc said from the driver's seat. "Get on, kid. Time to go."

"What about Lancelot and Zoe?" Gwen climbed onto the wooden cart beside him.

"Since we had already split up, they had already gone far enough that they likely did not hear the commotion." He snapped the reins, and the two horses eagerly began to trot as they quickly made their way out of the town and back toward the woods for cover.

Glancing back behind them, it looked like Grinn was sleeping or unconscious. She frowned. "I don't know if we can run far enough that Mordred won't be able to find us."

"You're most certainly right. We aren't running." Doc smiled grimly. "We're putting distance between us and innocent civilians."

She supposed that was fair. She wrapped her wings around herself, still not sure quite what to do with them. But at least they were warm and acted a bit like a cloak. "You could have warned me."

"Could have. Didn't."

"Why not?"

He sighed. "Because sometimes bad things have to happen for a chance at better things. But only sometimes. And we have to take that chance every single time. Because *sometimes* it might work. Even though it generally doesn't. Like this time probably won't."

She stared at him, flat and unamused. "Thanks."

His smile was cheerful in the face of her sarcasm. "You're welcome!"

Turning her attention to the sky that was slowly filling with clouds, she frowned. It'd be harder to see a dragon approaching if it was overcast. "How pissed do you think he'll be if—when—he finds us?"

Doc only snickered.

And honestly, he didn't need to say more than that.

I am so fucked.

* * *

"Where *is* she?"

Mordred slammed the man to the wall, his clawed gauntlet around his throat. The villager's feet were barely touching the ground as Mordred squeezed. "Do not make me repeat myself a third time."

The man gagged. "They killed—"

"I know what was done." He tightened his grasp enough to dig his nails just enough into the villager's skin as to break the surface. "And I do not care. Heed my warning, little man... I am in no mood to tolerate simpletons."

The villager pointed down toward a road leading out of Aercester and into the nearby glade. The man coughed. "But—the knight—"

Mordred dropped the man enough that he could place his feet on the ground and breathe. "The knight?"

"Lancelot and the Gossamer Lady were with them. They split up. Dunno where they went, prince, please—" The man was shaking in terror. Mordred had an overwhelming urge to snap his neck, simply from his foul mood. But the villager, to his credit, had not done anything wrong.

With a heavy sigh, he let go of him and stormed away. Flicking his wrist, an iron stallion lifted his head and trotted over from where it had been waiting with his other knights. They had flown in on dragonback, but it would be difficult to see Gwendolyn through the cover of the leaves. Climbing atop the steed, he headed from the town toward the woods—but more importantly, away from the listening ears of the town. His knights followed. He had summoned them all—or rather, all who remained in his service.

Galahad, Percival, Tristan, Gawain, and Bors, each atop their own steeds of metal. Mordred's jaw ticked. He would have to split his own forces to pursue the traitor Lancelot and the demon Grinn.

But he did not wish to start a war with the Gossamer Lady. Not yet. Letting out a sigh, he said, "Our foes have split. Grinn has taken Gwen—and perhaps the mage of the ruins—into the forest. Percival and Tristan, you will ride with me. Galahad—take Gawain and Bors in pursuit of Lancelot. I wish for him to be brought back to me alive."

"Yes, my prince." The Knight in Gold bowed his head before speaking again after a pause. "Does he ride alone?"

"No. He does not." Mordred knew Galahad would not betray him. Of all of his knights, of all his so-called *friends* over the centuries, he almost trusted the Knight in Gold. And what he was offering Galahad was obvious to them both—*bring me Lancelot, and you decide what becomes of the Gossamer Lady. Whether she joins us or walks free.*

As he rode into the woods with Percival and Tristan behind him, he did not bother to look back. Though he was certain that Galahad would fight his best to succeed, there was no guarantee of it. Galahad was a fearsome warrior, but so was Lancelot.

Even with the aid of Gawain and Bors, there was no certainty of the Knight in Gold's success over Silver. Especially with the Gossamer Lady at Lancelot's side.

Mordred was fairly certain that Zoe would not murder Galahad. But only fairly. Time, and the Crystal, could change many things.

There was not much thought or energy he could spare for Galahad and Lancelot. He had a demon of his own to fight.

Urging his horse faster, he rode into the glade. It had only been a few hours since he had confronted Gwendolyn in her fugue state after killing the soldier. They could not have gone far. But if Grinn was smart, he would know that the fledgling fire elemental was now too much of a risk to be worth hauling about as an ally or prisoner.

Questions flooded him.

Were they in cahoots? Was it Grinn who inspired Gwen to betray him? Why did the demon keep her about, when he was known for hating the company of all others? What was his plan? How did she play into the demon's lying low?

Soon, he would have his answers. If the demon did not kill him, of course. Their last clash upon the battlefield had ended with Grinn trapped within the Iron Crystal.

This time, he would have the demon's head. Damn the council of elementals to the pits, he cared nothing for their opinion on the matter. Grinn would die.

No matter the cost.

* * *

Gwen was getting more and more nervous as they rode. She kept glancing behind them on the road, expecting to see horses or a dragon bearing down on them at any point. It was only a matter of time.

Grinn was still out cold, though it looked like the bleeding was slowing down. She shared in his pain. Literally. She kept expecting to look down and see blood. He'd live because she did —but if Mordred found them? Who could say how long that'd last.

When they reached a field, the grass cut low, she finally gave in to what she knew she had to do. She sighed. If they stuck together, Mordred would catch all of them. And once he realized he couldn't kill the demon, but that *she* got hurt every time *he* got hurt? That'd ensure that Mordred would kill her.

If Doc stayed behind on his own, Mordred wouldn't stop.

If Grinn stayed behind? She looked at the curled-up, very injured cat. She knew he was really a demon and didn't really deserve her help, but she had a very hard time leaving his unconscious body on the road. It just didn't feel right.

And besides, it wouldn't stop the fact that her heart was pulling her back toward the Prince in Iron. Even if it was going to get her into a lot of trouble. "Stop the cart. I..."

"I know, kid." The wizard pulled the cart to a stop. "They'll be here in about half an hour."

"Could've said that." She glared.

"You looked like you were going to crap yourself enough already." He smirked. "Your plan's risky. If he kills you, Grinn's still too weak to bounce back."

She sighed. "Then I guess there's no more demon problem, huh." She jumped off the cart. Eod lifted his head, watching her with that expression that said the dog had already figured out way more than what he had any business understanding. When she walked around to the back of the cart, the big hound pawed at her. It broke her heart.

"Take the damn dog with you, for fuck's sake." Doc sighed, exasperated. "He isn't going to hurt his own mutt." He clicked his tongue at Eod, who jumped off the cart, tail wagging and tongue hanging out of his mouth like they were about to go for a romp in the park.

"You don't know that."

"I know Grinn has a much higher likelihood of eating that dog for lunch than the Iron Prince does of raising a hand to him." The wizard looked back at the wounded cat. "I can handle this prick on my own."

"How do you know you'll be safe with him?"

The mage barked a laugh. "Oh, you sweet spring child." He cracked the reins of the cart. "We'll see you soon enough! And you won't be happy when you do!"

With a sigh, she looked down at Eod and patted him on the head. "Well, here we go, I guess. Time to be bait." Either she would slow Mordred down enough that Doc and Grinn could get away, or Mordred would rip her head off and unwittingly kill two elementals with one stone.

Unfurling her wings, Gwen sat on a stump by the side of the road and waited for the sound of hooves or the creak of a giant metal dragon.

Doc was right. They hadn't been far away. Three men in full armor rode from the woods atop metal horses. There was no mistaking the one in the lead. "Stay here, good boy." She patted Eod on the head. He whimpered but did as she asked as she stood and went to the center of the road.

The last thing she wanted to do was get Eod hurt.

Taking in a breath, she held it for a second, and let it out, igniting into flames as she did.

Time to face the music.

FIFTEEN

Gwen kept her hands tight into fists. She was shaking. It took everything in her to hold back a panic attack. As the three armored men approached on their horses, it became more and more of a struggle. But she held on. Somehow. Barely.

For now.

Mordred pulled his steed to a halt a dozen feet in front of her. The stallion snorted angrily and stomped a rusted iron hoof into the packed dirt of the road. His opalescent, glowing eyes glared at her as if it clearly understood she was the reason why he had been ordered to stop.

The Prince in Iron dismounted, looking like a perfect monster from a nightmare in his full plate armor and helm that hid his face. It was impossible to know what he was thinking as he approached her. But when Caliburn appeared in the air beside him, floating and waiting at the ready, she had a guess he wasn't thrilled.

"Where is he?" Mordred's voice was tinny and hollow from inside the helm. It added to how inhuman he looked.

"I don't know." She squared her shoulders. It was the honest truth. If Doc was clever, he would have gone off the path or taken an unexpected route away. Staying on the main road was probably suicide if Mordred didn't buy her stall tactic and decided to just flatten her and be done with it.

"Why are you protecting him?" He clenched his fists.

That was a really good question. She couldn't tell Mordred the truth—*if you learn we're connected, you'll murder me to get to him.* So, what was she supposed to say instead? Her silence as she struggled to come up with a good fib was apparently enough for him.

"More secrets. More lies." His hands relaxed, and that was somehow scarier to her. "Very well. Stand down, Gwendolyn Wright. Surrender now, so that I may hunt that bastard demon down and ask him myself."

Taking in a deep breath, she held it for a moment, steeling herself for what was about to follow. She winced as she imagined it. This was going to hurt. "No."

He cracked his head from one side to the other. "Gwendolyn, stand down."

"No." She spread her wings, blocking off more of the path from him.

"You cannot win."

"I know I can't." She chewed her lip. "That's not the point."

"I see." He grasped the hilt of Caliburn and pulled it from the air. It seemed he planned on doing this personally. At least he wasn't going to just run her through and call it good. "You look lovely with wings."

"I wish they were prettier." She glanced at them. They were made of fire now, just like the rest of her. She supposed they looked nicer like that. "I was hoping at least for *feathers* or something. Zoe has butterfly wings. I get"—she spread them a bit more and then relaxed—"ugly-ass leather dragon wings."

"Do not say that near my own dragon. I think they are beautiful."

"I wish I knew how to use them." She chuckled.

"Perhaps that will come in time." He paused. "Shall we begin?"

It was going to be like their training sessions. Only way, way more painful for her. She nodded. "Yeah. I guess so." Her job was going to be to play defense. To keep him distracted for as long as possible. It would just be a matter of whether or not she could do it for long enough that Doc managed to get far enough away.

Winning was out of the question. But like she had said—that wasn't the point.

Mordred strode toward her. She blasted him with fire, and it had the same effect as it had when they were in the courtyard that day. He simply walked through it, the edges of his armor glowing from the heat, as though it hadn't happened.

Man, she really hoped this wasn't over in seven seconds.

She jumped away from him as he swung his sword for her. It didn't seem like he was trying to hit her with it. That was a relief. But what he was trying to do was keep her off her footing. She wished she could summon a sword. Or anything solid. But all she had was fire, and fire didn't do *shit* to him.

Jumping back, she instinctively flapped her wings, sending her another ten feet back than she had intended. She squeaked in surprise and nearly fell over. "Holy shit—" She laughed. "That was awesome! Did you see that?"

Mordred stared at her for a moment and then simply shook his head as if to say *youth*. He came toward her again, and she blasted the ground in front of him, trying to create a super-heated trench. Something that might hurt iron. The fire blazed white hot. He stopped for a moment on the other side of it, first eyeing the trench, then her.

"That would work under normal circumstances." He stepped over it as if it wasn't there. "But you forget the laws of Avalon. I am not simply made of iron—I am the *antithesis* of this island. I am the counter to all magic—including yours. Surrender, Gwendolyn."

"No. I can't." She was shaking again.

"Tell me why you are protecting him."

She shook her head. She wouldn't lie to him. But she wouldn't tell him the truth either. She didn't want to die. She *really* didn't want to die. And certainly not at his hands. "I'm sorry."

"Very well." He swung his sword for her, and the dance began again. She managed to get behind him at one point and blasted a fireball at his left knee. It knocked his leg out from under him and, for the briefest moment, he staggered.

Hope filled her heart.

And was instantly gone a second later when he threw an elbow toward her, sending her reeling and staggering into the field of cut grass. It instantly began to blacken and burn. *Great. I'm a forest fire machine. Smokey Bear, can you ever forgive me?*

Before she lit the whole field on fire, and before Mordred could get over her, she rolled back into the road and scrambled back to her feet. She wished she knew how to fly—she really did. Maybe she could just circle around and blast him with fire.

But he had a flying sword.

And a dragon.

She was so, so screwed.

Swing, dodge. Swing, dodge. Swing, dodge. He was bigger than her, stronger than her, but she had one thing on him—she was faster. And he didn't seem to be trying very hard to hit her.

It was too late when she realized what he was doing.

It was too late because, by the time she realized his ploy, it had already started working. He was tiring her out. She was struggling to catch her breath as adrenaline and her constant ducking and rolling took their toll on her.

And the big iron bastard didn't even look like he had broken a sweat. For fuck's sake, he was carrying himself with all the mannerisms of a man who was *bored.*

She knew it was going to be hopeless.

But it was another thing to experience it.

Gathering her strength, she threw another blast of fire at him with a shout. It knocked him back half a step. But that was it. A second time, and he flicked his cape up to deflect it, the panels of fabric turning to iron like a shield. A third, and she felt like she was running out of gas.

Her shoulders slumped.

He stepped forward and swung his sword for her head. She dodged again, but just a second too slow. With his other hand, he caught her by the upper arm and threw her roughly to the ground.

When she rolled onto her back, the point of Caliburn was already hovering over her throat. It was over. She put out her fire. There wasn't a point in it anymore. He'd won. "Are you going to kill me?"

"No." He reached down and grasped her by the throat with his clawed hand. She could feel the points of his talons digging into her skin. "But I am a man of my word, Gwendolyn Wright —I have found you, and now you are *mine.*"

"I—"

One word left him. She couldn't even figure out what it was. But whatever he had said, it must have been magic. Because with that single sound, the world went dark.

* * *

Mordred sighed as he picked up the unconscious young woman. When he had used his magic to force her to sleep, her wings had dissipated. They were not yet fully part of her sense of self. But at least it would make her easier to transport.

She had truly been a thing of beauty. So frightened of him,

with her wide eyes and frantic efforts to evade him. She would be a true force of nature in a hundred years when she had the experience and the full mastery of her power. She could rule the isle if she wished to.

A shame she would spend those hundred years in chains. He was relieved to have her safe with him once more, though the anger that boiled in his soul over her continued deception threatened his temper. Why was she protecting the demon Grinn? *Why?* What sway did he hold over her?

She could not possibly agree with the monster's goals. She was too empathetic to the plights of those around her. Far too empathetic. Was he lying to her, spinning some sort of tale to keep her as his ally? No. Mordred knew the demon well—and an actor, he was not.

So *why*?

He would learn the truth. And he would keep her as his prisoner until he did. His dragon landed in the field beside them with a heavy *thud*, the wind from his wings putting out the small fire that Gwen had started.

"What of the demon, my prince?" Tristan called. The Knight in Tin. He was the most youthful of the bunch, despite having as many years behind him as any other. Always brash, always hopeful, always naive. "Should we pursue him?"

"No. He is with the wizard. And if that lunatic has decided to aid the demon for whatever reason, there is little chance we will catch them now." Mordred sighed as he dismissed the iron steed back into the ether from where he had summoned it. Clicking his tongue, he summoned Eod. The dog had been sitting by his horse, watching the fight with deep concern. The dog eagerly jogged up to the dragon, barking a happy hello.

"The two of you should seek out Galahad. He may need your assistance in dealing with Lancelot and the Gossamer Lady. Return to the keep when all that has been resolved. We will wait for our enemy to make his next move." At his silent command, the dragon lowered his head to the ground and opened his jaws like an alligator. Eod climbed into the maw of the beast and lay down. It was not the first time he had traveled in such a way. Mordred trained his pups to be useful.

Settling down onto the back of the dragon with Gwen still in his lap, he ordered the creature to fly. He would return home with only part of his goal completed. He had wished to return with Grinn's severed head as a trophy as well. Now, he could only hope that Galahad was more successful in his defeat of Lancelot.

He doubted it. Galahad was the stronger knight, but Lancelot was far more ready to use dirty tactics to win. The Knight in Gold held his honor above all. It would be his undoing someday.

Looking down at the woman asleep in his arms, Mordred could at least take consolation in the fact that the day had not been a total loss.

There was too much that she was still hiding from him.

I was kind to you once before, Gwendolyn Wright. I was patient.

We shall see if I have the heart for it a second time.

* * *

Galahad slowed his horse to a walk as he entered the glade to where Lancelot and the Gossamer Lady had fled. Or, at least, so the townsfolk had said. He had not resorted to fear and threats of physical violence in exchange for the information. He was unsure if that made the knowledge more or less reliable.

He supposed he would learn soon enough.

Lancelot was a clever man. He would know that even with Zoe at his side, he was outmatched two to three. Gawain and Bors, the Knight in Cobalt and the Knight in Nickel, were not the strongest fighters of their order, but they were both wily and intelligent in their own right.

Subterfuge and stealth would be the tools that Lancelot would use against them, Galahad was certain of it. He would lie in wait and seek to ambush them. So, Galahad would ride slowly and ensure he had as much time as possible to see where the Knight in Silver might be hiding.

When he reached a clearing that would be a prime location for such an ambush, he stopped at the entrance to it. He could almost smell the magic in the air. There was an enchantment upon the clearing. "You forget that I would know her magic were I rendered blind and mute, Silver Knight." The magic that had been placed on the clearing shimmered and popped like a soap bubble on a sunny day.

Galahad kept his tone calm, though his heart was lodged in his throat.

He had been so very certain that he would never see his love again.

But she was *here.* Though he did not blame her for hiding. He was sworn to service to the Prince in Iron, one way or another.

"I was hoping you would be an idiot for once in your life." Lancelot emerged from behind a tree. "It was worth a try. I assume Mordred sent you after me?"

"Yes." He let his helm melt away. "It is good to see you are well."

Lancelot laughed. "Yes. And free of that bastard's magic. I finally have the chance to get revenge on him for what he has done to us—what he did to Avalon."

Galahad dismounted and pulled his steel and golden sword from its sheath. While a sword of solid gold would be pretty, it would be entirely useless in practice. "I wish you luck in your endeavor. But you know what I must do."

Lancelot drew his own sword. "Just like old times."

The moment that steel was to meet steel, a voice stopped them both in their tracks. A voice that Galahad had heard every night in his dreams.

"Stop."

The Gossamer Lady.

SIXTEEN

"C'mon you stupid"—*rattle, rattle*—"fucking"—*rattle, rattle*—"piece of shit!"

It was pointless.

Gwen let go of the chains she had been yanking on, and released a long, heavy sigh. This sucked. This sucked immensely. Waking up in a jail cell hadn't exactly been a surprise, but then again, she had really been hoping for a million other things. But here she was, right back where she had been before—in the same damn cell, no less—but this time she was *chained to the fucking wall.*

Iron cuffs were around her wrists, fitted tight to her skin as if they had been made for her. Because, of course, they probably had been. Matching iron chains connected the loops on the cuffs to a ring on the wall.

At least the chains were long enough that she could lie down without a problem and walk around most of the cell. Her biggest issue was going to be tripping over them or getting tangled up. She had almost cracked herself in the teeth with one of the links when she had woken up on a hay-stuffed mattress.

What ensued was a series of extremely disappointing

attempts to free herself. She couldn't pull the chains off the wall. She couldn't burst into flames because of the iron chains. She couldn't even summon her wings anymore. She couldn't reach the door, so it didn't matter if it was locked or not.

She was really running out of options.

She even checked to see if there was a keyhole in the cuffs that would release her. Nope. It was like they had been forged in place. So, she couldn't even pick the damn things with some straw. The only place for a key she saw was where the chain met the ring embedded in the wall. There was an oldey-timey padlock on it, but she had nothing to pick it with.

Not like she really knew how to pick locks, but—whatever. What else was she going to do with her time? But regardless, even if she got the chain off the wall, she'd still be without her power and locked in the cell. She'd have to get past a ton of guards with no ability to protect herself.

She was going to have time on her hands.

Shit.

To make matters worse, it was cold in the jail. A kind of humid, insidious chill that didn't seem so bad at first but slowly worked its way in until she couldn't deny how uncomfortable it was. She wished she had socks. Or a coat. Or anything other than the chainmail outfit she was still wearing.

Slumping down on the mattress, she at least got her bare feet off the cold stone. "This sucks."

She was the only prisoner in the room, which was both a relief and a bit of a disappointment. A relief because she wasn't stuck next to Doc, Grinn, Lancelot, or Zoe. A disappointment because it meant she had nobody to talk to. She was alone. She really didn't deal well with being alone.

The only other "person" in the space with her at all was a single metal guard standing by the door. He was odd-looking, even in comparison to all the other hollow-armor-people that Mordred created.

One of his arms was floating next to him, the joint where it met his shoulder having rusted away to jagged fragments. Part of his face was smooth while the other had features, making him look almost like a sketch that had been abandoned halfway through. He held a spear in his hand that was missing two fingers. There was that faint, telltale opalescent glow from within his chest.

Gwen supposed that answered the question about what happened to Mordred's people—they were still around. Which was good news, she supposed. She had hoped that Maewenn was all right, even if she was made out of the stolen bits of magic taken from other people. How she had been made didn't make her any less of a friend to Gwen.

She shivered, goosebumps spreading over her. "Excuse me? Mr. Guard, sir?" She assumed the creature was male by its proportions, but honestly, she didn't quite know. The guard turned its head toward her with a creak but said nothing. After a pause, she smiled, a little unnerved by his silence. "I'm cold. Would it be possible to get a blanket or a cloak or something?"

The guard looked down at the ground, then up again, then nodded with another *squeak-squeak-squeak*. He turned and left the room, the large wooden door closing behind him. She was pretty sure that leaving her entirely alone made him a terrible guard. Or it meant the iron chains were super effective and he wasn't at all concerned. Either way, she was happy for the assistance.

So, she wrapped her arms around her legs and rested her head on her knees and waited. Not like she had anything else to do. Stupid demon. Stupid Mordred. Stupid Doc.

The door opened, and she looked up, expecting to see the half-finished guard walking in with a blanket.

Her heart dropped.

It was Percival, the Knight in Copper. He walked up to the cell and, lifting an old iron key, unlocked the door. It swung open with a creak. He stepped inside. "The prince would like to see you."

Not like she could argue. But it sent her stomach twisting into knots. Nodding, she stood and waited. Percival stepped forward and undid the padlock that linked her to the wall. He walked away, leaving her to follow him. He apparently trusted her not to make a fuss or attack him. Or run.

Then she remembered she was half his size, a tenth his age, and had no ability to really do any damage. With a sigh, she followed, twisting the three-foot length of iron chain around in her hands. It was heavy, but not obnoxiously so. At least it gave her something to fidget with.

"If I had my way, you'd be dead." Percival's tone was bland as they walked through the halls. She didn't know where he was taking her. She supposed it probably didn't really matter.

"Thanks." What the fuck else was she supposed to say to that?

"It was bad enough when you were a distraction. Now you're a traitor *and* a distraction."

"Says the guy who mutinied and tried to kill Mordred back in the day."

He glanced over his shoulder at her. He was stocky and still reminded her of what a fantasy dwarf might look like if he didn't have a beard. Only a little taller, she supposed. His expression was dour.

"What?" She smiled sarcastically. "Pot, kettle, that's all I'm saying. Oh, wait, I'm sorry—you probably don't understand that phrase since you've been stuck here for the past sixteen hundred years having to lick the boots of the man you hate. *Sorry*." She grew up having arguments with strangers on the internet. She wasn't going to just bend over and take it from some angry so-and-so for no good reason.

Percival mumbled under his breath and shook his head, turning his attention forward, clearly giving up on talking to her. Which was fine by Gwen. He took her through hallways to an area of the keep she had only been in maybe once before, when Mordred had been giving her a tour.

But when she walked through the doors behind Percival, she knew this was a room he had skipped. It was a throne room. Rows of stained-glass windows lined each side, some cracked and some missing—likely from the blast when the Iron Crystal shattered. It was dark out, the moonlight streaming in, with flecks of color from the remaining glass scattering across the stone floor. It fought with the amber light of the fires that burned in large metal braziers attached to the columns that stretched up high overhead, disappearing into the darkness of the ceiling.

Soldiers stood like so many suits of armor on display—but she knew they were alive. The telltale opalescent glow coming from their eyes or gaps in their breastplates told her as much. The throne itself at the far end was made, unsurprisingly, entirely from iron. And sitting there, looking entirely bored, was Mordred. His arms were covered in armor, as they often were. But his clothing wasn't as casual as it usually was. He was wearing a coat that was split down the middle, the black fabric woven with thread that matched the unruly and tangled vine-like motif of his armor along the seams.

Caliburn, in all its terrible glory, was leaning against the arm of the throne beside him.

Percival brought her to a point in the center of the black carpet that ran up the middle of the room. "Kneel before your prince."

She stared at him flatly. "You've got to be kidding me."

"If you would like me to force the matter," the knight said under his breath, his expression turning grim. "I will happily break both your kneecaps."

"Leave her be, Percival," Mordred interjected.

Percival walked away, taking his position to the right of the throne. Another knight, one she hadn't met before, was standing to the other side. His helm was off, and his boyish appearance caught her by surprise. He looked barely any older than she was, with a bright-eyed farm-boy expression that almost reminded her of her old boyfriend Mick. His armor was made of an oddly tinted, shiny silvery metal that might have been tin, but she wasn't sure.

Mordred was watching her, expression unreadable. "You are accused of treason, Gwendolyn Wright. Of betraying my hospitality, my trust, and conferring with our enemy, the demon Grinn. How do you plead?"

"I—whoa, wait. Hold on. Am I on *trial*?" She blinked, stunned.

"It is not much of a trial, believe me." He began to tap his claws on the metal arm of his throne. *Tick-tick-tick-tick. Tick-tick-tick-tick.* The sound of it carried eerily in the enormous stone room. Oh, he was *pissed.* "How do you plead, Gwendolyn Wright?"

"I—I didn't know who he was until after the Crystal was shattered. I would have told you if I'd known." This was bad. This was very, very bad. Would Mordred sentence her to death? Would she find the answer to the question of what happened between her and Grinn if her head was chopped off? *Fuck fuck fuck fuck—* "I'm sorry, Mordred. I never meant to hurt you."

"You have not harmed me, young elemental. It was I who broke the Iron Crystal, if you recall. Not you. Your betrayal of my trust broke the laws of Avalon. I am certain I needn't remind you how highly we value adherence to those rules of hospitality which protect our guests?" His voice felt like it reverberated in the room itself. "They also protect the host."

Gwen's heart was racing. She fought against the panic attack that was welling in her chest. She nodded numbly. She remembered. How could she forget? Mordred had snapped the neck of the mayor who had broken those laws on her very first day in Avalon.

"Tell me why you continue to aid the demon." *Tick-tick-tick-tick* went his claw on the arm of the throne.

She shut her eyes, feeling tears streaking down her cheeks. This was it. This was how she died. She bowed her head. "I'm sorry. I can't."

"And why not?"

"It—it's complicated."

"You do not argue that you continue to help hide him, protect him, and aid him in continued attempts to overthrow my rule and seek my ruin?" His tone stayed calm and untouched. It scared her more than if he had been shouting at her.

"I'm stuck in the middle—I don't want to be." She stared down at the carpet in front of her, feeling herself start to shake from adrenaline and fear. She struggled to keep her breathing calm and normal. She didn't want to faint right now. She really didn't want to. "I'm not his friend. I'm not his ally. But I have no choice right now."

"Why?"

"I—I can't tell you, I'm sorry." She shut her eyes. *Because you'll kill me to get to him. I know you will. Because you'll sacrifice anything and everything to protect Avalon.* She felt so small. So little. She bowed her head. "But I won't help him hurt you either."

"And why should I believe you?" Mordred's tone was as cold and unflinching as the element he represented. It cut her deeper than it should have. "What have you done to keep my trust?"

She shook her head numbly, not knowing how to express how she felt. She cared about him deeply. She had missed him while they were apart. But in front of his soldiers, in front of his knights, kneeling in the middle of his throne room like the prisoner that she was? She didn't know how to say it.

Shutting her eyes again, her tears redoubled their efforts. She gave up. Her shoulders slumped. "Nothing. Absolutely nothing."

He sighed, and his voice went a little softer, even if the words themselves were just as firm. "If you are unable to provide me any reason as to why you continue to aid the demon, then I shall be forced to treat you as his cohort and spy, Gwendolyn Wright." He paused. She waited for him to order her execution. "You shall remain here as my prisoner until the stars blink out from the sky."

She looked up, shocked. Percival was staring at Mordred in disbelief. The young Tin Knight looked oddly relieved.

Mordred ignored the two knights beside him. His gaze was locked on her with an edge of sympathy. "You have lost all rights to freedom for your unabashed betrayal of my hospitality. Moreover, you will no longer be afforded any kindness from myself or others until you confess to me the details behind your inexplicable connection to the demon."

"My prince—" Percival started to argue.

Mordred lifted a hand to stop the Knight in Copper. "She is an elemental. I am unable to take her head as a trophy without the agreement of all the others who remain free. And as we are unable to call a tribunal at this point in time, her life shall be spared." His tone left no room for any further complaints. "Unlike *you*, she does not serve me by right and, therefore, is not subject to my whimsy as to whether she lives or dies. Do we understand?"

Percival looked as though he had gone two shades paler. The threat was very clear. "Yes, my prince."

"Good." Mordred placed his hand back down on the arm of the throne. *Tick-tick-tick-tick*. He sighed again. "Take her back to her cell."

Two armored soldiers came forward and half shoved Gwen out of the room. They pushed her back into the cell and attached her chain to the loop on the wall. Then they left her alone. Even the broken soldier by the wall was gone.

But folded up on the bed was a single, rather threadbare blanket. Sniffling, she flopped down on the hay-stuffed mattress and wrapped herself up in the gift from the soldier. It wasn't much, but it was something.

And she'd be grateful for anything at this point.

Like her life. She wasn't dead. Mordred wasn't executing her. He was just keeping her prisoner. What was she expecting? To be welcomed back with open arms like she had never done anything wrong? To have him just laugh off the fact that she was protecting Grinn?

No, this made sense. This made perfect sense. And it was about as forgiving as she could expect him to be. But it was still *shit.*

Lying down on her side, she shut her eyes and let herself cry.

It wasn't like she had much else to do.

SEVENTEEN

Galahad felt his heart hitch in his chest. He had wished for three hundred years to have a single moment again with the woman he loved. He cared not if Lancelot used this moment of weakness against him.

Zoe's eyes were filled with tears as he approached her. "My knight. My dear, sweet knight."

He fell to one knee before her, his throat too tight to form words. He bowed his head, fighting back his own urge to cry.

Her arms draped around him in a gentle embrace. Her touch was too much for his resolve, and he felt his tears escape and streak down his cheeks.

"How I have missed you," she whispered to him, her lips pressing to the top of his head. "How I prayed in that cold darkness that you were well. It brings me such joy to see you again."

Carefully, as though she were a fragile wisp of smoke in a breeze, he wrapped his own arms around her. Though he was certain it was not the case, he feared that she was only an illusion—a dream that might shatter with first light, or that she might simply dissipate if he held her too tightly. "My love..."

He was exposed, turning his back to Lancelot. If the Knight

in Silver were heartless, he could easily use the moment to his advantage, even with Gawain and Bors waiting for orders. But all three of his kin seemed content to let him have this exchange.

One he thought would never come again.

After basking in the bliss of the moment for as long as he could, he stood and caught her lips with his. His heart ached, both broken and overfull at the same time. Broken, for he knew what was inevitably to follow. When he ended the kiss, he stroked his fingers over her cheek, brushing away the tears that had slipped free from her as well. "Come with me to the keep. Mordred has extended his hospitality to you. You would be our guest."

She smiled in the way that one does when it is both in gratitude and in apology. "You know I cannot. The Prince in Iron must fall. His reign must end. You know this."

Yes. He supposed that was true, however much it brought him grief. His relationship with Mordred was... complex, to say the least. "You know I cannot stand against him."

"Yes. I do. And I would not ask you to do so." She placed her hand on Galahad's chest over where she knew the embedded crystal lived—that leash that kept him tethered to the prince, no matter his opinion. "Must we always find ourselves caught betwixt such warring souls? Will he not release you?"

"You know what the answer would be, were I to ask him." He stroked her dark hair, loving how it curled about his fingers as though caught adrift in water. How he missed her.

"Perhaps his heart has changed."

He smiled faintly. "Perhaps it has. I shall ask again." It was true—Mordred was enamored of the young elemental from Earth. Despite her entanglement with the demon, it was clear that the Prince in Iron did not have the heart to reject Gwendolyn outright for it. If he could coax Mordred to take pity on the young woman, perhaps he would find it to release Galahad from his enslavement and allow him to be free to be with his own love.

But Mordred did not have a penchant for putting empathy above duty.

So, while there was a glimmer of hope within Galahad's heart that perhaps things had changed... he did not have much faith.

And there was still another matter to deal with.

He kissed his love once more, savoring it, before turning to face Lancelot. "I thank you for allowing me that time."

Lancelot nodded. "You would do the same for me."

Yes. He would have. He stepped into the clearing and put his hand on the hilt of his blade. "I have been ordered to take you to the keep. Alive."

"Well, I suppose that last bit is somewhat a relief." Lancelot smirked. "I refuse to go peacefully."

"Very well." He drew his sword. "Then I shall request a duel between us to settle the matter."

"What, you will not leverage your greater numbers?" Lancelot drew his own blade.

Galahad took no pride in the following statement. It was quite simply true. "I will not need them."

Lancelot grinned. "We shall see, old man."

* * *

Lancelot staggered and nearly fell as Galahad's sword impacted his with so much force his hands stung. Lancelot knew he could not win this fight on his own. Nor would Zoe raise a hand to fight her husband—and that was likely why Mordred had sent the Knight in Gold in the first place.

Gawain and Bors were too afraid of Mordred's wrath to risk mutiny in front of the most senior-ranking knight as well.

No, Lancelot was going to lose. And painfully so. Galahad,

for all his lankiness and size, moved with a speed and a simple brutality that left Lancelot forced to stay on the defensive. He should have run from this fight, but Zoe would not be swayed. And it was not in his nature to avoid an honorable fight.

He could simply pray for a stroke of luck.

Galahad swiftly knocked Lancelot's sword from his hand, sending it flying. It landed in the brush at the edge of the clearing. It did not take Lancelot long to wind up on his back in the grass, with the tip of the Knight in Gold's sword resting against his throat.

Lancelot laughed quietly. "You've always won."

"Yes. I have." Galahad sighed. "Will you come peacefully now? Or must I restrain you?"

"We have been friends for ages, have we not?" Lancelot shut his eyes. "Kill me now. Deny that rusty bastard the pleasure of taking my head."

"No."

"Tell him I left you no choice." He hardly wished to die. But if he had to go, a death at Galahad's hand would be far more merciful. "I am certain Gawain and Bors would not disagree." He smirked. "As they would wish the same in my place."

Galahad sighed. "I—"

Something hit Galahad so quickly and with such force it seemed for a moment as though the Knight in Gold had simply disappeared. It was only when there was a *thunk* from a nearby tree, that Lancelot lifted his head to see what had transpired.

Galahad had been thrown across the clearing and the sound was his armored body impacting the tree's trunk. He half slumped to the ground, struggling to pick himself up from the blow.

"Begone, iron servants." A figure was standing beside Lancelot. He was dressed in barely anything at all, a scrap of leather wrapped around his waist in a sarong. His pale, nearly white skin was tinted a faint green. Long, dark hair that only glinted evergreen in the sunlight was pulled back in a braid that reached down to his waist. He was handsome and appeared to be no older than perhaps his mid-twenties. But Lancelot knew he was one of the most ancient elementals that lived upon Avalon. Old enough that Enin himself did not recall his age. The faded tattooed markings upon his arms and chest harkened back to some ancient and lost people, forgotten to the sands of time.

Lancelot furrowed his brow. "Enin?" The Lord in Green's arrival was certainly a surprise, though not an unwelcome one.

Enin ignored him, instead choosing to glare at the other knights. He held out his hand, and Lancelot watched as a spear of tangled wooden vines grew from nothing at his command. That must have been what had struck Galahad. "Leave here."

Galahad picked himself up from where he had slumped against the tree and wiped a bit of blood from the corner of his lip. There was a dent in his breastplate that was already mending itself. Gawain and Bors had drawn their swords, though the forest elemental did not seem to notice.

"Enin the Green, I have no quarrel with you."

"Yet I have a quarrel with your master." Enin held firm. His voice left no room for argument. "You will leave, if you value your lives." The forest around them creaked dangerously, the trees themselves echoing Enin's words. It might appear that the Lord in Green was outnumbered—but only to a fool.

And Galahad was no such thing. He bowed his head. "As you wish."

Zoe took the moment to rush to his side, touching her fingers to the Golden Knight's wound. The shimmering of magic was like the buzz of a storm before it broke, humming through the air as she healed him. He whispered something to her. She kissed him.

And for the life of him, Lancelot wanted to cry. It was such a terrible thing to see true love shattered by war. And Zoe and

Galahad had never once been given the chance to live in peace. Pulling himself up to his feet with a grunt, he brushed himself off. "Thank—"

"Shut up." Enin cut him off.

Well. All right then. Letting out a sharp exhale, Lancelot shrugged and went to fetch his sword from where it had landed. By the time he turned back around, Galahad had mounted his horse, and the three knights were turning away and riding back from whence they came.

Lancelot was surprised to be alive and not imprisoned. Surprised, but grateful.

Zoe floated over to Enin, her feet barely touching the ground. "You came."

"Yes. I heard your whispers in the trees." Enin looked tired, the weight of his age weighing on him. "My time to stay away from the quarrel has ended. I can no longer watch the suffering in silence."

Lancelot sheathed his sword. "You will join us then? I am surprised. You despise warfare."

Enin shut his eyes. "The demon and the prince must both be stopped."

"The prince must go first." Lancelot was glad to have another ally. "The demon cannot be felled as it stands without taking an innocent life. Not without Mordred's death preceding it."

Enin nodded and asked for no explanation. "Very well. The prince dies first." Without another word, he took two steps away and disappeared into a swirl of leaves that drifted away in the wind.

Lancelot sighed. Elementals. The older, the stranger, it seemed. *The older, the more removed from their humanity. If that creature was ever human.* He wondered if he would become so esoteric in his old age.

Heh.

Like he would ever survive long enough to find out.

"I fear it is time for us to depart." He clicked his tongue, his silver horse trotting from the underbrush. "We have an army to raise. And precious little time to do it."

* * *

Gwen had decided she was going to braid the strands of hay in the corner of the room into intricate patterns. She had nothing else to do, being locked in a cell on her own.

When the door opened, she jolted in surprise, nervous for a split second that it was going to be one of the knights. Or worse, Mordred himself. But it was none of the above. She blinked. "Maewenn?"

"Aye, the one and only." The cook was being let in by the rusted, half-finished guard with the detached and floating arm. She was carrying a tray of food. Nothing elaborate, but Gwen was hungry enough that she couldn't complain. The guard let her in, and Maewenn bustled into the cell and handed her the tray. "Oh, my poor dear. Are you all right? Look at you."

"I'm okay." Gwen smiled half-heartedly back at the cook and took the tray. Bread, cheese, some cured meat. Breakfast of champions. "Thank you so much."

"It's the least I can do." Maewenn sighed. "It's all I really *can* do. That bastard Mordred... I don't know what he's thinking."

"At least I'm not dead."

"That rusty fool—if he thought killing you would solve anything, I'd smack him around the head."

Gwen glanced nervously at the half-finished guard.

"Him? Pah." Maewenn waved a hand at the soldier in question. "I can run my mouth around him all I like. He's mute—never been able to say a word, that one. Mordred only keeps him around out of sympathy, I think. He was the first of us, you see. It's like—it's like baking. The first attempt at a new recipe always comes out a bit odd."

"Oh." Gwen frowned. That explained the guard's half-finished and neglected appearance. He was just a prototype. Somehow that made her sad, especially seeing how dismissive Maewenn was of him. She picked up a piece of cheese and broke it in half before eating some of it. She really was starving.

"I hope he lets you out of here soon. I'm sure he will. I don't think he can stay mad at you for long." Maewenn was clearly trying her best to sound hopeful, though the way she was wringing of her hands in front of her told Gwen otherwise.

"Is... is Eod all right?"

"The mutt has been sniffing and barking and running in circles trying to find you. But he's quite fine, trust me." Maewenn chuckled quietly. "He'll scratch a hole through that door as soon as he figures out where you've gone. Not like Mordred to hurt an animal."

That was a relief. "And Lancelot?"

"Couldn't say. I will tell you that five knights left here. And five came back—with you and a dog." Maewenn sighed. "No sign of Lancelot or pieces of him, for better or worse."

Gwen nodded. That was hopefully a good thing? She assumed they'd bring back his corpse if he was dead. Or a prisoner if he wasn't. "I hope he's okay."

"Me too. He's a cad, that one, but means well." Maewenn's shoulders fell with a quiet clink. "I do not know how everyone gets out of this in one piece."

"Neither do I." She stared down at her tray of food. "I shouldn't have ever tried to destroy the Crystal."

"Don't think like that, dear. No, you did the right thing. You had the bravery to stand up to Mordred. He's too set in his ways—been at this for far too long. He needed someone to hold up the mirror to his actions. This chaos has been a long time in the making."

"Thanks." Gwen smiled but wasn't really feeling it. "I'm just glad you're okay. I didn't know what had happened to you and the others."

"Oh, it was a right awful day, let me tell you! I was standing in the kitchen, minding my own business, and all of a sudden, all the pots and pans were falling and flying about, and—"

The guard rapped his knuckles on one of the bars of the cell.

Maewenn shot the guard what Gwen would assume would be a glare if the woman's face, y'know, moved. "Oh, calm down, you useless tin can."

The guard knocked his knuckles again. *Clang clang clang.* He wasn't going to take no for an answer.

"It's all right, Mae." Gwen smiled. "Thank you for coming. And thank you for the food."

"Of course. I'll bring you more for dinner. And maybe the pup can join me, if this rusty old piece of junk here will take pity on the poor animal." Maewenn walked from the cell with a *harumph.*

Gwen chuckled but couldn't help but feel entirely hopeless about the whole ordeal. And a little sad for the silent guard. Maewenn left the jail, and the guard took up his position by the door once more.

"Hey," she called out to him.

The soldier turned his head.

"Thank you for the blanket yesterday." She smiled. "I really appreciate it."

The soldier looked down at the ground for a moment, then nodded with a squeak, and went back to what he was doing. Which was just standing and staring.

She finished eating her breakfast and slid the tray aside. With nothing better to do, she lay back down on the mattress and dozed. Then she got up and paced. And then she dozed.

And then she paced. And braided hay. And paced. And braided more hay.

Being a prisoner was going to get insanely boring.

There sounded like there was action going on outside the cell window, like someone rolling heavy machinery around. The creak of wood and metal. Gwen tried to hop up to see what was going on, but the little barred window was way too high up for her to reach even by jumping. She sighed. She really wished she could have at least had a view, if she was going to be locked in a damn cell.

This sucks. After that, she even resorted to some push-ups. Wasn't that what people did in prison to pass the time? Not like she really knew.

She also had no idea how much time had passed. Maybe an hour. Maybe twelve. The soldier hadn't moved—it didn't seem like they needed to sleep. She figured that must be convenient. There were more sounds of heavy machinery and hammering, but... she couldn't see shit, so there was no telling what was going on.

The door opened. She wondered if it was going to be Maewenn and Eod. Or maybe even Percival, come to drag her off somewhere again.

No. She wasn't so lucky.

Her heart hitched.

It was Mordred.

EIGHTEEN

Gwen scrambled to her feet and pressed her back against the stone wall behind her. Once again, Mordred looked like a living nightmare—a shadow figure in a black cloak over twisted armor, the hood pulled up to hide his features.

Was he going to torture her for information? What would he do when he found out she healed too quickly, even for an elemental? It wouldn't take long for him to figure out that something was linking her to Grinn.

The door to the cell opened for him without a key, the iron simply clicking open at his silent command. She was shivering as he approached her, though she tried to swallow the lump in her throat and be brave.

"We have to stop meeting like this," she said, with no idea where she got the balls to joke. She supposed it was her last line of defense. She had nothing else.

What she could see of his expression was hard and unreadable as he approached, looming over her. He reached over her head, grasping the chain where it connected to the wall, and she watched as he simply pulled the chain free, the links melting through the bolt that it connected to the wall before solidifying on the other side.

That would never stop being fascinating.

Mordred dropped the chain in front of her. "Come." He turned on his heel and left her standing there as he headed for the exit.

Why had he come to fetch her? He had knights and soldiers. He'd always sent them. But he came personally. Why? Chewing her lip, she followed after him, afraid of angering him any further. And also, because she was entirely certain he'd drag her to wherever they were going if she put up a fuss.

He brought her to the room with the large circular table, dominated by the map of Avalon. It made a lot more sense, now that she had seen more of the island in her pretty-much-entirely-pointless adventure. She had some things to reference. Mordred walked up to it and placed his gauntleted hands on the surface of the map. "Where is he?"

"I don't know. I really don't. We didn't really have a plan." That wasn't entirely true—they did *kind of* have a plan. They were going to wait for Lancelot to raise his army and then attack all at once. And she had a suspicion that Grinn must be close. He had told her that they couldn't get too far apart without it causing them both pain. He might have been lying. But if he wasn't, she felt fine. Okay, she felt bruised and cold, but that was Mordred's fault.

He lifted a claw and beckoned her closer. She hesitated, but with one firm glare from him, she let out a wavering breath and approached.

He moved to stand behind her, his presence there making her shiver harder. When his fingers trailed through her hair, it forced the air out of her lungs.

"Where is he?" he asked again.

She shut her eyes. "I don't—"

The hand in her hair tightened into a fist, stinging her scalp.

She cried out as he pulled her back against him, craning her head in his grasp. He stepped forward, pinning her to the edge of the table with the length of his armored thigh. "I do not believe you, Gwendolyn Wright. Where did he go?"

"Somewhere nearby—I think—"

"Why?" His voice was a baritone rumble. It was full of danger and *power*, and it sent something that felt like cold lightning crashing through her.

She felt helpless. Usually, she hated it.

Right now?

Right now, she was extremely conflicted.

His hand tightened harder, mistaking the reason why she was hesitating again. "Why, Gwendolyn?"

Give him something. Anything. Anything that doesn't get you killed. "Lancelot is raising an army of elementals to storm the keep. Grinn wants to join him to take you down." She wouldn't tell him about Caliburn or her link to Grinn.

"And Zoe is aiding him," Mordred said. It was a statement, not a question. He sighed. Without stepping away from where he was pinning her to the table, he let go of her hair. "Show me the path you took. Show me precisely where you went."

"Why? I—"

"*Do it.*"

She flinched and swallowed; her mouth going dry again. "What happens if I don't? Will you torture me?"

"Do not test me, Gwendolyn." His hand settled on her back, his thumb on one side of her throat and his fingers on the other, the points pressing into her skin just firmly enough to remind her how deadly they were. "The ice you stand upon is thin enough as it is."

She supposed that was more than fair. With a trembling hand, she picked up a few of the iron markers from the surface of the table and placed them along the path they had taken to the mountain and then to Aercester where she had killed a man.

She had to lean forward to do it, resting one palm on the table as she did. The chain that connected her cuffs together rattled as it slid across the surface. The hand on the back of her neck slid between her shoulder blades, the metal of his nails scraping against the chainmail fabric of her shirt.

"Why did you seek the wizard?"

"We needed his help." Her head was reeling. This shouldn't be *doing* things to her. She should be terrified. And she was, which was only making her strange physical need all the more confusing and complicated. God help her, she wanted him. Not in spite of his darkness and his power—but *because* of it.

"And did he provide it?" His hand on her back trailed lower.

"N—no." She stammered like an idiot.

"Why?"

"He couldn't."

Slowly, agonizingly, his hands grasped the bottom hem of the chainmail tank top and pulled it off over her head. She lifted her arms to accommodate the action, the cold air and the brush of those gauntlets sending a wave of goosebumps across her skin.

"Tell me what you sought from the wizard." Mordred leaned over her, his lips pressing to her shoulder, hot and slow. The sensuality of his touch was in such sharp contrast to his words, it was making her head spin.

"I can't..." Her voice was little more than a whisper. "I'm so sorry..."

"Why not?" He began to feather kisses along her shoulder, up her neck, and closer to her ear. "Tell me why you aid my enemy, Gwendolyn Wright."

"Because if I tell you, you'll kill me." She shut her eyes. Knowing that he might kill her on that alone. "And I don't want to die."

"I will ask you one more question, firefly." His voice was

like the boom of thunder on the horizon. A quiet rumble that promised a storm. "And in this, I need you to speak the truth." One of his hands slid to her stomach, the points of his claws scraping at her skin, sending another shiver of electricity through every nerve in her body. He splayed his fingers wide. "Will you join the demon to seek my downfall? Do you wish to see me destroyed?"

"No." In that, she was absolutely certain. "Never. I—" She didn't know how to say it. She didn't know how to tell him how she felt. Everything was too complicated. Too heavy. Too messy.

Thankfully, he didn't wait for her to finish. He turned her head to his and captured her lips in a kiss. It was full of fire. Of frustration. Of anger. And of *need.* He was rightfully furious with her. And if this was how he wanted to vent it... she wouldn't argue. His hand twisted in her hair again, yanking her head back.

She cried out, her lips parting, and his tongue danced with hers, invading her mouth like the warlord that he was. She moaned, unable to help it, her eyes sliding closed as he simply took over.

God, it felt so good.

Claws trailed up her stomach, making her moan again as he grasped her breast and kneaded it harshly. Firm, but not painful. Rough, but not cruel. This wasn't a fight she could win. This wasn't a fight she *wanted* to win.

He parted from her, finally allowing her to desperately fill her lungs with air. Those molten, rusted eyes met hers. He waited in silence for her to protest again—to tell him to stop.

She trusted him.

He might kill her when he learned the truth, but damn it, she *trusted* him. And more importantly than that—she needed him. And deep down, somewhere in a place she didn't know how to admit existed... she cared deeply about him.

Shutting her eyes, she surrendered.

Mordred pressed her face down onto the table, the cold of the metal surface redoubling her goosebumps. His hands roamed her slowly before finding the circular scar on her back where the arrow had gone through her. He hesitated.

It should have killed me, but it didn't.

He'll see that.

No words were said, though, as he undid the clasp of her chainmail skirt and let it slide to the floor at her ankles, leaving her naked and bent over his table—her cheeks were hot from embarrassment at the sight she must make.

He grasped her ass in his hands and squeezed it hard enough to draw a mewl from her, though she tried to swallow it back. He wasn't her knight in shining armor. And she didn't want him to treat her like one.

There was a moment of hesitation as he stepped an inch away from her. She tried to turn her head to look back at him, but a fist caught her hair and pinned her down again.

"*Stay.*"

She wouldn't argue. Pressing her cheek against the cold metal surface of the table, she waited. She didn't have to wait long. He pressed against her again, and she felt him there at her core. She groaned quietly, shutting her eyes and biting her lip as the pressure began to build.

With one harsh movement, he filled her. If this was how he wanted to punish her, she'd thank him and ask for another.

She cried out, pleasure arcing through her as the wonderful ache that came with his size somehow only added to it all. She whacked her fist into the table. He snarled over her, using a fist in her hair to both keep her down and balance his weight as he gripped her hip with his other hand, claws digging into her skin.

He was angry with her.

And it showed.

And she loved every goddamn second of it.

With him, nothing mattered. There were no demons. No war. No nothing. It was just him, and her, and what they were like when they were together.

He was relentless. Inhuman. And God, between breathless cries and gasps for air, she was begging him for more.

Free.

She was *free* when she was with him. Even wearing iron chains.

Pleasure crested and built into a crescendo for them both. The snarl that left him was almost animalistic as he buried himself to the hilt and stayed there. He doubled over her, kissing her shoulder as he shuddered from the aftermath of his own bliss.

She was going to be bruised. And he might have broken the skin on her hip with his claws. But she couldn't find it in herself to care in the slightest. She was shivering as he slowly pulled himself away from her, gathering up her chainmail clothes and redressing her. She was too shaky to do it herself.

He tilted her head up to him and kissed her one more time, his touch tender and gentle. When he broke away, his expression finally held something in it other than cold rage—sadness. Perhaps regret. But for what?

"Tell me the truth, firefly." His words were quiet. Pleading, almost.

Shutting her eyes, she fought tears. "I can't..."

He kissed her forehead. "Very well. We shall talk again tomorrow. And every day after that until you do."

"Is the interrogation method always going to be the same?" She fought for a smile. It almost stuck.

He chuckled but said nothing. He stroked the back of a claw down her cheek. Wordlessly, he scooped her up in his arms. She leaned her head against his broad shoulder and shut her eyes. To her surprise, he didn't take her back to the cell. He brought her to her old room and set her down on the bed.

She looked up at him, curious and confused.

"You remain in chains. And you are not to leave this room unless you are escorted by me or one of my knights. Mark me, firefly—you are my prisoner. And do not mistake this for kindness." He headed to the door. "It is a convenience for both of us if you do not freeze on a stone floor."

His harsh words were somewhat deflated when he opened the door and Eod came charging in, barreling up onto the bed at a million miles an hour. He didn't waste a second before he was licking Gwen's face with the vibe of *I never thought I'd see you again!*

Mordred let out a long sigh. "I suppose that was inevitable."

She tried to shoo the dog away. "Wait, Mordred, I—"

He shut the door behind him and was gone.

Frowning, she accepted the dog's affection. There wasn't anything else she could do. "I missed you too, boy." She hugged the animal, who draped his head over her shoulder, his tail thumping on the bed.

At least she wasn't alone. At least she wasn't freezing in a jail cell, chained to the wall. At least this room had a privy.

But she felt hollow inside, all the same. Lying down on the bed, she shut her eyes. Eod cuddled up next to her, his head on her hip.

It was two hours before sleep came for her, her thoughts troubled and conflicted. Mordred was soon to be the target of a massive war. She was bound to his sworn enemy. But there was one thing she couldn't deny any longer.

Whether or not she should. Whether or not it would matter.

She loved him.

NINETEEN

Being trapped in a bedroom was at least a little less boring than being trapped in a cell, Gwen decided. But while she wasn't chained to the wall, she was still chained to herself and that made certain things—like changing her clothes—entirely impossible. Or at least her top half.

And Eod was getting just as antsy, but for a very different reason. He was sitting by the door, whining. With a sigh, she went up to the door and knocked on it. "Excuse me? The dog needs to go out."

Silence.

She rubbed a hand over her face and almost cracked herself in the teeth with the iron chain that connected the bracers on her wrists. "Look, I don't need to go with him. But unless you want to be cleaning up dog shit from the carpet, the animal needs *out*."

Another long moment of silence. Then the lock clicked, and the door swung open. Standing on the other side was that same, half-finished guard that had been standing in her cell.

She smiled. "Hi. Good morning."

He just stared, unmoving.

The dog walked into the hallway, then turned to look back at her, wagging his tail.

"Sorry, boy. I have to stay here. Go and do your business." Gwen smiled.

Eod's ears drooped.

"I know. I know. It's okay—you're good. Go on out."

His tail slowly stopped wagging. God damn it, dogs knew how to pull the heartstrings. Smiling, she knew what would work. "I bet there are *squirrels* outside."

Ears perked up, tail flying back and forth, Eod turned and ran down the hall, nails scrabbling on the wood as he beelined toward the front door.

Chuckling, she smiled. "Dogs. Simple creatures. Gotta love 'em."

The soldier nodded with a *squeak-squeak-squeak.*

She studied him for a moment. "Do you have a name?"

He shook his head. *Squeak-squeak-squeak.*

That was depressing. "Mordred really needs to get better about naming his creations. Would you like a name?"

A nod. *Squeak-squeak-squeak.*

"I'll think of a good one for you." She smiled broader at him. "When the dog comes back up, you can just let him in, right?" She walked back into the room. "Thank you!"

The door shut quietly behind her. It looked like a beautiful spring day out. It took her a little time, but she figured out how to open the windows to the room. They swung on hinges. Looking over the edge, the cliff was a sheer drop all the way down. Maybe if she'd still had her wings, she could have managed it. But as it was, she'd fall to her death.

And if not death, well, terrible mangling. It didn't sound fun at all. No, she was going to be stuck in Mordred's keep until he saw fit to let her go. Which might be absolutely never if what he said was true.

Not like she really wanted to run away either. She bristled

at the idea of being his prisoner—who wouldn't? But she... loved him. She really seriously did.

Sitting down on the thick stone sill of the window, careful not to risk falling out, she watched the clouds drift lazily along in the clear blue sky. She could hear the quiet crash of waves against the cliff below.

She loved Mordred. *The* Mordred. It was probably going to get her killed. No, screw that, it was absolutely going to get her killed. The question was just how long it took and how it went down.

She didn't want to run away. But she didn't want to be his prisoner either. Maybe over time she could earn his trust again. But that was time that she didn't know if she really had. Lancelot and Grinn would be building their army and storming the castle. A war would break out. And if Mordred lost...? Well, he'd be gone and her heart would go with him.

And if he won?

He'd have to kill her to kill Grinn. And she knew that Mordred's hatred of the demon ran thick and deep—there wasn't going to be any dissuading him.

Gwen suspected that Mordred cared about her. He hadn't ever said the words, but the way he fretted when she was injured, with such fear in his eyes at the idea of losing her, she knew he felt something.

But would it be enough? Was his attachment to her deeper than his hatred for the demon?

She didn't know.

And that was the problem.

She didn't know.

Sticking her finger into a proverbial live socket with Mordred was stupid enough the first time around, with the whole Iron Crystal debacle. She sure as shit wasn't going to do it again. For now, she'd stick to the plan—keep her soul bond to the demon a secret for as long as possible.

The current trick was to get Mordred to forgive her for not telling him the truth about Grinn. She hated the idea of him being mad at her, even if the result of him being "mad" was having epic sex.

She snickered. She was never going to look at that map table the same way again.

The door opened up and Eod bounced back in, proudly carrying someone's knee-high sock—or stocking, or whatever—in his mouth. Laughing, Gwen climbed from the windowsill. "Where did you get that? C'mere, give me that."

He danced around happily with it. He clearly had no intention of giving it up. What ensued next was a mixture of wrestling and tug-of-war that rendered the sock well and truly useless. But after about twenty minutes of games, Gwen was laughing so much it was hard to breathe. She rolled onto her back with her eyes shut as she tried to fill her aching lungs.

"Perhaps I made a mistake. It seems your imprisonment is far too much fun."

She blinked her eyes open. Standing over her, upside down and looming, was Mordred. Eod was at his side, tail wagging and tongue out, clearly proud of all the hard work he had just been doing.

"Oh—I—" She sat up. "I didn't think—"

"I am joking with you." Mordred patted the dog on the head. "I assume you would want to eat breakfast."

Climbing up to her feet, she brushed herself off. "Sure." Things felt so awkward between them. "Mordred, I..."

But he was already walking away. With a breath, she followed after him. Eod was trotting alongside the Prince in Iron, obviously knowing what the word *breakfast* meant. She just plodded along behind them until they reached Mordred's study. It was set up for two, with food already laid out.

He gestured idly to her chair and took his own. She sat, not knowing what to say. And it seemed, for a long moment, neither did he.

"I must apologize." His jaw twitched as he reached for his tea, easily grasping the mug in his claws. She was always impressed at how dexterous he was with them. "I wish for you to understand that any sort of..."

"Sex. The word you're looking for is sex." She smirked.

"Yes." He let out a huff that was a weak attempt at a laugh. "I wish for you to understand that you are not required or expected to have sex with me. This is not a condition of your imprisonment. Last night I acted rashly."

"I didn't tell you to stop." Quite the opposite, actually.

"But you are my prisoner." Grimacing in disgust, he shut his eyes. "I did not make it clear that your safety and well-being are not contingent upon further providing me—"

"Stop." She reached out and put her hand on his metal wrist. "Just stop."

Mordred watched her, uncertainty etched on his face, his brow furrowed. But he said nothing.

"I... look. I know you might think that I was just using you—using whatever this is between us to get you to lower your guard. And I mean, I guess, partially—" She cringed. She wasn't helping her argument a whole lot.

He fought back a smile.

"I'm not good at this shit. I'm sorry." She let out a sad laugh and scooted her chair a little closer to him, turning to face him. "Mordred, it wasn't about tricking you. It wasn't about using you. I care about you. I honestly and truly do."

"Says the traitor in league with the creature trying to burn down the world."

"Yeah, I *know*." She sighed and stared down at her lap. "I know you have no reason to believe me."

"You are right. I have no reason." The side of one of those jagged claws tipped her head back up to him. "But I believe you nonetheless." His gaze softened, just a little, as he lowered his hand back to the table. "Even if it makes me a fool."

"I wish... I wish I could take it all back. If I had known who he was, I never..." She picked idly at the plate of food in front of her as she talked. It gave her something to fidget with. "I never wanted to hurt you. I never wanted to get involved in any of this mess. And I certainly don't want to be stuck helping that mammoth asshole of a demon. I just don't have a choice."

"Because you believe if you tell me the truth, I will kill you."

She nodded.

The sigh that left him was so heavy and full of defeat that it summed up her mood just as nicely as his. "Gwendolyn, why do you not trust me? Even after all this? Have I not shown myself to be reasonable?"

"You have. But I also know what kind of a threat Grinn is, and how much you hate him. I know you want to protect Avalon at all costs. Even if it means..." She trailed off. She was already giving him too much.

"Even if it means killing you."

"I guess, really, I've already given you enough reason to kill me anyway." Folding her arms on the table, she put her forehead down on them. "I hate this shit. And I'm really bad at it."

"You are." He chuckled, resting a hand on her head and gently stroking her hair. "You will have to tell me, Gwen. Sooner rather than later, I expect. If what you say is true—if Grinn and Lancelot are raising an army to stop me—you will have to take a side. And I fear there will be no sparing Lancelot this time."

"I know." It broke her heart. All of it did. She didn't want Lancelot to die. She certainly didn't want Mordred to die.

The jury was out on Grinn.

The path of Mordred's hand over her hair shouldn't have been as comforting as it was, considering what it was made from. "For what peace it may give you, I will not seek violence. I shall not hunt them down. If they wish to wage war against me, I will defend myself. But I must give them the ability to choose this path. Otherwise, there would be no shred of my honor left to which I could cling."

She wanted to blurt it out. Just to tell him everything. And most of all, she wanted to say *I think I love you.* But she summarized it all into one thing that she also couldn't deny. "I'm just so scared." Scared for herself, sure. But also scared for *him.* An army was coming. And she didn't know if one guy and five knights could take out a horde of elementals. Even if they did have big metal dragons.

"I know. And it is for that reason I do not blame you for your actions." Mordred paused. "Come here."

Raising her head, Gwen was confused for a moment. She was sitting next to him. But when he opened his arms to her, she smiled faintly. She moved to sit in his lap, and let herself rest her head against the crook of his neck and his shoulder as he held her.

"Whatever this is between us, whatever it becomes, I do not wish to lose it. I do not wish to lose *you.* Not to the demon. Not to a new Iron Crystal. And not to myself either." He kissed the top of her head.

They stayed like that for minutes. She lost track of time. She just basked in the feeling of him—the security of it. The strength in his frame. Finally, though, she broke the silence. "Does this mean I get to walk around the keep again?"

"No."

She snickered. "Damn."

"Nice try."

Lifting her head, she kissed him, loving the feel of his lips against hers. He was addictive—not nearly as stern or unflinching as she would have expected him to be. He reacted to her every touch like a starving man might react to the taste of food.

She didn't know how she was going to make things right. She didn't know how they were going to get out on the other side of this in one piece. But damn it all, she knew she didn't have a choice.

She just *had* to.

Or else there wouldn't be anything of her on the other side of it at all.

TWENTY

Lancelot fought the urge to scream. He kept a smile on his face, and prayed to God that his irritation with the four elementals in front of him was not visible. They were four that had been known to travel in a pack—and also had been known to lay waste to whole towns when angered.

Isha, Mirnin, Niva and Olgon. Olgon was the most visually intimidating, as he had long since given up his human form and instead preferred to roam the countryside *as* the countryside. The giant collection of boulders was unpredictable, but at least slow-moving. He was currently serving as a perch for Isha, a lava elemental who had long since claimed Olgon as hers.

While she was less impressive in size, she was the one that truly worried Lancelot. He had once seen what she was capable of, long ago.

Niva and Mirnin were both air elementals and tended to stay close to Olgon and Isha for protection. That said, he would not discount anyone who commanded wind and lightning. Both were exceedingly dangerous—especially when one was, as Isha was always quick to point out, a lightning rod.

All four were watching him with wary suspicion at best, and in Isha's case—molten violence. He knew the only reason he wasn't a smoldering smear on the grass or buried under a boulder was because Zoe was floating beside him.

"And why would we help *you*?" Isha sneered. "Once a traitor, always a traitor. If you would betray Mordred now, why would you not betray us later? How can you prove this isn't a trap?"

"Simple. Because I have hated that bastard far longer than you." He held his head high. "I have been his prisoner for sixteen hundred years; you have only been so for three hundred. And while you were trapped in that *misery*, I was forced to lick his boots." Grimacing, he let his hatred for Mordred show plainly on his features. "I wish to free my brethren. I wish to make sure he pays for his crimes."

Olgon grunted, a sound that resembled more of an avalanche of rocks than anything a human might make. He had long since given up the ability to speak. It seemed Isha had no problem understanding him, however. "Why have you come to us?"

Mirnin flickered into existence, his crackling, static-like form disappearing a moment later and reappearing on the other side of the clearing. "Yes—speak—" He was an impatient sort. "Now!"

Lancelot let out a breath. Zoe might be able to keep the other elementals from killing him if things went poorly. *Might.* "I seek to lay siege to the keep. Drag Mordred out and put him on trial for what he has done. If he refuses to yield, then I seek to part his head from his shoulders and be done with it. I need an army for that. Enin the Green has already joined our cause, as have ten others."

Isha let out a thoughtful hum. "And do we get to reduce that castle of his to molten ore when we are done?"

"I would love nothing more than to see that place wiped from the face of Avalon." Lancelot smirked. "Along with all his iron abominations."

That seemed to convince Mirnin, who blinked out and reappeared standing by Niva. Niva looked for all the world like a ghost, made only of translucent wisps of air and whatever leaves and bits of grass were caught up in the whirling wind that was her body. Mirnin leaned over and whispered to Niva, who was intently listening.

"And what of you when all is said and done?" Isha sniffed. "Do you seek to rule in his stead?"

"I seek to live out the rest of my years in peace. I am done with soldiering—for myself or for others." Perhaps Gwendolyn might join him if she survived the fray. But deep down, he knew her heart belonged to Mordred, however tragic that might be. He shook his head. "I seek my own road, far away from all this nonsense."

Olgon let out a long sound that might have been a hum or just a vibration of stone on stone.

Isha watched him for a moment, and for the life of Lancelot he could not understand how the two communicated. Olgon's face was a collection of unmoving rock, and it seemed that any expression he tried to make would crack the surface and harm him. It was not uncommon for the Lord in Stone to simply choose not to move for *years*, moss and wildlife growing atop him as though he were nothing more than any other outcropping of rocks.

But Isha seemed to know what he was trying to say without fail. "If you are certain, love."

Lancelot tried not to ponder the details of how the two might consummate their relationship. He was happier not knowing.

Isha turned to him and flicked a lock of her chin-length hair out of her face, sending a bit of lava falling to Olgon's enormous shoulder. It hissed and turned cool and became part of the Lord in Stone, as if it had always been there. "As you wish, Knight in Silver. Olgon and I shall join your cause."

"As shall we," Niva said, her voice resembling reeds brushing on each other in the wind. It was a whisper of a thousand sounds, not one. "We shall see him brought to justice."

Smiling, Lancelot bowed.

"We rally at the keep in five days. We will march upon him at dawn."

* * *

"I thought I wasn't allowed out of my room." Gwen wasn't sure why she was giving Mordred shit for asking her to go on a walk with him. She should be thankful to get out of the keep, and to give the bored-ass dog a chance to stretch his long legs and go for a run.

Mordred was silent for a long moment. "I thought perhaps you should understand the seriousness of what is about to occur."

Oh, great. Just great. She was in for a guilt trip. Wrapping her arms around herself, she tried to ignore the presence of the three-foot chain that connected her wrists. It was another fantastic reminder of the trouble she had gotten herself into.

"There will be death. It is inevitable in war," he explained, as they walked from the keep out into the open area before the walls.

She blinked. It looked a lot different than the last time she had seen it. Giant, trebuchet-looking things were set up and aimed out at the field. Guards were carrying large, spiked spheres made of rusted iron in buckets—clearly what the trebuchets were meant to launch. She cringed, picturing the spiked wrecking balls coming down on some poor elemental. As they were all vulnerable to iron, she figured it would be instant death, regardless of how big they were or what they were made of.

It was horrifying to think about.

The ramparts were being set up with spears and cauldrons. Gwen furrowed her brow. They looked more like forges with the way they were set up. "What're the cauldrons for?"

"Molten iron. If we are beaten back to the walls, and the attackers attempt to climb them, my soldiers will dump the iron on them." Mordred's tone was flat and matter-of-fact. As if nothing about that disgusting image was out of the ordinary.

"Holy shit."

"You have never seen war, firefly." He began to walk up the stairs to the ramparts. "I am simply trying to prepare you for what you may witness."

Following, Gwen had to step around soldiers and guards who were setting up, readying for a siege that may or may not come any day. "You're going to let me out?"

"No. But should the keep fall—should I be killed—you will need to defend yourself." Again, Mordred was talking about dying like it was no big deal.

"I... I really don't want you to die, Mordred." She reached out and took his elbow, perpetually covered in the armor he wore up to his shoulders. "You know that, right?"

"Yes. I do." He smiled down at her, a bit mournfully. "Yet you are not on my side either."

"I—" She wanted to say that she was. She really did. But she couldn't say it with a straight face when she was still hiding the truth of her connection to Grinn. "I don't want anybody to die." That much was true. Even for as much as Grinn was a total ass to her, she didn't think he deserved to be executed over it.

"You are young. Naive. You come from a world that has

been spared this level of destruction and mayhem." He stroked a clawed gauntlet over her hair gently. "I wish I could spare you the reality of our situation, but I cannot. You are protecting those who will, in short order, attempt to kill me. My soldiers will certainly fall in battle, their magic and their souls shattered. My knights are at risk—some may die, but they all will if I fall. And as for me, well. I am obviously their target." He shook his head. "I will fight upon the front lines in hopes of minimizing the risk to you and those within the keep."

Gwen knew better than to try to argue with him. She nodded, swallowing the lump in her throat. Tears were threatening to build. "I'm so sorry, this is all my fault."

"No, firefly. It is not your fault." He brushed the backs of his knuckles over her cheek. "This has been inevitable, I suppose. The Crystal would not have lasted forever, and when it finally broke apart, the reckoning for my actions would come. The others are not likely to see the sense in my choices. Some may—but enough will rise against me to see me undone. You may have been the catalyst for these events, but they were bound to come in time."

That didn't make her feel better in the slightest. Looking out at the field, she tried to picture it filled with bodies, and mud, and blood.

As if knowing what she was doing, he stepped in closer and rested his clawed hand on her shoulder. "It is not the sight that will haunt you, firefly. It is the sound that will linger with you."

"You're not making me feel any better."

"It was not my intention to upset you. My intention was to prepare you."

She laughed weakly and rested her forehead against his chest. He was wearing a black linen shirt, so at least she didn't thwack her head on his armor. "I just wish... I just wish everything could be peaceful."

"As do I. Believe me, that has been my only goal in all this.

But it is not the way of Avalon." He pulled her into his arms. "And I grieve the uncertainty of our future."

She believed him. Sniffling, she let out a wavering sigh. "I'm just so sorry, Mordred. I didn't want any of this to happen. I really didn't."

"Gwendolyn, I must know the nature of your relationship to the demon. It is crucial before I enter the fray to know what I am up against. Please." Despite his words, his embrace stayed the same—tender and caring.

Shutting her eyes, she thought it over. It would make her life a lot easier—namely because she'd be dead. Mordred's commitment to seeing the demon gone was a death sentence for her, simple as that. "I'm sorry. I can't."

He kissed the top of her head. "I will not stop asking."

"I know."

"Come, firefly. There is much more to show you."

She should be happy to be outside and out of her cell or her room. She should be loving going for a stroll with Mordred while Eod ran about and sniffed every new thing and barked greetings at several of his guards.

But it was hard to enjoy anything when she knew that the sound of birds and the whisper of the wind would soon become the screams of the dying and injured, and the sounds of clanking armor would be replaced with the clash of weapons and cleaving flesh.

There was a twist in her stomach that made her want to be sick. She wasn't cut out for this shit—but it didn't matter. She was smack in the middle of it anyway. *This sucks.* It wasn't an eloquent way to express her feelings. But it was all she had at the moment.

This really sucks.

* * *

Lancelot sighed and rubbed his hand over his face. He knew what he was getting into, trying to raise an army of elementals. It was the only option for defeating Mordred. It wasn't like he could just summon an army out of thin air in any other way. He wasn't nearly strong enough.

But damn it if the process wasn't going to drive him *insane.*

The bickering.

Dear God, the bickering.

Enin and Zoe stood beside him, both of them having just as little patience for the mayhem that was going on in front of them. Four elementals of water were all shouting at each other about whether or not they should join his force to take down Mordred.

So far, it was an even split, two against two. The real issue was that two of the water elementals were twins, and they did everything together. And they were currently divided in opinions.

"Enough!" Lancelot couldn't take it anymore. "Enough. Please. Spare my aching head."

The four elementals glared at him.

"I seek the continued freedom of all of us. I was placed in that Crystal the same as you. Stand with me or leave, I do not care. To stay idle is to stand with *him.*"

"Why do you think we will succeed now, when we failed before?" A man with the lower body of an octopus sneered.

"He has grown weak over the past three hundred years." Lancelot shook his head. "And you have allies now that you did not have before."

"You?" the air elemental scoffed.

"Yes. And one other. The demon Grinn."

All four elementals grimaced in unison. One of them, a woman, swore in some ancient foreign tongue that Lancelot did not recognize, though he didn't need to understand the words to get the drift.

"I know, I know. I hate it as well." Lancelot sighed. "But we have no choice. Our first step should be to defeat Mordred. Then, we can contend with the demon. But he was a prisoner like you, all those years—the first to go into the Crystal. Perhaps he has changed his ways."

Silence.

All of them burst into laughter.

One of them who had been resistant to the idea tapped her chin. "Perhaps you speak wisely. To stand together now, before Mordred can ready his defenses, might ensure our success. And if we moved together, one elemental of fire would be weak."

Another elemental shook her head. "No. I shall never side with that demon. Not after what he did. I will stand by your side when his time to die has come. Until then, I shall not join you."

Lancelot nodded. That was fair. Three out of four was not bad work. Slowly, but surely, his army was growing. But he knew time was of the essence. "We must move quickly. The longer we wait, the more he will be ready for us. Meet us at the keep in one week. Five days at dawn."

The elementals disappeared or flew off into the sky, leaving Zoe and Enin behind.

Lancelot ran his fingers through his hair, scratching his scalp. "This is taking too long. We should split up." He knew, sadly, where he was most needed. "I should go and ensure that Grinn is neither dead nor busy terrorizing the countryside. I should learn what has become of him and Gwendolyn." After a pause he added, "And the wizard, I suppose." Lord above, he hated wizards. Shifty bastards.

Zoe chuckled. "I can send you to him. Enin and I will rally as many others as we can find." She opened a portal through space. "Five days at dawn."

Enin nodded once curtly. The Lord in Green was not a talkative fellow.

Letting out a breath, Lancelot kept his hand on the hilt of his sword and stepped through the portal, not knowing what to expect on the other side. But he knew one thing.

His headaches at the hands of elementals had only just begun.

TWENTY-ONE

Damn it all, Gwen was *bored.*

She hadn't seen Mordred in a day, as he was busy continuing to prepare the keep for war, and everyone else seemed to ignore her existence. Hours and days fell into the same pattern —wake up, let dog out, wait, let dog in, sit around, poke at things in the room, eat what was brought to her, let dog out, wait, let dog in, sleep.

There were books in her room, but one of them looked like it was in Old English—so it was pretty much gibberish—and the other one was in Latin. Which was as good as gibberish. The only person she had to talk to was the guard that was stationed outside of her room.

And he couldn't talk.

This time, when Eod was let out in the afternoon, she sat down on the floor on the inside of the jamb into the room and waited. It was just nice to have the door open for a bit. It made her feel a little cramped.

"Y'know, I've been thinking," she said to the unfinished soldier. "I shouldn't name you. You should name you."

He tilted his head to the side slightly with a squeak.

"You should have the right to pick your own name." She smiled. "I'll list off a bunch of choices, and you can stop me when you find one you like. First—would you like a boy name?"

A nod. *Squeak-squeak-squeak.*

At first, she tried to list all the names she could think of in alphabetical order. "Aaron, Alex, Andrew—"

Nothing.

Then, she kept remembering other names and quickly gave up on the idea of doing them in order. She just decided to jump around at random. "Ben, Mac, Jon, Jake—"

Nope.

"—Lorcan, Jeremy, Brennan—"

Nada.

"—David, Jim, Garry, Dillon, Isaac, Michael, Don, Eagan—"

Zilch.

"Tim—"

He raised his hand. She paused. He thought it over for a second, turning his head away. Then he nodded emphatically.

"Tim?" She smiled. "I like it. Tim the Tin, although... I guess you're technically made of iron and all." She pushed up from the ground and stuck her hand out to him. "Nice to meet you, Tim."

He stared at her hand for a moment as if not knowing what to do with it before carefully putting his hand into hers. It was missing a finger, like it had rusted away or hadn't been drawn at all. It didn't bother her. Shaking his hand, she couldn't help but feel a little proud of herself. It wasn't fair that he was so neglected. She'd have to lecture Mordred about taking better care of his creations next time she saw him.

Speak of the devil, and there he was. Mordred rounded the corner of the hallway and saw the exchange. He arched an eyebrow. "Am I interrupting?"

"Meet Tim." She smiled and pointed at the metal guard. In

response, Tim straightened his back and puffed out his breastplate in pride.

Mordred stared at her flatly. "You really must stop naming everything."

"Never." She grinned.

He shook his head. "Eod has decided to continuously bark at me, rendering me unable to focus. I believe the dog is scolding me for leaving you locked away. Would you care to join me for dinner?"

"Dude, you could ask me to do your laundry right now, and I'd be game. I am *bored to tears* in here." Heading out of the room, she felt a weight slide off her shoulders. Smiling back at the guard, she waved goodbye. "See you later, Tim."

Mordred let out a quiet sigh. But when he turned his back to lead her away, she couldn't help but catch a faint smile on his features.

"I do have a request." She jogged to catch up with him and fall in line beside him.

"You are my prisoner."

"I know, but... It's for your benefit too." She lifted her hands to show the iron chain that connected her wrists. "I'd really like to change my clothes, and this stupid chain makes it impossible. I won't ask you to take the cuffs off, but this is getting super irritating. I keep hitting myself in the face with it."

Mordred fell silent for a long time. "When you are in your room, I will remove the chain. When you are being escorted, however, it will remain on."

"Deal." She smiled. That was progress. She could be happy with that.

"You are in a cheerful mood today."

"Someone has to be." She stuck out her tongue at him. She wasn't sure why she was feeling so feisty. It was probably from being cooped up in a room for thirty-six hours with an antsy dog.

He chuckled. "Yes, I suppose so." He brought her to a room that was smaller and cozier than where he usually hung out. Eod was upside down, asleep on a sofa by the wall, his legs sticking out in all directions.

A small fire blazed away in a hearth by one wall, filling the room with a wonderful warmth and smell of woodsmoke. A table that looked like it wasn't usually set up in what looked like a reading room, sat in the middle on a carpet. It was set for two. All in all, there was only one word for it—romantic.

She blinked. "Is this a date?"

"If I knew what a 'date' was, perhaps I could tell you."

"It totally is." She smiled and hugged his metal arm. She'd hug him around the waist, but the stupid chain definitely wouldn't go all the way around, and she'd just end up embarrassing herself.

He hummed. "I suppose this is my way of attempting to entertain you after leaving you alone for so long. I apologize. But defensive wards needed to be put in place."

"I get it." She rested her cheek against his armor. It was cool to the touch. "And you don't need to apologize. This is my fault."

"No, it is not. The demon is to blame, not you." He turned her to face him and rested a hand on her shoulder. "You are caught in the midst of a battle that has been waging for a millennium and more. You are right to be wary of the depth of hatred between him and me. I do not fault you for your distrust, though I wish it were not so."

She smiled faintly. "You're a good man, Mordred."

He snorted.

"Well, okay, you try." Her smile bloomed.

"I will accept that." He was smiling back down at her, though there was a twinge of sadness in it. The mirth did not reach his eyes. "Come. Dinner is growing cold."

She was shocked the dog hadn't eaten it while he was out of

the room, but both of the plates were under those metal dome-thingies that they used to use. Cloches? She thought they might be called cloches.

He pulled out her chair for her, and she sat down. It was so damn cute, even if she was, y'know, chained up. He poured her a glass of mead. "Oh no," she said with a playful tone of dread.

"Pace yourself." He kissed the top of her head before taking his own seat. All it took was the lifting of the cloches and Eod snorted awake, rolling over in a tangle of long limbs. He was soon sitting beside her, head resting on her lap, already in full beg mode.

She couldn't blame him. The food looked *amazing*. It was steak and potatoes, with a side of green beans and tomatoes. "You know how to butter up a girl."

"I..." He stared at her. "I assume that's a metaphor..."

That cracked her up. Laughing, she put her hand on his. "Yeah. It is. I mean, unless you're into that kind of thing, in which case we can have a talk about it, but—"

Now it was his turn to laugh. "I would rather not. I feel as though it might make a mess." He paused. "Besides, I can think of better ways to spend our time."

Her cheeks went hot as she blushed. It was a second later that the melancholy settled over her with the reality of what was happening.

"No. None of that." He must have seen her mood fade. He turned her head toward him with the gentle crook of a talon. "Our time may be short, firefly. And I will not waste it on fears for the future."

"But..."

"No. I forbid it."

She arched an eyebrow. "You're ordering me around now?"

His smile was just a little bit wicked. "If that is what you wish, then yes."

If it weren't for the iron she was wearing, she'd worry she'd have burst into flames with how hot her cheeks were. "Damn it, Mordred."

"Eat. Do you play chess?"

"Miserably. I know the rules, but past that I'm a four-year-old at the game."

"Then I will teach you." He picked up his knife and fork and began cutting up his dinner.

"If you teach chess the way you teach sword fighting, I'm scared." She winced.

He smirked. "I expect you might end up with a few less bruises."

"I *might*?"

"It depends on how poorly you play, I suppose." He chuckled and gestured at her meal. "Eat, firefly."

Her stomach rumbled, clearly agreeing with him. With a smile, and a hope in her heart that maybe things could be normal between them—as normal as things *could* be, given the situation—if they had enough time.

But she didn't think time was on their side.

* * *

Lancelot wasn't entirely certain how he was going to find the demon and the sorcerer, hiding somewhere in the wilderness by Mordred's keep. Luckily, he knew the terrain like the back of his hand. He'd had sixteen hundred years of wandering about the island, and three hundred of those with all the magic of Avalon trapped in the Iron Crystal. It had left him nothing better to do except wander.

So, as he puzzled over exactly how and where *he* would go to hide, there was one clear answer that came to mind—a cave by a river that pointed away from the road and the keep itself. It would be protected enough from the weather, had a source of fresh water, and he would be able to burn fires without the fear of being spotted by any onlookers.

He rode along on his silver steed, enjoying the fresh air and the wonderful spring weather. The world had come alive again—finally freed from the terrible clutches of a perpetual autumn. That depressing point in the season where it was clear that the celebration of fading life had ended, and the winter was only minutes away.

God, how he loved this island when it was as it should be. The chaos and the fighting were simply the cost of such a wonderous, beautiful place. It was a worthy price to pay. He would not allow this world to return to the Crystal—or he would die trying.

Normally, his money would be firmly upon the latter. But with the aid of Grinn and a growing pack of elementals, he had hope he might succeed. And if Gwendolyn was still with the demon and the wizard, they had another powerful resource at their disposal.

Not because he suspected the young lady was a useful fighter. Far from it, at this point in her life. No—because she was a weakness. Mordred would not stand against her; Lancelot was certain of it.

For a thousand years, and a half again, and more, he had suffered the presence of the Prince in Iron. He knew the man, whether he liked it or not. And it was painfully clear to him that Mordred was in love.

The idea was almost laughable. Indeed, if anyone had suggested it to him in passing, he would have laughed and called them a fool. But Lancelot had seen it himself, firsthand. It was undeniable.

And it might be the only thing that saved the sacred isle from suffering more of the bastard's cruel reign.

Lancelot had been riding through the countryside, sticking to the roads as best he could but avoiding major towns, as he headed back in the direction of the keep. Zoe's magic had put him close to his destination, but not quite there.

There was hope in his heart that Zoe and Enin would be successful in finding more elementals. There was only so much he could do on his own. Despite his newfound freedom from Mordred, Lancelot knew he was likely a deterrent not an aid when begging for support from those who had been imprisoned in the Crystal. He was, after all, a knight and elemental of metal. Who was to say that he was not setting them up for a trap? And now that he had others to help him, he was likely best served to help wrangle the demon.

Sadly, it was best to let the Gossamer Lady and the Lord in Green do the convincing for him. Though he disliked the idea of what would come in a few days when it came time to rally the forces and only a measly number of elementals emerged for the fight.

That would be a bridge he crossed when they came to it.

He found himself smiling, despite his dark thoughts, as he rode through the woods. He remembered riding through this very glade with Gwendolyn. In another life, perhaps, he could have wooed the girl to his side and spent eternity with the fire-haired young woman. But his duty was to the isle, above all.

Moreover, his duty was to see Mordred removed of his head.

As he approached the cave, he was glad to see that his suspicions had been right. Two horses were grazing off to the side. A wooden cart was resting on its yoke. Lancelot could smell cooking food. A fire was crackling out in front of the entrance to the cave.

"Hail," he called to whomever was inside.

"Took you long enough." The mage emerged from the entrance, brushing his hands off. "I *hate* camping. Hello, knight."

Lancelot frowned. "Are you here alone?"

"I wish." The mage jerked a thumb behind him into the cave. "Grinn is still recovering. You think he's cranky normally? Try putting up with him when he's been riddled with musket balls."

Lancelot's concern deepened. "I heard the chaos erupt in the town, but we were too separated to reach you in time. What of Gwendolyn?"

"Taken by the prince." The sorcerer shrugged. "She's fine."

Lancelot did not bother to ask how he knew. He had spent enough time in the company of Merlin to understand that it was futile to question what sorcerers did and did not know. It was a waste of time. He had been smacked with the old man's walking stick more than once for asking "stupid questions."

Dismounting his steed, he approached the other man with a heavy sigh. "I am glad to hear that she is unharmed. I am... honestly surprised."

"Mordred doesn't know the details between her and Grinn. I suspect that's the only reason she's still attached to her limbs. And I suspect she knows that." He smiled sarcastically. "Or maybe, we're all reading the prince wrong. Who knows. I made chicken soup, want some?"

Lancelot blinked at the sudden change of topics. "Yes, thank you."

"Finally, somebody with manners," the mage grumbled, as he walked back into the cave. "Wake up, *your highness*, we have a guest."

The baritone grumble from within the cave told Lancelot that the demon was awake and in his usual mood. He could not help but place his hand on his sword as the monstrous creature lumbered out from the cave, still limping. There were bandages wrapped around his midsection, stained a dark black from the creature's inhuman blood.

The demon sneered at him. "What took you so long?"

Lancelot rolled his eyes and ignored the goading. "We have

two more days until we will be joined by whatever army we have managed to muster. Will you be whole by then?"

"I will be whole enough." Grinn lay down by the fire. "If you do not plan on stabbing me, that is."

"I am rather tempted." Lancelot let go of his sword. "But no. There is no honor in fighting a wounded opponent. And you and I, for the time, have a common enemy."

Grinn let out a quiet grunt but said nothing. The wizard went about spooning soup into two mugs and one wooden bowl for the demon. The odd, eccentric mage seemed content to just ignore the conversation entirely.

"And when Mordred falls?" Lancelot arched an eyebrow. "What will your path be then? To scorch the ground and render this place a wasteland?"

"What does it matter?" Grinn sniffed dismissively. "If I were to tell you my plan was to retreat to a remote corner of the isle and finally be left alone, you would not believe me. What is the use in asking me in the first place?"

He had a valid point. Lancelot shook his head. "You have lost the right to be cynical toward the opinion others have of you. There is too much blood on your hands."

"You mistake me for someone who cares, knight." Grinn shut his eyes, seemingly unimpressed with whatever threat Lancelot might pose to him.

By the savior, he *hated* the demon. "I will stand beside you in this war for the greater good, Ash King." He put a heavy emphasis of sarcasm on the final word. There was only one King of Avalon, and he was long dead and dust. "But once Mordred has fallen, you and I will have matters to settle of our own."

"I will eagerly look forward to squaring our mutual distaste for each other on the battlefield, once I have my power back and Mordred is dead." Grinn's one good eye opened to fix a glowing red stare on him. "I will enjoy making a rug from your skinned flesh."

It was Lancelot's turn to sneer. "I look forward to watching you try."

The wizard interjected cheerfully, as if he hadn't heard a single word of the conversation. "Soup's up!"

TWENTY-TWO

Mordred could not help but find himself somewhat enraptured by the young woman who sat beside him. He watched as she valiantly tried to rally her mood again and again, only to have it dulled by the foreboding cloud of *what will be* that they had found themselves in.

He could not say he blamed her. It was certainly not his place to judge someone for dreading the future. It had become a large portion of his own personality over the centuries, after all. But he found himself smiling all the same as she tried and failed to pace herself on the mead he had served with their dinner.

While he did not intend letting her get dangerously drunk, he wished to see her smile and laugh. To see a little bit of the joyful creature he knew lurked inside. He had witnessed it before—mostly when she was interacting with the dog who was begging successfully for bits of dinner at her side.

And occasionally when she looked at him.

Her fire-colored eyes would light up. She would smile, almost shyly, and a slight pink tone would hue her cheeks. He was afraid to give a name to what it was that they shared, as it was likely to shatter before the week was out. Likely when he wound up with his head on a pike.

But that was tomorrow or the day after. Tonight, they were together. And tonight, they might forget everything that was to come. Even if the chain connecting her wrists was a constant reminder as it rattled along the edge of the table.

He loved her.

By the Ancients, how he loved her.

But how could he trust her, with the seriousness of what she was still hiding from him? She was in league with the demon. With *Grinn*. And while he knew that what she had told him thus far was not a lie, it was the secrets she kept that needled them both.

Whatever it was, whatever the nature of her strange alliance with Grinn might be, she thought it would spell her demise at his hands. He wished to fall to his knees before her and pledge his heart and soul to her. To promise her that nothing—absolutely *nothing*—could lead him to do such a thing.

Yet deep down inside, he knew that would be a lie.

She was right to be wary. To think that he might put Avalon first ahead of her safety. It was not out of the question. Without all the facts in front of him, he could not say what he might do. For where would they live, how would they exist, if the isle were destroyed around them?

There was always a line that could not be crossed. And anyone who would say otherwise was either dishonest or a fool.

But for now, for this night, he would not have to choose between his duty and the woman he loved. Dinner was finished, and Gwen was already a glass and a half into the mead. She was quicker to smile than she had been a moment before.

Eod, realizing he wasn't going to get any more treats, clambered back up onto the couch by the wall and started snoring.

Standing, Mordred picked up the bottle of mead and offered Gwen his hand. She looked up at him quizzically for a moment before taking it and letting him lead her from the room. He kept hold of her hand, not caring what others might think as they passed, and he brought her to his favorite place in the keep.

The tower observation deck was often where he went on lonely nights to think. The ceiling stretched high overhead, disappearing into the darkness above them. Floor-to-ceiling windows were open to the outside air on all sides, revealing a balcony and the most stunning view of the isle that the keep had to offer.

Gwendolyn gasped. She headed to the balcony through the open archway door. He followed behind her, smiling as she took in the sight.

The clouds had cleared, and the sky was alive with the dancing flicker of stars. The moon was high, casting the forest beyond in a pale glow. Even from this distance, Mordred could make out the blink of fireflies in the field and in the darkness of the forest beyond. Avalon was once more alive.

She leaned on the stone balustrade. "Wow..."

"I had missed this. I did not realize how much until it returned." He stood beside her, resting his own arms on the stone rail. "I do not wish to rebuild the Iron Crystal."

"Really?" She glanced up at him for a moment before turning her attention back to the view.

"I will if I must. But I do not want to see this world muted and broken once more. I do not enjoy that which I must do to protect Avalon." He shut his eyes. "I would weep to see such beauty broken once more by death... I do not know if I could stomach total war a second time. Yet I do not know if fating it to the Crystal is any less damning. What am I to do, firefly?"

When her fingers touched his cheek, he almost jolted in surprise. She turned him to her with the slightest of movements.

Such a sweet creature.

"Take this fucking chain off me."

He blinked. That was not what he was expecting. "Pardon?"

"I want to *hug* you, you big, stupid, rusty freight train." She poked him in the chest. "Take the chain off."

Chuckling quietly, he shook his head. "Yes, fine." Taking the chain in his hand, he willed the links to detach from her wrists before vanishing it into the ether complete. "But it goes back on when—"

He never finished the sentence. She threw her arms around his neck, having to leap up until her feet were no longer touching the ground. He caught her reflexively as she kissed him.

* * *

Gwen's heart had never been more broken or more full at the same time before in her life. She wanted to cry for him—she wanted to hold him and tell him it was all going to be okay. That she loved him, that she understood him, that she wanted to never leave his side again.

But what would be the point, if one or both of them was going to be dead soon?

The dread that filled her was beyond anything she'd ever felt before. War was coming. And it was coming *soon.* It had been three or four days since she had parted ways with Grinn and Doc, and that meant, any second now, all this would end. Which meant she had only one thing to do.

She couldn't stop the war. She couldn't stop people from dying. So, she vowed to enjoy tonight for what it was. Savor the moment. That was what he was trying to get her to do. So damn it all, she was going to do exactly that. When she broke the kiss, she smiled at him and ran a hand through his iron-gray hair. It was so damn soft and had no business being anything of the sort. It was right then that she realized she hadn't really... touched him. Not exactly. They'd had sex a few times, but it was all with him driving the bus and her being along for the proverbial ride.

She stroked her fingers along his cheek. The slight rasp of a day's worth of stubble was prickly against her palm, but she found she liked it. He was a brutal warlord when it came down to it. He should feel like one.

He rested his forehead against hers, clearly basking in her touch. It was fascinating to her how much it clearly meant to him. How lonely had he been for so very long, with no one who cared? No one who was brave enough to get close. Or no one he let try.

"I'm not nearly tipsy enough," she murmured to him. She'd need some liquid courage for what she was planning.

Chuckling, he let her back down onto her feet and gestured to a stone bench by the wall. The balustrade had railings, so it didn't do much to cut off the view. She sat on it, smiling, and patted the spot next to her.

Silently, they sat there beside each other, passing the bottle of mead between them as they gazed up at the stars. "Are there other worlds out there?"

"I am certain there are. But while I have seen other worlds, and met visitors from them—I do not know if they live out in our stars, or somewhere else. Perhaps they are just a facsimile to fill the sky and keep this isle from being that much more bleak." He took a sip from the bottle and passed it to her.

"Yeah, it'd be pretty sad to see a sky with no stars."

"Almost as sad as it would be to only see clouds."

There was something in his voice. It wasn't disappointment. It was a softness she didn't expect. Turning to look up at him, she was caught by the expression in his eyes.

It reflected something neither of them seemingly wanted to name. And likely for the same reason. Because tomorrow might spell the end. Why make the pain worse than it already would be?

But tonight was about them. Standing from the bench, she took his metal hand and wordlessly led him from the tower. She was learning the layout of the keep well enough that she could navigate it largely on her own. At least to the major landmarks.

She brought him to his room, neither of them saying anything.

When he closed the door behind him, it took seconds before he caught her lips with his, picking her up to even their height. Wrapping her legs around his waist to support herself as best she could, she met the embrace with a passion that surprised her.

He walked them to his bed and placed her down on her back, caging her in as he continued to devour her. After breaking the kiss, he straightened up, and she watched in awe as he stripped naked.

God, he was such a work of art. The way his muscles moved, the way the scars on his skin seemed to make him... she didn't know. Human? Touchable? Reachable? The marks of a hundred battles. She supposed she had one of her own now—though she hadn't really earned that. It had just kind of happened.

He knelt down on the bed, taking the hem of her chainmail top and pulling it off over her head. The skirt went next. When he leaned down to kiss her again, she put her hand in the center of his chest to stop him.

He paused, his brow furrowing. She sat up, urging him to lie down instead, then straddling his lap as he lay back on the sheets. A clawed hand settled on her ass as she leaned over him to kiss him once more, wanting to feel the slight scrape of his stubble and the firmness in his touch.

She had never been so bold in her life. And it felt incredible.

It was her turn to set the pace. And damn it all if she didn't want to savor the sensation of him as she sank him deep into her. She had to rest her weight on his chest, her eyes sliding half-shut, lost in the moment.

It wasn't about a physical need. Oh, there was that—she had a veritable demigod of a man beneath her. But she needed to feel connected to him. Needed to have him there, guiding her motions with the grasp of iron at her hips.

I love him.

It wasn't even a question anymore. It was simply truth.

Mordred didn't seem to want to rush the moment either. He lay there, gazing up at her almost in awe. As if she were something special—something precious.

When it all ended, she was in his arms as he kissed her. And she knew that was a place she never, ever wanted to leave.

Too bad that choice would probably be snatched away from her.

It was the middle of the night that she had the proof of her suspicion. There was a rough knock on the door that jerked them both awake.

"My lord. They have arrived. We have spotted fires in the woods."

Mordred was up and dressing while she was still blearily wiping the sleep from her eyes.

Shit. Shit shit shit.

"Dress and return to your room, Gwendolyn." Mordred summoned his armor. It flowed over him like liquid before hardening into shape. "Do not argue."

Gwen nodded.

Fear twisted and tangled in her stomach like angry snakes. She wanted to cry. But it was like a tornado warning—you just did what you had to do. You just went into action mode.

The others had come. It was about to begin.

War.

TWENTY-THREE

It was almost dawn on the seventh day, and Lancelot was nervous.

He was pacing. And he hated pacing. It was useless. Especially when he was not trying to reason his way through a problem. No, he was simply pacing because he was *waiting*. And he hated *waiting*.

But here he was—doing exactly that. Waiting and pacing. Pacing and waiting. He kept his gaze locked on the structure in the near distance—Mordred's keep. The building he had called home for over a thousand years.

And one he now planned to burn to the ground, along with all the cursed, corrupted magic that the rusted bastard had stolen and put into his *creations*. But while Mordred himself was immune to elemental magic—his guards were merely resistant. They could be destroyed.

He weighed the sides and tried to calculate the odds for success. Elementals were more powerful than an iron soldier in a one-on-one fight. The Prince in Iron had about a hundred guards. And six dragons.

Lancelot had his own dragon that he would summon when

it came time to reveal their location. But one versus six was not a brilliant strategy, especially when Lancelot himself was likely to be on the front lines personally. It would make him an easy target, and he might fall quickly to a lucky shot.

Enin and Zoe had arrived with their recruits, and so had those that Lancelot had spoken to personally. That gave him twenty-one in his ranks. But Lady Thorn had yet to arrive, and there was still time for stragglers to appear.

Would Lady Thorn arrive at all? Would she come with ten? Twenty? Zero? How many even remained to recruit at all?

Of the seventy or more that went into the Crystal, how many had been driven mad or drained of their own being to be turned into those hideous iron soldiers?

There was no way for him to know.

Hence, the pacing.

It was just as the sun began to peek over the horizon, casting rays of amber light across the field, that he heard a voice from behind him.

"Knight."

He never once believed that he would feel relief at hearing Thorn's voice. But as he turned toward the harsh greeting, he felt exactly that. She had come. And she had not come alone.

Standing behind her were at *least* thirty more elementals of all shapes, colors, and sizes.

He could not help but smile. That gave him hope. That gave him something even near certainty.

"The bastard dies today." Thorn spat on the ground in front of her. "I am sick of waiting."

"As am I." Lancelot whistled, getting the attention of the others. "Prepare yourselves! We march!"

Someone bumped his elbow. The wizard was standing beside him, offering him a cup of coffee. "Drink it, you'll need it."

"I hate this vile substance." He took it all the same. Sipping it, he made a face. It didn't stop him from taking another sip a moment later.

"It grows on you." The mage sipped from his own mug, looking out over the field at the keep beyond.

"Where is the demon?" Lancelot had noticed Grinn's absence, namely because the angry dark cloud was missing.

"He mumbled about needing to 'fetch something' and fucked off." The other man shrugged. "Probably for the best if he's off the battlefield anyway. He's just going to protect himself and not help the others."

That was quite true. The demon's disappearance was cowardly, but not unexpected. The bastard had been known to run when the odds were even. Which brought up another question that Lancelot could not help but ask. "What will happen? You must know."

"I know what's likely. I don't know what's real. It's like a—"

"Lighthouse. I've heard the speech."

"Have you?" He hummed. "I don't remember."

Wizards.

Lancelot was convinced at this point in his life that he had the patience of a damnable mountain. "You do not remember much."

The wizard snickered into his mug of coffee. "*Yeeeahh...*"

"Will you stand with us, or against us?"

"You know me. I stay neutral. I'm merely here to observe and watch this fuckery play out in real time." He smiled, but there was an odd, faraway look in his eyes. As if he could see exactly what was going to happen, and he simply wasn't telling Lancelot the truth.

Knowing all that was and all that is led quite quickly to a person, in Lancelot's humble opinion, being entirely insane. He did not bother to ask what the wizard's prediction was. He already knew the answer.

More than fifty elementals had answered his call and rallied to see the Prince in Iron brought low. A force that the island had not seen in a very, very long time—if ever.

We are going to win.

Mordred is going to die.

* * *

Mordred stood upon the rampart and gazed out at the woods beyond. He knew today would be the day. He did not know how, precisely. But he could sense it. After a millennium and a half suffering Lancelot's presence, he could predict the knight's actions as well as his own.

And something about this day—about the weather, about the feeling in the air... There was an urgency to it. Perhaps it was his own link to the magic of Avalon and the lingering gifts from his mother Morgana.

Cracking his neck from one side to the other, the tension releasing with a series of loud pops, he braced himself for what would inevitably follow.

An army would come from those trees—how many in number, he did not know. But he supposed it did not matter. He would have the advantage of numbers and six dragons, where Lancelot would only have the one and whatever elementals he could cajole to his side.

Would it be all seventy-something who had once dwelled on the island? Or zero? Mordred hated the uncertainty.

There was one person he could add to his own ranks, perhaps... Gwendolyn. A fire elemental would be useful. But... she would remain in her room, in chains.

He was concerned for her safety on the battlefield. It was one thing to learn to pick up a sword and stand properly—it was another thing to actually *fight.* He would also be distracted by the need to ensure she was safe. And he had to focus in the thick of a battle.

But that was only one side to his thinking. The other was that he simply did not trust her.

She had been convinced by the demon to betray him once before. Who was to say she would not do it a second time? With the nature of her strange attachment to Grinn still a mystery, he simply could not risk it.

No. She would stay in her room where it was safest for *both* of them.

The late morning sun added nothing but a false cheeriness to the sight before him, the breeze rolling over the long grass in waves, giving it an almost waterlike appearance. It was beautiful.

Too bad it would soon be filled with the screams of war. Of the dying. Of fallen iron soldiers and corpses alike.

Galahad, Percival, Tristan, Bors, and Gawain were already prepared for the fight, their dragons lurking nearby and ready to enter the fray. Mordred was uncertain how many would make it through the day. He hoped all his knights survived.

Save for one.

His hand tightened on the hilt of Caliburn where it was sheathed at his side. One knight would die this day. There would be no mercy granted, no quarter given, no pleading from the woman he loved to convince him to spare his foe.

Today, Lancelot would fall.

And this time, Mordred would put him in his grave where he belonged.

A horn sounded from the woods. The blast to signal the rallying of forces.

Mordred grimaced.

It was time.

* * *

"In."

"Hey!" Gwen glared at Percival as the knight shoved her unceremoniously into her room. Mordred had reattached the iron chain connecting her wrists once she had the chance to change into a new dress, finally ditching the metal clothes for the time being. "You don't need to push me around, you—"

The door slammed shut in her face. Percival clearly hadn't cared to listen. Tim was standing guard at the outside of the door, watching the whole ordeal in silence. Idly, she wondered if the poor soldier had been left standing there for the day and a half she had been out of her room.

Probably.

People seemed to overlook him at the best of times.

"Asshole!" she screamed through the door. No one answered. She figured the knight was already long gone.

She hadn't bothered to ask to be let free to help. She knew what the answer would be. Mordred might have forgiven her for what she had done—but he certainly didn't trust her yet. So she would be left to her own devices, locked in a room like the so-called "princess" that she was, and wonder who was going to live and who was going to die.

A whimper from behind her told her at least she wouldn't have to wonder alone. Turning around, she saw Eod lying on the bed, his head on his paws, those big soulful eyes asking her if everything was going to be okay.

"Hey, doggo." She walked up to the bed and sat down next to him. He was quick to plop his heavy head into her lap. She petted him and the coarseness of his fur had a grounding effect on her. She knew Mordred had put the dog in the room specifically to console her.

And damn it if it wasn't already working.

Someone was going to die today. A lot of people were probably going to die today. The question was simply—how many and who.

Would it be Mordred? Would it be Lancelot? Would it be

her and Grinn? What about Galahad and the rest of the knights? Percival could go get wrecked as far as she was concerned, but she didn't think even his shitty behavior was enough to deserve death.

But it wasn't just going to be one person who fell.

Off in the distance, she heard a trumpet.

A moment later, and it felt like the whole keep had come alive. Something shifted in the air. She shivered as magic rolled over her like the buzz of electricity. The fur on Eod's back stood up, and he growled.

"I know, baby. I know." She kept petting him for both their sakes. "I'm scared too."

The creak of enormous metal wings filled the air. The building shook as something large landed on it. A dragon, she had no doubt. Either Tiny or one of the other knights' enormous monsters.

Her family had gone to a baseball game once. They had traveled to Kansas City for a packed game against the Cardinals, the Royals' sworn enemies. She had heard the roar of thirty-seven thousand people cheering and jeering, and she wondered if that wasn't just a little bit like what an Ancient Roman colosseum must have sounded like.

Or a medieval battle.

At the time, it had been thrilling, to shut her eyes in that stadium and imagine what it would be like to hear the clash of weapons and the battle cries of opposing forces, fighting to the death for victory. She had wished she could have been there to witness it.

But as she heard it for real, the sounds muted and far away as they drifted in through the open window?

She very much regretted having made any wishes at all.

TWENTY-FOUR

Lancelot rode onto the field, his sword drawn, his drake circling overhead. He had fifty elementals at his back. Nearly half of those who still lived, he expected. Less than his target, but more than he had expected. It gave him hope. It gave him certainty in his mission. He was not the only one who knew that Mordred needed to fall.

He only prayed to God that it was enough to see him through.

Fifty elementals, himself, and his dragon. Versus Mordred, his iron guards, six knights, and six dragons. Though he had the greater power on his side, he did not discount the Prince in Iron. He had the defensible position.

But where *was* he? There was no sign of Mordred's soldiers as Lancelot marched his meager regiment onto the field. The rumble of the earth beneath him was a strange comfort, reminding him he was not alone.

The doors to the keep swung open, and from it rode one man, unmistakable even from a distance. A monster of a man atop an equally nightmarish steed—rusted and jagged, and holding an enormous blade in one hand as though it weighed nothing to him.

Mordred.

But he was alone. No soldiers fell in file behind him. Mordred rode thirty yards from the front gate of his keep and then stopped, his stallion angrily digging its hoof into the ground. Lancelot frowned behind his helm but continued his march along the path. There was no sign of an army. No sign of a counter-offensive.

It made him nervous. Extremely nervous. But perhaps Mordred was surrendering—or attempting to broker peace. Cautiously, waiting for any sudden movement from the Prince in Iron, Lancelot approached and came to a stop some ten yards away.

"Surrender." Lancelot gripped his sword tight in his hand.

Mordred ignored him. "Return to your homes and dwellings, elementals. Begone from here. I have no quarrel with you."

Isha laughed from atop a molten lava steed—something that resembled a giant hellhound far more than a horse. "And yet we have a quarrel with you, *warden.* Did you think we would so easily forget what you have done to us? Forgive you, for all those years you left us imprisoned?"

"No. I did not." Mordred's voice was as cold as the metal he wielded. "But an opportunity lies before us to start anew. To seek peace."

"*Now* you wish for peace?" Lady Thorn snorted from where she stood at Lancelot's side. "Do not insult us. You only seek peace because the Crystal is gone, and you are without any allies that you do not force to stand at your side."

"I never wished to imprison the magic of Avalon. I only sought to protect this place from complete destruction. I am hoping a lesson was learned." Mordred's tone was even, flat, and emotionless. His steed, meanwhile, seemed ready for battle. It snorted and shook its head, desperately wanting to wreak havoc. "I entreat you all—begone from here. Seek not to end your lives so soon after they have been restored."

"And how do we know you will not simply seek to imprison us again?" a wind elemental asked.

"I do not act without reason. And if I am given none to seek your incarceration, then why would I?"

"Because you wish only for power! This noble act of yours is a farce—it has always and only ever been about seizing the crown you feel was denied you," Thorn said through a grimace, her teeth bared like a wild animal's. "You will die here, usurper."

None of the elementals seemed swayed by Mordred's request. And the Prince in Iron did not seem surprised. "Very well. If it is war you want, it is war that you shall have."

"I see no army, Mordred. I have more than fifty elementals with me." Lancelot sneered beneath his helm. "Each one capable of destroying a legion of your soldiers. You stand no chance against us with only your guards and your remaining knights."

Mordred was silent for a long moment before he laughed quietly. "Your idiocy will never cease to amaze me, Lancelot."

"I admit that six dragons will—"

Mordred interrupted him. "Do you not remember the army I commanded three hundred years ago, when we captured the magic of the isle? Do you not recall where it was they went, when their work was done?"

Lancelot furrowed his brow. "It has been three hundred years. They must be nothing but rusted—"

"Perhaps if I had not been using my strength to keep them maintained. Do you not think that I realized this day would come? That it was only inevitable that the Crystal would break and you would all come for your petty revenge?" He shook his head. "Truly, Lancelot, you are a fool."

Mordred reached out a hand in front of him, fingers jagged, rusted knives, and clenched it into a fist. "Rise."

No. No, it wasn't possible.

Lancelot yanked on the reins of his horse as the ground rumbled around them, and not because of Olgon the rock elemental's lumbering form. "Retreat! Retr—"

It was too late.

Twisted soldiers of rusted iron began to climb from the dirt like corpses from their graves. Dirt and mud, blood, and muck, fell from their forms as they pulled themselves free and up to their feet.

They pushed up, limbs jerking back into place as they were commanded to life once more by their master, dormant opalescent glowing eyes flickering as they straightened themselves up from their shallow graves and lifted their weapons.

More importantly, the vast army of Mordred's soldiers was now standing in rows *behind* Lancelot and his elementals.

He was pinned between the keep and Mordred's forces.

Swearing loudly, Lancelot reeled his horse back toward Mordred, deciding to take the front assault of the keep. "Elementals, attack!"

Lancelot did not know how he would win the day.

He prayed that he could.

But it was in the hands of God now.

* * *

Mordred watched as his iron army climbed from the dirt where they had lain dormant for so very long. He had hoped—he had prayed—that the elementals would act wisely and turn to leave. That they would take his offer of peace. But they refused it. Their hate and anger ran too deep—and he supposed he could not blame them. If their places were reversed, if he had been placed inside the Crystal and did not understand why,

Mordred could not say that he would not be fighting alongside them.

But such was the way of life.

And Lancelot—oh, that poor idiot—had played right into Mordred's trap. The moment his army rose from the ground, the trebuchets began to fire, lobbing their spiked munitions high over the walls of the keep. They were aimed precisely where Mordred had put Lancelot and his elementals.

Trapped between Mordred and his army.

The elementals scattered—those who could flee quickly did so, leaving those who could not in a tightly packed circle as they were attacked from all sides. Mordred kicked the sides of his horse, and that was the signal to his knights to attack—most from the backs of their dragons. But joining him in the fray on horseback would be Galahad and Percival.

For a moment, Mordred hoped that his victory would be quick and relatively painless—for him at least.

But elementals were an unpredictable bunch. Despite his hopes that the trebuchets would make quick work of his opponents, it seemed to be only mostly the case. The enormous stone elemental knocked one of the projectiles from his trebuchet away as though it were nothing more than a fly, sending it rolling through rows of his soldiers, destroying them in the process.

Shadows fell over the landscape as the dragons circled overhead. Lancelot's great silver steed was attempting to distract the other dragons from the fight, to keep them occupied while avoiding a direct conflict. And it seemed to be working.

Damn.

He had surprised Lancelot. But the Knight in Silver had the more powerful soldiers—even if they were disorganized and chaotic.

One of the other earth elementals came for him, sending vines and tangling weeds that overtook him and his steed.

Mordred's horse ripped at the vines, but they were growing faster than he could slice them away. He had to jump from the animal to fight on foot, swiping and ripping through the growth with his claws and Caliburn in equal measure.

It was Enin the Green.

Mordred sighed. "I have no quarrel with you, old one." The vines could not hurt him. Such was the way of iron. "Begone."

"No." The man with the green skin lifted his head in defiance. "I stood and watched last time. I will not make that mistake again."

"So be it." Mordred sliced through more of the greenery, fighting his way toward Enin. It was slowing him down, but it would not stop him. He swung Caliburn at Enin when he was in range, only to have the elemental dodge and summon swords of his own.

This was the life that Mordred knew. This was all he had known as a mortal man—fighting, and war, and death. As an elemental, it was the same—centuries of incessant violence. It was familiar to him, both abhorrent and strangely comfortable.

This was his world.

The sound of screams. The smell of blood and fire.

The chaos.

Enin fought well. He was as old as the isle itself, by Mordred's measure. When his swords shattered with one hard swipe of Caliburn, Enin summoned himself a spear instead. It snapped within moments.

Mordred knocked Enin to the ground with a sweep of his foot, sending the old warrior to the dirt.

"Will you imprison us again, Mordred?" Enin's breaths were coming heavy and hard, exhausted from the fight. "Am I doomed to return to that place?"

Mordred turned his blade over. "No."

And Enin shut his eyes, accepting his fate.

Mordred drove the blade through Enin's chest, straight

through the heart. The man grunted in pain but did nothing else. Wrenching the blade free, Mordred watched greenish-black blood drip from it onto the ground.

"Rest well, old one."

Enin dissolved, his body disappearing into the wisps of pollen and the seeds of trees, carrying off in the wind. Mordred did not take pride in his victory.

"You *monster*!" Lancelot hollered from behind him. "Stand and face me!"

Yes, that was an opponent he was far more interested in fighting. Mordred turned to face his former knight—his former "friend." The companion he had trusted, long ago, only to be betrayed.

"Only one of us will leave this battlefield alive," Lancelot snarled.

"For once, you speak true." Mordred cracked his neck from one side to the other loudly. "Let us begin."

* * *

Gwen was hugging Eod, her face buried in his fur, listening to the animal periodically growl at the sound of the war going on outside. Now and then the building would rumble as something struck it. There was no way to identify what was happening by sound alone. It felt like when her family would have to cower in the basement in the dark as a tornado swept through the countryside.

The noise. The fear. The helplessness.

The inability to do anything but *wait and see.*

It was a long moment before she realized she should be having a panic attack. That if she were home, hiding from a tornado, she would have been hyperventilating and passed out within minutes. But here she was, clutching Eod, her heart racing, but otherwise... she was okay.

I told Dad we should've gotten a dog.

Something about it made her laugh. Quiet and sardonic, sure—but a laugh nonetheless. Of all the random revelations to have, at all the possible terrible times, here she was. Discovering that all she needed to cure her panic attacks was a puppy.

A big, murderous, adorable attack puppy.

But still a puppy.

She kissed Eod on the top of the head and ruffled his ears. "You're the best, doggo."

He lifted his head and licked her cheek.

"I love you too, buddy." She smiled at him. His tail wagged once or twice, thumping against the mattress.

"Am I interrupting something?"

The voice instantly made her mood worse than it already was. Looking up, she glared at the black cat sitting on the chair by the fireplace. Grinn.

"Where the *fuck* have you been?"

"I am fine and recovered from my wounds, thank you very much for asking." Grinn bared his one fang as Eod growled at the demon. Probably half out of the instinct to hate cats, and half out of the instinct to hate the demon.

"I figured, seeing as I'm not also dead." She rolled her eyes. "What do you want? Shouldn't you be fighting with Lancelot?"

"Yes, well, that is why I'm here." Grinn looked away, pausing for a moment. "Mordred is fatally wounded."

"*What?*" Gwen was on her feet in an instant. So much for not having a panic attack. "What do you mean?"

"I mean what I said, girl." He let out a quiet version of that air-raid siren sound that cats could make when angry. "Lancelot struck him down in single combat. The centuries have made the prince cocky. He is dying."

"No—no, you're lying to me—" Tears stung her eyes. He had to be lying. He had to be. Didn't he? "No, no, no, no—"

"Lancelot wants to give you a chance to say goodbye. So,

I'm here, out of the *kindness of my own heart*, telling you that if you want to see him before he dies, you need to escape." Grinn swished his tail angrily. "Ugh. I cannot believe Lancelot was right. You've fallen in love with Mordred, haven't you?"

"I—" She couldn't breathe. She forced herself to slow down. She put her hand atop Eod's head, using the dog to ground her.

"It doesn't matter. He'll be dead soon. Most of the guards are out on the field. They'll be dead with him. But you'll need to get past the one at the door if you want to say goodbye. *Peh.*" He huffed. "Disgusting. I must go back to the field to fight the remaining knights."

With that, the demon disappeared.

She gave herself a few seconds to slow her breathing. Otherwise, she'd make it two steps before collapsing in a heap. Tears were already clouding her vision when she went to the door and knocked on it. "Tim—Tim, it's an emergency, please open up."

The lock clicked and it swung open. The half-finished guard tilted his head at her in his silent question.

"Mordred is—Mordred is dying. I need to go see him. Please." She moved to step forward.

Tim blocked her way, shaking his head with a *squeak-squeak-squeak.*

She wanted to scream. Threading her fingers into her hair, she clenched the strands, trying to use the sting to center herself. "Please, Tim. Please. I need to see him. I need to."

Another shake of his head.

She was still chained and shackled. She couldn't force the matter. She couldn't jump out the window and fly away. She had to get past Tim.

There was only one card she had left to play.

One thing she could try.

But it meant she would have to say it aloud.

Shutting her eyes for a moment, tears streamed down her cheeks. Her words were almost broken in a sob. *Please, no, don't let me lose him. I don't know if I can take it.* "Tim, I—I love him. Please. Let me at least say goodbye. Let me at least tell him how I feel. He doesn't know."

A small clank as Tim's shoulders sank. He looked down the hallway for a moment, then back to her, then back down the hallway. He sighed, breathlessly as it was... and then began to half run half walk down the hall toward the entrance. He waved at her to follow.

She followed eagerly, grateful for the escort. The other few guards who were stationed through the keep watched them as they passed, but with Tim leading the way, none of them moved to stop her.

They would all be gone when Mordred died. Maewenn and Tim with them.

Eod had run ahead, barking and snarling, ready to join the fray. She was worried sick about the dog, but there was nothing she could do to stop the animal from doing his job. She could only pray she didn't lose him too.

The keep had never felt larger in her life. Each second the dread and panic and horror grew. The only hope she had that there was still time to tell Mordred she loved him was because Tim had not dropped to the ground in a pile of parts and pieces. If he lived, so did Mordred.

There was still time!

For now.

Please, please, please—hold on, Mordred. Please, I'm coming!

It didn't take her long to get outside. Seeing a normal war would have been one thing. Seeing an *elemental* war was something else entirely, Gwen decided. "Holy shit—" She stopped just outside the gate to the keep.

It was total mayhem. Fire roared off to one side of the field, charring the ground. Sections of the grass were frozen solid into ice. There were rocky structures where there shouldn't have been, and if she wasn't mistaken there was a twenty-foot *boulder giant* lumbering around some hundreds of feet away.

The ground was littered with bits and pieces of armor.

And corpses.

Putting her hands over her mouth, she could only gape at the horror. Of the blood that mixed with the dirt. Of the empty, staring eyes that looked upon the cheerfully colored sky that they could not see. Nor would they ever see again.

One thing was clear, however—Mordred's side was winning.

But where was he? Where had he fallen?

Eod was standing a hundred feet ahead of her, barking and snarling, warning the chaos not to get too close to his home and his human.

Tim put his hand on her shoulder. It was hard for her to tear her eyes away from the disaster before her. But finally, she looked up at him. The half-finished soldier pointed into the field.

There was no mistaking him, even in the sea of clashing metal and blasts of magic.

He was almost seven feet tall, after all.

Mordred. The polished sections of his armor glinting in the sun, the rusty portions dull and lifeless, his helm resembled the skull of a dragon.

He was standing.

And he was very much alive.

But—

Something smashed into Tim so hard that the soldier went flying, hurtling some fifty feet away before hitting the ground with a heavy *ka-thud* and rolling to a stop.

"What the—"

A monstrous demon loomed behind her, his scarred and broken face pulled into a gleeful sneer. "You really are an idiot."

She didn't have time to shout at him. She didn't have time to scream or kick or run away. Grinn snatched her by the chain that connected her wrists and hefted her up off the ground, dangling her some four feet in the air.

He straightened up to his full height, increasing the distance between her and the dirt as he stood on his hind legs and bellowed.

"Prince in Iron—surrender, or the girl dies!"

TWENTY-FIVE

Mordred's heart skipped a beat. He stared at the demon who had somehow appeared behind his ranks, and at the young woman who dangled from the chains in his fist. He stormed away from Lancelot, not caring for what the knight chose to do. Summoning his steed, he barely broke his momentum as he mounted his horse and kicked it into a gallop.

All the while, he did not know if he breathed once. The pounding of heavy hooves into the dirt drowned out the pounding of his heart in his ears. Gwendolyn was in danger. Gwendolyn might die.

If she did not... he would.

Did he want to live in a world without her at his side? Did he want to live in a world where he knew he had sacrificed her for his own pathetic life? Could he die, knowing he doomed the world to burn—with her in it—simply to spare her in this moment?

"That is far enough, *prince*." Grinn sneered, falling down from his raised position. He dropped Gwendolyn into a heap and pinned her to the ground, flat on her face, underneath a massive hand. "Unless you want to hear what it sounds like when I shatter every bone in her ribcage."

Mordred yanked on the reins, commanding his steed to stop. It reared, angry at the sudden change, pawing furiously at the air before slamming back down and tossing its head. "Leave her alone, demon. Your fight is with me."

Gwendolyn was shouting, but the sound was muffled and Mordred could not make out the words from this distance.

"It is. But here I have a wonderful toy at my disposal. *Your* toy, I believe." Grinn laughed, baring his long remaining fang. "What stands before you is a simple choice. Her life for yours."

Mordred paused, choosing his words carefully. "And who will protect this world from you in my absence?"

"It certainly would be of no concern to you." The demon snorted. "You would finally be dead."

Glad the demon could not see his face, Mordred fought the urge to scream. Sensing his need for violence, his horse pawed at the ground, shifting from side to side. There had to be another way. There *had* to be.

"Your life or hers. Make your choice." Grinn shifted his weight, and Gwendolyn cried out in pain.

"Enough. Stop."

Grinn's laughter was mocking and cruel. "I *knew* it." He leaned back, easing the pressure. "You truly do care for her. How disgusting. How disappointing."

But Mordred ignored the demon's gloating. His heart was still shattering in his chest. He could not sacrifice himself—Avalon would follow shortly behind him. And she would join the dead shortly after he did, he was certain of it. "I shall not surrender to you. I shall not doom this world to the cinders you would reduce it to in my absence. No matter the cost."

The demon did not move. Gwen was crying into the grass. The din of the battle behind him seemed to die away. All that existed was this stretch of time where he wished above all else that he could tell her how he loved her. That she would take his heart to the grave.

But that he could not put his own happiness or her life above the lives of the thousands upon thousands who called Avalon home.

"Well..." Grinn tilted his head a little in thought. "Perhaps we are simply negotiating on price. You wish for me to spare her life, do you not?"

"Yes."

"But not enough that you would sacrifice your own."

Mordred would not dignify that with an answer.

"Very well. My next offer is this, *prince*. Give me Caliburn. Surrender your sacred sword, and I will let her live." The monster smiled. It was an unnatural expression at best.

"What use do you have for a sword?"

"None. I simply do not wish for *you* to have it." Grinn laughed. "Anything to weaken you for the fight. Besides... how utterly embarrassing for you, don't you think? Sacrificing the only thing Arthur gave you because you were outplayed by me? I think I will enjoy that for a very long time."

If Mordred's claws could have punctured his palms, they would have. As it was, the metal simply creaked at how very hard he was clenching his fist. The idea of giving up Caliburn violated every natural inclination he had.

But Gwendolyn...

What was he to do?

* * *

"You lying fucking piece of shit son of a bitch!" Gwen kicked desperately at Grinn. But she was hanging in the air by the chains around her wrist—which *hurt*. "Put me down!"

"Shut up. He's coming," Grinn snarled. "Play your part. This is how I get Caliburn and how I am finally free of you."

"You're going to break my hands you motherfucker, put me down!"

"Fine. He's getting close anyway. Keep your mouth *shut*, girl." Grinn dropped her to the ground. Gwen grunted as she hit it, feeling both her ankles shout in protest as she toppled down. A second later, she was squished flat in the grass.

She could swear and shout all she wanted, but it wasn't going to do any good. The demon weighed as much as a school bus, and he was currently parked on top of her.

All through the conversation between Grinn and Mordred, she tried to scream for Mordred not to do it. That the demon was bluffing. Not to give over the sword. But she could barely breathe, and after Grinn tried to crush her once, she decided she was going to just lie there and sob.

Eod was barking, snarling at Grinn, but he was smart enough not to get too close to the enormous demon.

"None. I simply do not wish for *you* to have it." Grinn laughed. "Anything to weaken you for the fight that is about to follow. Besides... how utterly embarrassing for you, don't you think? Sacrificing the only thing Arthur gave you because you were outplayed by me? I think I will enjoy that for a very long time."

Mordred was silent.

Don't do it. Please, don't do it. I'm not worth it—and he can't kill me anyway. Please, Mordred!

"Very well." Something thumped into the grass nearby. "Caliburn is yours. Let her go."

The weight eased off her back suddenly. Gasping for air, she rolled onto her side in a coughing fit. That demon could seriously go get fucked.

"Trick—" she wheezed. "It's a trick—Mordred—" But it was too late. She was too late. Her vision was a little bleary as she watched the demon step forward and pick up the sword in his palm. It looked ridiculously out of scale for him, like a grown adult holding a kid's plastic toy sword. But he wasn't planning on using it—not for that.

"Finally!" Grinn cackled. His long fingers began to glow a vicious, unnatural shade of red as he closed them around the blade. The sword itself crackled and seemed to fight back—a whitish-blue glow clashing against the red.

"No, stop—" She slowly managed to climb to her feet, wavering, but vertical. "Grinn, stop!" But the demon didn't listen. She couldn't say she was surprised. She took a step toward him.

It was too late.

The air began to taste like ozone as the power from the two snapped and popped, like electricity splitting the air. With one final roar, Grinn clenched his fist tight around the blade. The shift in the air around her was so strong that it made her ears pop.

Grinn dropped the broken, empty shards of Caliburn to the ground.

And then she saw it.

A thread, glowing and translucent, connected her and Grinn. She stared at it for a moment in awe, unsure of what to make of it. It was both real and not—if she stared directly at it, it disappeared. But out of the corner of her eye, she could make it out. The magic that bound them.

Grinn snatched it in his hands and yanked, and Gwen felt a terrible, searing pain in her chest.

It hurt so much she couldn't even make a noise. She just fell back to her knees. She couldn't think. She couldn't scream. She couldn't breathe.

Grinn broke the thread.

Something felt like it had been torn out of her spine.

She blacked out from the agony.

* * *

Mordred rode to Gwendolyn as fast as he could. Caliburn was no longer of any concern to him—it was as good as dust, its magic drained by the demon. But whatever Grinn had done, he was certain it must have killed the young woman.

He dismounted the horse and rushed to her side, ignoring the laughter coming from the monster only a dozen feet away.

Crouching, he vanished one of his gauntlets to search for a pulse. *Please, by the Ancients—please—let her be alive!*

He let out a rush of breath in relief as he found it. Faint, but present. Standing, he summoned his own sword, one he had not used in thousands of years. It was an enormous broadsword, rusted and neglected, the blade jagged and broken off at the tip. It was not as powerful as Caliburn. But it would be plenty enough to murder the treacherous demon.

He turned to face his foe and paused.

Fire arched from the demon's mane, and his mouth was a glowing forge of embers, causing the air to steam as it curled from his maw. The grass beneath the demon was already blackened and burned from his presence.

Mordred had not had the time to notice that the flame had been missing from Grinn a few moments prior. Glancing back down at Gwendolyn, he noticed her hair was no longer the color of fire—but a chestnut brown.

No longer an elemental.

But human.

All at once, it became clear to him what had happened. Somehow, by some means, they had been bound together. Gwendolyn's fire was not her own but had belonged to the *demon.* Rage and betrayal ripped at him, nearly turning his stomach.

This was her secret.

This was what she had been hiding.

He faced the demon. The danger had not yet been dealt with. There was still a war to win. "You are whole, I see."

"Indeed!" Grinn looked overjoyed. He stood up on his hind legs, his sunken ribcage glowing with fire from within, as if his bones were molten rock. He truly was a nightmare from hell itself. "That is *such* a relief! Can you imagine having to live tied to that idiot girl?" He huffed and dropped back down to all fours with a thud. "One would truly have to be a fool to desire such a thing."

Mordred did not bother justifying the insult with a reply. He took a step toward the demon, holding his sword at the ready. "Then why not settle this between us once and for all?"

Grinn chuckled, and took a few steps back, the grass beneath his feet instantly charring and crumbling to, well, ash. "I think not. That was hardly pleasant for me either. No, prince. We shall not fight this day. I will go lick my wounds before I end you once and for all."

Mordred sneered beneath his helmet. "You always were a coward."

"Is it cowardly to know when one will lose? Hardly." The demon laughed, more smoke rising from between his broken teeth. His one good eye blazed. "I will look forward to the day when I can finally crush your skull in my fist."

Before Mordred could force the matter and attack, Grinn disappeared in a swirl of fire. Snarling in unspent anger, Mordred forced himself to breathe. Gwendolyn was injured and unconscious. And *human.* The demon had fled.

Lancelot and the elementals were still warring with his own soldiers.

There was still a battle to be won. He would deal with Gwendolyn and her secrets when the dust had settled, and the bodies were accounted for.

Whistling, he called Eod over. "Protect Gwendolyn." He pointed at the young woman on the ground. "Stay."

Eod moved to stand over her, ears forward, alert for any new danger.

Mordred had a desperate need to cause someone a great deal of pain. Luckily for him, Lancelot was riding toward him. It was time to settle the issue of the Knight in Silver once and for all.

Caliburn or not—Lancelot was about to meet his end.

At least *one* traitor would suffer this day.

Mordred would see to it personally.

TWENTY-SIX

Gwen woke up feeling like she had been hit by a literal truck. Someone was licking her face with the exuberance and socially unacceptable nature that told her it had to be Eod. Or rather, it had better be Eod. "Good boy," she mumbled, trying to push the head away from her. Her words slurred together.

Everything ached.

Literally everything.

Her limbs were trembling as she pushed up to her knees. A strand of her hair fell in front of her face. She almost brushed it aside before realizing it was brown.

Her hair was *brown* again.

That only meant one thing. Letting out a wavering breath, she tried to calm her rampant nerves. She was human again. She wasn't an elemental anymore. And that meant she was now extremely fragile in this world of superhuman creatures.

Speaking of which—it looked like the return and prompt disappearance of Grinn had shaken the elementals. They had turned and fled for the forest, opting to retreat.

The crash of metal on metal very close to her quickly pushed her attention elsewhere. She could worry about being a squishy mortal another time. Because right near her were two men fighting to the death.

Two men she knew very well.

Lancelot and Mordred.

To the tune of the concerned whimpers from Eod, she struggled up to her feet. She had to stop them. She *had* to. Otherwise, one of them would die. And her money was on Lancelot. She tried to step forward, but a hand caught her arm.

"Don't bother." It was Doc the wizard. He was watching the fight with a grim expression. "This is inevitable. And has been for a very long time."

"But—"

"I know. But you can't save everyone. And right now, I'd worry about saving yourself first." He sighed. "I, for one, am impressed you're standing. Adrenaline. It's a hell of a drug."

"I can't just stand here and do nothing." She tried to step toward Lancelot and Mordred again, but the wizard kept her back. Not to mention Eod was now standing between her and the violence like he was a sheepdog and she was his flock.

"You'll just be putting yourself in pointless danger. Those two need to end things in the only way they know how." He handed her his walking stick to lean on. "Stay here with me."

She was human, after all—and still chained up. There was nothing she could do to make the two men stop. And knowing her luck, one of them would accidentally kill her. There was a lot of sense in what Doc was saying, she just didn't like it. She leaned heavily on the wooden stick. "This is stupid."

"Yup. Welcome to Avalon." Doc finally let go of her arm. "You might want to sit down before you—"

Her knees gave out abruptly without warning, and she found herself quickly sitting once more in the grass. "Ow."

"—collapse." The wizard huffed a laugh. "You poor thing, you've been through the ringer today, huh?"

She ignored his casual banter. "Tell them to stop. Get them to stop. Please."

"I wish I could, kid. I really do."

"What am I supposed to do?" Tears were filling her eyes again.

"Watch and wait." His hand fell on her shoulder. "Even if it hurts."

Sniffling, she didn't bother fighting the urge to cry. She figured she had a damn good reason already. And it was about to get worse.

* * *

Anger had finally gotten the better of Mordred. Like the blinders on a horse, all he knew was that which was in front of him. Lancelot would die. This was all *his* fault. Grinn never would have convinced the elementals to rise against Mordred.

"You made a deal with *Grinn*," Mordred snarled, as he brought his ancient sword down on Lancelot's, forcing the Knight in Silver to stagger backwards. "You knew he was scheming to hurt Gwendolyn! You *knew* he was after Caliburn —didn't you?"

"I didn't know what he was going to do." Lancelot dodged out of the way of Mordred's fist.

"Liar! You knew what the demon was capable of. And you would rather that monster be free upon the world."

"I had a chance to ensure only *one* monster walked Avalon —and I took it." Lancelot brought his sword up for a strike.

Mordred knocked it away with a sweep of his arm. There was little to nothing in this world that could hurt him when he wore his full armor. "Your hatred for me has doomed this isle. And the woman you claimed was your friend—one that sought the destruction of the Crystal for *you*. You have betrayed her and all the people of Avalon."

"No. This was for their sakes, not mine." Lancelot grimaced. But doubt flickered in his silver eyes behind the visor of his helm. "This wasn't about revenge."

"Yes. It was. And it is a shame you cannot see that." Mordred brought his elbow forward, striking Lancelot in the helm with a loud clank.

Lancelot's head snapped back, and he staggered. Unable to catch his balance, he fell to the ground. The only knight who could stand toe to toe with Mordred was Galahad. And Lancelot's prowess was a far cry from that of the Knight in Gold.

It was time for Lancelot to die. Once and for all. Mordred stepped over Lancelot and pinned him to the ground with a boot in the center of his breastplate. Lancelot fought, punching at his leg, trying his best to move Mordred. But it was no use.

Mordred lifted his broken blade. It was a horrifying-looking thing after so many centuries of misuse, but it was still as strong as any other. It was a far more fitting blade for him than Caliburn, he had to admit. "Goodbye, Lancelot. I wish I could say that it has been an honor."

"Wait, wait! I—"

Mordred did not wait.

* * *

Gwen covered her mouth with her hands to muffle the pained wail that escaped her as Mordred brought his huge, terrible sword down upon Lancelot and through the man's neck. Lancelot twitched, hands weakly grasping at the blade. But it was too late.

Gwen had only ever seen Mordred kill one other person before—the mayor. That felt a world away and so very different than watching Lancelot be executed. He had been her friend. She had tried to save him.

She had tried to free him from the Iron Crystal.

And for what?

What good had it done?

Nothing—if anything, she had caused *more* harm in the process. How many other elementals were dead in the field? What kind of terrible suffering would everyone endure now that Grinn was free with all his power returned to him?

This was all her fault. Lancelot was dead because of her. Her vision was starting to cloud with tears as she wept. She was going to hyperventilate. She could feel her head already swimming and her limbs tingled as she went numb to the world.

Good.

Let it happen.

The darkness was better than this.

Lancelot's hands fell from the blade that jutted from his throat. Blood pooled in the grass. His head went limp, rolling to the side. Gwen was glad he was wearing his helm. She didn't want to see his face, caught in a last expression of fear and pain.

He was dead.

Lancelot was dead.

And it was *all her fault.*

* * *

Mordred yanked his sword from Lancelot's corpse. He felt no joy for having done it. He felt no relief. Only the calming of his rage. Out of the corner of his eye, he saw Gwendolyn faint. Eod was lying beside her, ears down and whimpering. And the wizard was there too. How charming.

It was no matter. He had business to attend to. "Enough of this. Enough of *all* of this."

The fighting in the field was over. The elementals, seeing their captain fall and the demon abandon them, had quickly fled. His knights were quick to chase them off into the woods on the backs of their metal drakes. He would leave it to them to finish defending his keep.

Mordred shut his eyes and tried to keep from screaming in frustration and rage. He had won, but it felt as though he had been robbed of so very much. Gwendolyn's terrible secret had now come to light. Lancelot was dead. And the demon Grinn was now restored to power.

Avalon would be thrown back into the grips of war. Bodies of iron and flesh, stone and water, fire and air lay strewn about the field before him, riddled with wounds and covered in blood and stuck deep into the muck. How many thousands more would join them before it was all said and done?

What could he do to stop it, when he had done all he could think of in ages past? Fighting only led to more violence. Trust only led to more betrayal.

Grinn would be his first target. The demon had to be stopped. There would be no imprisonment for him this time—the demon would die. But what then? What of the elementals? There were twenty or more loose in the world, likely waiting to see how Lancelot and the others fared in their siege.

Would they choose peace? Would they join him in his quest against Grinn?

Or would they do what they *always* did—resort to their warmongering ways?

Mordred knew there was only one way forward.

It was the only choice he truly had.

Turning on his heel, he headed back to his keep, stopping to crouch down and pick up Gwendolyn's unconscious form. He should snap her neck, he knew. Twice now, the woman had betrayed him. Twice now, she had caused immense chaos in his world.

But he loved her.

And he had vowed that once he had her again, he would never, ever let her go.

Mordred was a man of his word if nothing else.

* * *

Gwen was somewhere soft and warm and comfortable. She didn't want to open her eyes. There was a warm presence that she recognized quickly as Eod. She must be in bed.

It had all been a dream. A terrible nightmare. What a relief. Blinking her eyes open, she rubbed at her face with her hand. And didn't hear the rattle of iron chains. Maybe that had all been a nightmare as well.

"Welcome back, sunshine."

Squinting, still bleary from sleep, she lifted her head. The wizard was standing by her window, picking at a thread on the cuff of his robe. "Doc?"

"You fainted. Can't say I blame you. Mordred brought you back in. Took the cuffs off, since y'know, you're human now and there's no point." Doc shrugged. "Glad it wasn't just a kink thing."

"I—" She might have blushed if she wasn't trying to grapple with everything that was going on. Gwen sat up. More accurately, she tried. She fell back onto the pillow, her head spinning dangerously. Groaning, she put a trembling hand over her eyes. She felt woozy and feverish.

"I wouldn't. You're going to be in a bad state for a while. I'm surprised you're awake at all. Being split from a demon, especially like that. It nearly killed you."

She was human again. That meant it hadn't been a nightmare at all. "Lancelot...?"

"Dead. I'm sorry."

She cringed, trying to fight the tears. Eod whimpered and licked her hand, doing what he could to cheer her up. "What about Mordred?"

"In his war room, with the other knights." Doc sighed

heavily. "He plans to take his army and hunt down Grinn. He won't stop until that demon is dead this time. Although, I'm not sure that's a worse fate than being trapped in an Iron Crystal."

"The Crystal is destroyed."

"Is it?" Doc's sardonic question sent a chill down Gwen's spine. "Is it *really*?"

Oh, no.

"I have to stop him." She tried to stand up. She couldn't even get upright. Every time she tried to move, her body just noped right out, and she fell back against the mattress. Letting out a frustrated growl, she tried again and again to no avail. "I have to—" Now she really felt like she had a fever. She was shivering, and her stomach lurched.

"Stop." Doc sat on the edge of the bed next to her. He picked up a washcloth from a basin next to the bed and, wringing it out, put it on her forehead. "There's really nothing you can do. Not right now. Wait until you feel better. Wait until he..." He trailed off.

"Will he talk to me?" There was the other bit that she was afraid of. Mordred knew the truth now. All of it. Did he hate her? Was she only back in the keep so he could put her on trial and kill her?

Was the relationship between them over, now that he'd learned what she was keeping from him?

Doc sighed. "Yeah. He's angrier than a kicked hornets' nest. Give him some time to cool down. And you some time to heal, missy." He poked the end of her nose. "Doctor's orders." The lopsided grin he gave her was almost adorable.

"Why're you in here?"

"I told Mordred that you're mortal and injured, and I know how to help you. Hard to argue with that. Besides—he knows my type are generally neutral. Not to say he trusts me any farther than he can throw me." Doc paused. "I should use a different phrase for that. He could probably chuck me pretty far."

She'd have laughed if she didn't feel like she wanted to puke. Shutting her eyes, she let out a wavering breath, feeling utterly exhausted all of a sudden. "This is all my fault."

"No. It isn't." He paused again. "I mean, you made things a lot worse, but—"

She glared at him.

"What? You said it, not me!" He grumbled as he dunked the washcloth in the water again, wrung it out, and put it back on her forehead. "People always getting mad at me for shit *they* say."

"At least you're better than listening to Grinn yell at me." She shut her eyes again. The cool compress did make her feel a lot better, she had to admit. "Barely."

"Gee, thanks."

"Anytime." She smiled, but it didn't last. She wasn't in the mood.

"Get some rest, Gwendolyn. You still have a long road ahead of you." The wizard patted her arm. She felt the mattress shift as he stood and left the room, shutting the door behind him.

At least she was too tired to cry. At least there was that.

TWENTY-SEVEN

Mordred sat in the iron chair that was positioned at the circular table in his study. It had once been his war room, and now it had taken that purpose once again. Five other chairs sat around the large surface with the inlaid metallic map. Five, where there should have been six.

Gold, Copper, Tin, Cobalt, and Nickel.

But Silver was missing.

And in those five chairs sat five knights. Whose expressions were as grim and serious as the occasion required. Tristan, in particular, looked almost defeated, staring down at the surface in front of him with a level of grief that Mordred knew the others felt, but did not display.

"First, the matter of Lancelot," Mordred began. "He shall be buried with full honors beside Arthur in the ruins of Camelot."

A look of relief crossed Galahad's wizened features. Percival looked more than a little perturbed.

"He died in battle, fighting for a cause he believed in. And for that, he deserves our respect. Galahad, Tristan—see that it is done." Mordred shut his eyes.

"Yes, my lord," Galahad replied.

"We are gathering to go to war against the demon. We shall seek him out." Despite all his wishes, Mordred did not see a better way forward. "We must corner him—flush him out before he can fully heal and destroy him."

"He could be anywhere," Tristan interjected. It was not meant to argue, it was simply the "young" man expressing his dismay at the considerable nature of what was before them. Mordred did not hold it against him.

"We shall sweep out from here. He cannot hide forever." Mordred tapped his claws against the arm of the chair in a methodical progression.

"And what of the elementals we encounter?" Gawain arched an eyebrow. The Knight in Cobalt had chin-length, wavy black hair, a thick mustache that was often fixed into a frown, and equally thick and disapproving eyebrows. He was wary in all situations.

"If they wish to declare war against us, we shall pay them back in kind. Do not seek violence where there is none. But deal with it when there is." Mordred stared down at the map.

"And what do we do with the elementals we fight?" Bors, the Knight in Nickel, asked the next logical question. "Are we to break the laws of Avalon and kill them, or...?" He trailed off. He need not finish his thought.

Mordred understood precisely where the statement led. "No. We shall keep the laws of Avalon." He grimaced in disgust. "Save for the demon Grinn. He shall die at my hands. Should I be held accountable at a tribunal, so be it. As for the rest?" He hated to say the words. He hated to even think them. But he had no choice. "You know what awaits them."

Pulling the hood of his cloak over his head, he stalked through the hallways of his home, making his way down the winding stone staircases to the tomb where the shattered fragments of the Iron Crystal still remained where they had fallen.

The rest of the crystals that had dripped from its surface had gone dark, the magic seeping into the air and dissipating.

Shutting his eyes, he held his hands out in front of him. It took all his focus to pull the shattered Crystal back together, forcing his will upon it, melding it back to one piece. It rumbled and shook as the pieces rejoined, the chains creaking under the load as it rose back up to its original position.

The tiny crystals that had surrounded it bled back into its creator. He did not leave a single speck of metal behind as he completed his second "masterpiece."

What a joke of a legacy it was.

Was this truly all he would leave behind? A trail of corpses and prisons? Dead elementals and imprisoned warlords? No wonder the world despised him. He wondered what Arthur would think of his grand work—and then quickly decided he was better off not knowing.

His thoughts were dark enough as it was.

When his work was done, exhaustion knocked him down to one knee. It had been a grueling day. He was eager for sleep, though he wondered if it would grace him this night with its presence, or if he would be doomed to stare listlessly into the flames while his thoughts tormented him.

Looking up at that which he had created, he felt no pride in its jagged beauty. It was improved over the original. Perhaps this time it would be more stable in its making, and those put within it would not bleed out in the way they had before.

Or perhaps he would die before he ever put it to use.

He did not know which outcome he preferred.

Now, it was time to rest. For tomorrow, the hunt for the demon would begin.

To be continued...

A LETTER FROM KATHRYN

I want to say a huge thank you for choosing to read *To Bind a Dark Heart*. I hope you enjoyed it and are looking forward to the rest of the series! If you did and want to keep up to date with all my latest releases, just sign up at the following link. Your email address will never be shared and you can unsubscribe at any time.

www.secondskybooks.com/kathryn-ann-kingsley

There are several kinds of writers out there in the world—those who are happy to tell their story to a blank page, and those who thrive on hearing about how their readers engage with their tales.

I am definitely the latter.

I love to hear from you and hear what you think of the Iron Crystal series and Mordred and Gwen's adventures in Avalon. Please leave me a review or stop by one of my many social media spots!

I absolutely love hearing from my readers – you can get in touch on my Facebook page, through Twitter, my website, or even join my Discord (link to join on my website) to interact with both me and other fans.

Stay Spooky,

Kathryn Ann Kingsley

KEEP IN TOUCH WITH KATHRYN

www.kathrynkingsley.com

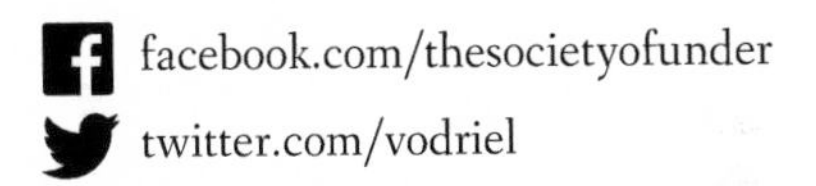

facebook.com/thesocietyofunder

twitter.com/vodriel

ACKNOWLEDGMENTS

I would like to take the opportunity to thank my three staff members for tirelessly bothering me and interrupting me in the course of my work. While I find their contributions disruptive, they are at least emotionally supportive of my endeavors. Mostly.

I just wish my marketing director, Nelson, and my HR director, Lilly, would stop getting into brawls that break the furniture. I have asked them to take this kind of nonsense into an area of the building that won't result in so much property damage, but I just received an explanation that "it was all in good fun."

Right. Sure.

My publishing agent, meanwhile, continues to sit next to me and judge me for every word that I type. I can feel her critical glare even now. I haven't had the heart to tell her that she's been replaced by a new publishing agent who is far better at responding to emails, but seeing as she has yet to notice that I've stopped paying her, I've decided it's better to let her live in ignorance for now. What Nutmeg doesn't know won't hurt her, after all.

Oh. I should probably mention my staff are my pets.

Sorry for any confusion this caused.

Made in the USA
Middletown, DE
13 December 2023

45379827R00156